ROSA'S SECRET

ISBN 978-1-8384560-9-2

louieelizabethparker.com

To Malcolm

Acknowledgements

My thanks to Jill Russell for proof-reading, editing and advising during the writing process. To Russ Naylor and Eileen Tucker for their support, proof-reading and commenting on completion of the work.

Also, my thanks to Lynne Emmerson, Carol McCoid and Carole Johnston, members of the 'Write Well' group, for their comments and continued encouragement.

PART 1

FRIENDS

CHAPTER 1

Anna

Summer 1996

Anna arrived on the island shortly after mid-day. She had set off from her home in Fort William early in the morning, looking forward to spending as much of the day as possible with her old school friend. It was ten years since Marie had moved to the island off the west coast and only now, both aged twenty-six, had the opportunity arisen to meet up. Yet, despite her excitement, Anna had an odd feeling that things were not quite right. Ten years, from the age of sixteen, is a long time. Had Marie changed? Had she changed? Would they be able to pick up where they left off?

The two girls had formed a bond on their first day at the High School in Fort William. Throughout most of their secondary education they were inseparable but, during their fourth year, as they prepared for the standard grade exams and looked towards their future, they had drifted apart, forming different friendships. Still, it was a sad day when they said goodbye. Anna was staying on at school to take her Highers, hoping to progress to university. Marie was moving to the Isle of Bute with her parents: she was anxious to secure a job, preferably outdoors. Although the two girls kept in touch, neither made the effort to visit the other. Not until she was older, with her own transport, did Anna consider the possibility of making the journey to Bute to see her friend.

On several occasions, Anna suggested they meet somewhere on the mainland – perhaps book into a hotel in Crianlarich to the north of Loch Lomond, and spend a couple of days walking. Marie was reluctant. Although she could drive, she was not used to busy roads or town traffic, her driving experience being limited to quiet country roads. *But,* Anna pondered, *is it just about the driving or is there more to it*? Perhaps her friend might suggest she stay with her on the island. Disappointingly, no invitation was forthcoming. In the end Anna invited herself using, what seemed to her, a legitimate excuse. She had booked a holiday to Spain, flying from Glasgow airport. Looking at the map and the ferry times, it occurred to her that she could drive to the island, cross at the north end and stay overnight at Marie's. If her friend was agreeable, she could leave the car there and take the ferry from Rothesay to Wemyss Bay where she could catch a bus directly to the airport. Much to her delight, the request achieved a positive response. Marie looked forward to seeing Anna – or so she said. She could stay for a night on her outward journey, and perhaps a little longer on her return.

Now that she had almost reached her destination, Anna was troubled. Had she done the right thing? In ten years they had only communicated by post – mostly Christmas and birthday cards with a note included – they had never spoken on the 'phone. Marie had moved to the island with her parents. Did she still live with them or did she have her own place? Only now that she was so close did it occur to Anna how little she knew about her former friend.

Thankfully, her doubts dissipated as she pulled up in front of Marie's country cottage. Her friend was there to greet her, to guide her round the side of the property to park her car, and welcome her into her home. The afternoon and evening passed quickly: they had plenty to talk about. Marie had left her parents' home several years earlier, taking on the rental of this cosy cottage with ample space for herself, and a small spare bedroom for a guest: it was ideal. Apart from disclosing that her mother was currently not in good health, she said little about her parents. Her lively chatter was focused on her work at the farm about three miles away; her free time spent exploring every corner of the island, and her main hobby of embroidery keeping her busy throughout the long winter evenings. Reading was also a significant pastime, making use of the local library. She borrowed books on foreign lands, travellers and explorers. It all sounded very interesting although, even as she spoke, it occurred to Anna there was something missing. Only later, after they had retired for the night, did she realise that, aside from the odd brief comment, Marie made little reference to friends. Neither was there any mention of a man in her life. For her part, Anna told her friend about her life at Edinburgh University, followed by her chosen career in teaching, as well as the friends she had made on the way. In addition, she revealed much about her latest boyfriend, the man she had arranged to meet at Glasgow airport to join her for two weeks holiday in Spain.

***

Early the next morning, Anna was woken by the sound of the telephone ringing. Dreamily, she listened to the scuffling and the sighs that ensued. A while later her alarm went off: it was six forty-five. As she opened her bedroom door to go through to the bathroom, she heard the back door close. She washed and dressed quickly then made her way to the kitchen. The table was set for breakfast but there was no sign of her host. She checked outside. Marie's car was still there. *That's odd*, she thought. Ten minutes later, when Marie failed to return, Anna helped herself to cereal, toast and tea. There was still no sign of her friend. Panic began to set in. What should she do? *Keep calm! Keep calm*, she told herself. *The telephone call must have been an emergency, probably something to do with Marie's mother. That's it!*

Anna reasoned that her friend wouldn't expect her to hang around waiting so she decided to set off walking to Rothesay to catch the ferry. It must be at least a mile which, with a suitcase and flight bag, would take time.

She had mixed feelings as she proceeded down the road: at first, a sense of guilt for leaving her friend, who must surely be facing some crisis. But as the luggage began to weigh her down, a different emotion took over: one of frustration and annoyance. *She could at least have left a note*, she cried out in anger as the struggle increased with every step. *I'll have something to say when I get back!*

Weary from the strain of the load, she arrived at the pier at last. Setting her suitcase on the ground, she slumped down on a bench to watch the ferry from the mainland as it approached the harbour. As soon as the boat was safely anchored and tied, the gangplank was secured and a hoard of foot passengers jostled their way onto terra firma. Many were school children and teachers making their way to Rothesay Academy; others, workmen heading for building sites in the town. A few white-collar workers were also in evidence. Anna considered the morning so far. Now that she had regained her composure, she was confused. *'What is going on?'* she asked herself. As the last of the passengers descended from the ship, the vehicles crawled out from the lower deck, making their way towards the road. The noise of the engines from the cars and lorries waiting to embark alerted Anna, waking her from her daydream. She stood, lifted her case, and steadily walked towards the gangway. Tickets could be purchased from the purser's office once the journey was underway.

With the ticket in her hand, Anna ascended the narrow stairway to the top deck where she stood, enthralled at the splendid panoramic view: the gentle rolling hills of Bute disappearing in the distance, the scattering of houses on the mainland, the community of Wemyss Bay looming up in front, and the dramatic mountains overlooking The Kyles of Bute behind. The scene around her presented itself as an idyllic landscape of tranquillity. She breathed in the fresh sea air, absorbed in the moment.

Buses from Wemyss Bay to the airport were frequent. The journey, though slow as passengers were embarking and alighting at every stop, did not seem arduous. Anna had plenty of time to spare. Her boyfriend had arranged to meet her at the main entrance at mid-day. Their flight departure was not until after four o'clock, but William had suggested they have a leisurely lunch, enjoying each others' company after several weeks apart. William West was a consultant psychiatrist working in Edinburgh. He was divorced with a young daughter, whom he often cared for at weekends. Getting away to see Anna was difficult.

Having arrived early, Anna found a café where she could relax for an hour before meeting William. Relaxation, nevertheless, eluded her. The prospect of the reunion sent waves of excitement through her body, which she found impossible to control. It was therefore with some relief that William was already at the airport entrance when she arrived.

"My dearest Anna," he greeted her with open arms, "I have missed you so much."

"Me too," she whispered, her heart pounding at his touch. They embraced; clinging to one another until an onslaught of passengers barged in through the doors, brushing past the amorous couple in their haste.

"Perhaps we should find somewhere quiet to eat," William commented, "It's too soon to check in."

"Perhaps we should," Anna agreed.

It would have been good to find a quiet corner to enjoy a meal and catch up on the last few weeks, but

14

airports are not conducive to such luxuries. They had to content themselves with a noisy self-service café / restaurant where families with young children struggled with cases, trying to find seats.

William sighed, "It's not going to get much better – that's the trouble with travelling from Glasgow during the Scottish school holidays."

For a fleeting moment, Anna experienced a sinking feeling in her stomach. As a teacher, she would never have the option to travel other than during school holidays. Of course she appreciated peace and quiet, but what did William expect in a busy airport during the height of the season?

"How have things been with you?" she enquired, determined to distract him from his present mood.

"Fine, things are going well with the job, apart from not having much free time."

"So tell me, what sort of clientele do you have?"

Having focused his attention, William spoke incessantly for the next half hour. He enjoyed his job, although it was stressful. The opportunity to talk to someone who knew nothing of his patients, where confidentialities were not compromised, was a relief. Anna listened intently for the most part, genuinely interested. However, she wished he would stop for a moment to draw breath and give her a chance to offload *her* worries. She would have liked to share her anxieties of the last twenty-four hours. But she decided that would have to wait.

The rest of the day went smoothly. The flight was on time and apart from the cheers of passengers as the plane landed safely – a reaction, which clearly irritated William – there were no further grumbles about the presence of unruly children. Nevertheless, Anna was relieved to be safely ensconced in their hotel room: time to themselves at last. As they cuddled down together for the night, Anna forgot her troubles. Only when she woke the next morning to find William already up and out for an early morning stroll, was she again disturbed by the mysterious disappearance of her friend the previous day. At least William had left a note.

Anna turned over and went back to sleep. She was tired after the journey the day before. When she awoke, about an hour later, there was still no sign of William. She showered and dressed, expecting him to return at any moment. Much to her annoyance, he did not appear. Adding to her frustration, he had taken the only key to the hotel room, probably so as not to disturb her when he came back. However, it meant that if she went out, she would not be able to get back in again. Hungry, and anxious to make it down to the dining room before breakfast was cleared away, she became increasingly exasperated. There were no tea-making facilities in the room so she couldn't even make a drink for herself. Another fifteen minutes passed. *Whatever is he playing at? I don't intend to spend my first holiday abroad stuck in a hotel room!* With this thought in mind, she stuffed her valuables into her handbag, lifted the latch on the door and headed for the elevator. If anyone went into the

16

room, the fact that William's passport was lying on the coffee table was his problem.

Before returning to the apartment, Anna requested another key from the receptionist. The room was as she had left it. There was still no sign of her missing beau. She was beginning to wonder if that was the correct term. So far, she'd had no chance to share her concerns about her friend on Bute. William had not bothered to enquire about her journey from Fort William, or the get-together with her old school friend that she had been looking forward to. Now that he had deserted her on the first morning, she wondered that he had any interest in her at all. Then, just as she had packed a bag ready to go down to the beach, William appeared. Seemingly oblivious to the anguish he had caused by leaving her alone for so many hours, he greeted her with a bright "Good morning".

"Where have you been?" she retorted, unable to disguise the sharp edge to her voice.

"I left a note," he quipped, stepping forward with arms open to gather her in his embrace. Anna moved back quickly. She was not in the mood to be consoled.

"I'm going down to the beach," she asserted, adding, "I've had breakfast," before bolting for the open door.

This wasn't the way that Anna had envisaged a holiday with the man she had so looked forward to spending time with: more time, aside from the brief encounters restricted by work commitments, that they had experienced so far.

CHAPTER 2
Anna and William

Anna and William first met, or rather came across one another, while at university in Edinburgh. He, a married man; a post-graduate student: she, a fresher, new to the university and to city life. He attended the meeting of first year students, ready to mingle and answer any queries following the introductory talk. Anna joined a group of fellow students listening to him giving reassurance about the coming term, and intimating he would be in the students' union bar most evenings between six and seven should they want advice, or simply the opportunity to chat. Although Anna often saw him around, she never had cause to approach him. She settled well, made friends within her year group, progressed with her studies and generally enjoyed life.

At some point, towards the end of her second year, she noticed William sitting alone in a far corner of the bar: not his usual position. Feeling rather downcast – she had recently ended a brief, though intense, relationship with a fellow student – she purchased a lager and wandered casually over to the lonely-looking figure.

"May I join you?" she asked, in a low tone, barely audible.

"Why y-y-yes, of course," he managed reluctantly. He didn't want to be disturbed, so why hadn't he bought a couple of cans of beer to take back to his room? *Too late now*, he thought. Normally, he was willing to listen to any student: to console them, to reassure them. Today, however, he was the one who needed to be consoled. When he had arrived home from university a few days earlier, an envelope bearing his name lay on the kitchen table. Inside, a neatly handwritten letter from his wife – a 'Dear John' – in which she expressed her appreciation of the happy times they had spent together, explained her sadness that they had drifted apart over the last year, and concluded with her 'carefully considered' decision to leave. The relationship, she insisted, had reached a point of no return. She was very sorry but …

In short – his wife had left him, taking their three-year old daughter with her. He was devastated.

Though desperate to relay her own troubles, Anna politely asked if he was all right. Her enquiry resulted in him relaying his marital problems – all of them, it seemed. Words tumbled from him in a torrent. Words that he had, so far, been unable to articulate. Since the fateful moment when he had read the carefully scripted note, he had felt thoroughly sick. It had taken every ounce of strength within him to summon the energy to get up in the morning and make his way to his place of work. Fortunately, being close to the end of the term, he did not have to lead any undergraduate lectures or seminars. He could concentrate solely on his research … except that he couldn't concentrate at all, on anything. Anna listened with a sympathetic ear, but it was not the right time to get involved. She would be returning home for the summer in less than a week.

Although they met for coffee from time to time during the next two years, the relationship went no further. William lectured at the university whilst completing a doctorate. Eventually he joined the psychiatric unit at the hospital. Anna gained an honours degree, and subsequently a teaching diploma, before being appointed to the staff of an independent school in Edinburgh, where she remained for the next three years. Things were going well until her relationship with the man she hoped to be with for the rest of her life came to an end. Dan had been offered work with a research team in America. Maintaining a relationship across the Pond was not practicable. The parting, though amicable, was heartbreaking for both of them.

Although she enjoyed life in the capital, Anna decided her heart was in the more rural setting further north... her hometown. She applied for a job in Fort William. Following a successful interview, she resigned from her post in Edinburgh and made preparations for the move.

As she was enjoying an end of term celebration with her colleagues, she came face-to-face with William. He expressed disappointment on hearing that she was leaving Edinburgh in less than a week. "Would you care to join me for a meal tomorrow evening – a farewell dinner?" he suggested. Without thinking through the implications, Anna agreed. She was delighted to be invited for dinner at one of Edinburgh's exclusive restaurants. Nevertheless, it was strange that William, whom she had not seen for more than three years, should go to these lengths. There had never been any romantic designs, certainly not on her part, and if he'd had ideas in that direction, he had not given any indication.

Much to her surprise and delight, William was the perfect gentleman. Aside from being outwardly attentive, he was attractive in a way that she had not noticed before. Maybe it was the dark suit and tie that emphasised his sleek appearance – his jet-black hair, dark brown eyes, and the hint of a smile that surfaced now and again as he held her in his gaze. When he escorted her home at the end of the evening, he kissed her gently on the lips. "Can we meet again before you leave?" he asked.

"Yes, I'd like that," she answered, with a depth of feeling towards him that she had not sensed before. They met twice more before she vacated her Edinburgh apartment. For their final meeting he invited her to his home, a spacious first floor apartment in the pleasant suburb of Corstorphine, for coffee. He fussed around her, voicing his devastation that she was leaving. "Why," he remonstrated, "do you want to return to the backwaters? Surely the city has so much more to offer."

"Maybe so, but Fort William is vibrant with tourists for much of the year. It is a beautiful part of the country. Perhaps I will meet the man of my dreams," she teased.

William's expression changed in response to this light-hearted quip. He was not amused. "And what about me?" he demanded.

Anna was taken aback. She had revelled in the time they had spent together over the last few days but knew it must end. Why had he assumed such an interest in her now? If he wanted a relationship why had he not made advances years ago, after his divorce?

"I want you. I want to be with you," he persisted. "Please," he begged, "please stay." He stepped towards her, held her in his arms and continued to plead.

Anna trembled. "I can't. I've given up my post here. I have a new job in Fort William. Please let go," she entreated, as she wriggled from his grip. Despite her strong words, her stomach was turning somersaults. She had feelings for this man, deep yet troubling feelings that she'd not anticipated when she had accepted his invitation for dinner. In a strange way, she was drawn to him.

Turning to the door, she hesitated. Pausing just long enough for him to think that perhaps all was not lost, he grabbed her by the arm. "I have some time off at the beginning of August. Please say you'll see me."

"I must go," she insisted. "I'll ring you when I've settled in."

As William accompanied her to her car, he managed to persuade her to give him her new address and telephone number. He wasn't taking any chances. When William West wanted something, he was not to be deterred.

***

That was a year ago. Since then they had managed a long distance relationship, of sorts. It was difficult. Most weekends William had custody of his daughter,

Bella. He also had commitments to her during school holidays, so times when he and Anna could be alone together were limited. Nevertheless, they found sufficient opportunities to take their relationship forward. They spoke on the telephone each week, and usually managed to spend at least one weekend a month together. Anna had reservations. The arrangement was dissatisfying in its limitations, yet she yearned for his company. Here was someone who appeared to want her... sometimes.

Since arriving in Edinburgh, Anna had had three 'serious' relationships, all of which had ended disastrously. The last, the most recent, was the greatest heartbreak of them all. Dan, she was convinced, was the right man for her. In the six months they had dated he had meant everything to her. The feelings she had for him, she was sure, were mutual. When he completed his doctorate and announced that he had been offered the opportunity to join a research unit in the USA, she was dismayed, but did not lose hope. Surely they could work something out? However, as the time drew close for him to leave, he broke off the relationship. "It's not fair on you," he insisted. "I'll be away for at least two years, possibly longer. You have your own career, your life is here." It was true: she had worked hard to pursue her chosen profession. They parted, both with tears in their eyes. The episode had caused her to re-think her future, coming to the conclusion that she would return to her childhood home. Edinburgh held memories of too many disappointments.

Now, settled into a flat close to the centre of the town and not far from her parents, she had mixed feelings, questioning whether she had done the right thing. The place felt right; her apartment was ideal; being close to her parents was a bonus. But what about this 'new' man in her life? Was William the one? Was this the person she had been waiting for? She hoped very much that that was the case, yet she was uneasy. The forthcoming holiday in Spain, her first time abroad, raised her spirits. It would be a real chance for them to get to know one another, perhaps discover whether things could go a step further, whether they were meant to be together.

Now, here she was, on holiday with the man she had yearned for all year and it had got off to a bad start. However, after that first hiccup, things did improve. William followed her down to the beach. He apologised. He had not considered how upset she would be at being left on her own. It was careless of him to take the only key. In an attempt at reconciliation, she explained that it wasn't him going out on his own that had upset her – after all, he had left a note – but the length of time he had stayed away. When several hours had passed, she had felt abandoned.

During the entire fortnight, Anna never did get the opportunity to relay the incident on Bute. Whenever she began to talk about Marie, he interrupted with some pressing concern of his own. It was almost as if he was jealous of her friendship with someone else.

The weather on the Costa Del Sol was warm and sunny, as they had expected for the beginning of July. Since the schools in England had not yet broken up for the summer holidays, the number of children was not as great as it would be later on in the season. They whiled away their time relaxing on the beach, swimming in the sea or the hotel pool, and strolling along the seafront. In the evenings they enjoyed Spanish cuisine in restaurants close to their hotel. It was a restful rather than an exciting holiday which, in a way, suited them both.

William could be very attentive at times, but not all the time. He liked to talk about his work – his passion – relaying, in depth, the problems of his clients and how he sought to help. He would ask her opinion but tended to dismiss her views as naïve. He was an expert, or so he claimed, and in regard to many of his patients he was probably right. His expertise, however, fell short in his personal life. Anna soon realised that he had little notion of the effects of his careless behaviour towards her.

As well as his obsession with work, he also had some odd ideas about his daughter. It was obvious that he doted on her, which was understandable, but when she was with him, he wanted to keep her to himself. He refused to allow her to have friends to stay, he avoided taking her to see relatives and, whenever Anna suggested that she would like to get to know the girl, he invariably found an excuse to avoid a meeting. He claimed he wanted to keep that part of his life separate. But how could he? If he were serious about his relationship with

Anna, then surely the two would have to meet at some point.

Anna tried to weigh up the positives in William's character against these worrying attributes. She was strangely attracted to him; she wanted things to work out between them, yet knew deep down that it was unlikely to end well.

When they boarded the plane for the return flight to Glasgow, Anna's mind turned to her friend, Marie. "I hope everything is all right with Marie," she sighed, as the plane cruised at its set altitude.

William shrugged. "Why wouldn't they be?"

Anna began to explain. "Well, the morning I left she dis…" A message from the steward on the loud speaker interrupted: a strong headwind meant they could be delayed by up to half an hour. When it ended, Anna tried once again to express her concern, but William was not listening.

"I hope we're not too late, I have to be back in Edinburgh to pick up Bella: she's staying with me for the weekend. I expect she'll be missing me – two weeks is a long time for a ten-year-old." He proceeded to impart what he had planned with his daughter, ignoring Anna's further attempts to divulge her worries.

As the plane circled Glasgow Airport waiting for Air Traffic Control to give the all clear to land, Anna tried one last time.

"The morning I left, Marie disappeared without a good-bye. I'm bothered about her," she persisted.

"Look," he responded, clearly irritated, "Don't you worry your head about it, everything will be fine. Your friend – what's her name again?

"Marie,"

"I'm sure Marie can take care of herself."

Tears sprang to Anna's eyes. Did he understand a word she had said?

CHAPTER 3
Detained

As they queued at passport control, William turned to Anna, and in a gentle tone whispered, "I've really enjoyed your company, Anna – it's been so good to spend time with you. When can we see each other again?"

Anna was distraught. How could his mood change so suddenly? Fortunately, there was no time for her to respond: it was their turn to move forward to the passport desk. William politely stepped aside for Anna to present her passport first. The officer took her passport, looked at her, studied her. He appeared to check with other papers in front of him before picking up a telephone. She heard him give her name. A few moments later, two police offices appeared. One of them addressed Anna, "I'm afraid I must ask you to come with us."

Totally flustered, she turned to William.

"I'll wait for you at the baggage reclaim," he stated.

"Are you with this woman?" one of the police officers questioned.

"Y-y-yes," William replied hesitatingly.

The policeman turned to the passport control officer. "Check his passport," he commanded.

"It's all in order," came the reply.

"We will need you to come with us: we must ask you a few questions. It shouldn't take long."

William followed the two officers and Anna through a door marked 'Private'. One of the officers escorted him to a small room at the far end of the corridor. "Look," William stated emphatically, "I really don't have time for all this."

"Just cooperate. You can go as soon as you've made a statement and we've taken your fingerprints," the officer affirmed, bluntly.

"I have to be in Edinburgh to pick up my daughter. The plane was delayed; I'm already running late." William's anger rose: he felt trapped. With a tendency to claustrophobia, he began to shake: beads of sweat appeared on his forehead.

Seeing that his client was indeed suffering, the officer leaned back in his chair. "I realise this has come as a shock to you but you must answer some questions." In a softer tone he resumed. "Your partner, or girlfriend, whoever she is, is in serious trouble. We need your help, if only to eliminate you from our enquiries. Please try to keep calm so that we can get this done as quickly as possible."

Feeling less threatened, William calmed down.

"What is your relationship to Miss Milne?" the officer began.

"She's just a friend," William responded, with a shrug.

"Have you been together for the last two weeks?"

"Yes."

"Tell me, when and where did you meet for the flight out to Spain?"

"We met at the airport a few hours before the flight was due to take off. We had lunch at one of the cafeterias before boarding."

"How did Miss Milne get here?"

"She drove down from Fort William… I think."

"Mr West – did she or did she not arrive here by car?" the officer queried, with a note of exasperation in his voice. *Surely this guy must know*!

"She said something about staying with a friend on the Isle of Bute," William responded.

"And, what is the name of this friend?"

William tried hard to recall the name. "M-M-Ma," he hesitated, "I-I-I think her name is Mary – something like that."

"Have you met this person, this friend?"

"No," William was decisive. "Look, where is all this leading? I don't know this woman. I don't know any of Anna's friends or relatives."

"Did Miss Milne drive to the airport from Bute?" the officer persisted.

"I don't know." Once again William was showing signs of agitation.

"You have just travelled back from Spain with Miss Milne?"

"That's right."

"You say you are going to Edinburgh. Was your friend intending to go with you?"

"No, no. She lives in Fort William. We were not travelling any further together."

"Do you want to see Miss Milne before you leave?"

"No," William retorted. "I told you, I have to be in Edinburgh to pick up my daughter."

"One moment please," the officer got up and left the room. Two minutes later he reappeared at the door. "Please come with me, Mr West," he ordered. William was taken to another room where he recognised his suitcase on a table. "Open the case," came a further demand.

William responded with a sigh. There was nothing untoward in his case. After his fingerprints were taken he was allowed to go, with a warning that he may be contacted for further questioning at a later date. With a sense of relief, he hastened to the car park. He was thoroughly annoyed at being detained: not a single thought for Anna's plight had entered his head.

***

As William was interviewed by one officer, Anna was facing a much more sinister ordeal. She had followed the other officer into a separate room, where a third officer was already waiting for them. He turned to Anna, "Miss Milne," he stated gravely. "I am detaining you for questioning in connection with the disappearance of Marie McInnes. You…"

Anna's knees buckled. She heard no more. When she came round, she was seated at a table in a small featureless room. A female sergeant was by her side, and the officer who had last spoken to her sat behind the desk. There was no sign of William.

"Where's William?" Anna asked.

"He's gone home," was all the explanation she was given. "Now then, perhaps you could tell us about your movements, starting from the time you left home more than two weeks ago."

Anna said nothing. She wasn't ignoring the question intentionally but needed a few minutes to compose herself. Her face was pale – drained with the shock. Her hands trembled. The investigator sat back in his chair. The sergeant gently told her to take her time. Eventually Anna began to relay her trip to the island the day before the flight to Spain. She recalled the events of the following morning, including her decision to make her own way to the ferry on foot. Although she admitted she'd felt uneasy about her friend's absence, she was sure there must be a valid explanation. After all, Marie knew of her intention to catch the nine o'clock boat from Rothesay. Her friend had also indicated that her mother was in poor health, so Anna had concluded that the telephone call in the early hours was an emergency, hence the reason Marie had rushed away without leaving a note.

"Can you prove any of this?"

Anna said that the ferry ticket from Colintraive to Rhubodach on the north end of the island was in the glove compartment of her car.

"And where did you leave your car."

"It's at the side of Marie's house. I'm going... was going to stay with her for a few days before heading home."

"Miss Milne," her interrogator interrupted, "Your car was found abandoned at Perth railway station. There was a suitcase full of clothes in the boot."

Anna gaped at the officer in disbelief.

"As you say, the ferry ticket across to the island was found in the glove compartment." He hesitated, as Anna nodded, before he continued... "As was another ticket, from the island to the mainland on the same ferry, shortly after eight o'clock on the morning you say you travelled as a foot passenger from Rothesay to Wemyss Bay". Again Anna gaped in disbelief.

"I left my car at Marie's," she insisted. "Wait, wait," she cried in desperation, as she fumbled in her handbag searching for the other ferry ticket to prove that she had been on the Wemyss Bay Ferry that morning. The ticket wasn't there. Neither was the flight ticket to Spain. "The hotel, the hotel in the Costa Del Sol. They'll be able to verify the duration of our stay." She looked pleadingly at her aggressor.

"Okay," he acknowledged, "That shouldn't be too difficult to ascertain."

For a moment Anna felt relief, but it didn't last long. "Now, Anna, are you saying that you did not *drive* off from the north end of the island, perhaps taking Marie with you?"

"No, no, I haven't seen Marie since the night before I left. I heard the 'phone ring, I heard her moving

34

around, I heard the door close. It was early. I didn't get up until my alarm went off about an hour later. There was no sign of Marie. I washed and dressed, had some tea and toast and made my way to the pier."

"Where was your car?"

"It was at the side of Marie's cottage. I left it there, as we had arranged."

"Are you sure it was there?"

"Yes, I'm sure."

The officer rose from his seat. "We need to take your fingerprints, collect your luggage, and get over to the police headquarters in Glasgow."

"I want to go home. I've not done anything wrong," Anna implored. "I don't know where Marie went."

"I'm afraid that's not possible, Miss Milne. You are the last person to have seen Marie on the island. We want answers."

Anna sank back in her chair. If she thought that the interrogation was bad enough, what was to come was worse. In another room, her fingerprints were taken; her case was searched; she was searched. It was the worst, most humiliating experience she had ever endured. What they were looking for, she had no idea. Towards the end of the morning she was bundled into a police van. On arrival at the headquarters in Glasgow, she endured further questioning before being escorted to a cell. *How can this be happening?*

Later, food was brought to her and she was asked if she would like to make a telephone call. It was suggested that she contact her solicitor.

"I don't have a solicitor," she snapped.

"We can provide you with one."

"N-n-no, that won't be necessary. I'd like to ring my mother."

It had already crossed her mind that she should have a solicitor but, since she had not yet been officially charged with an offence, she had not pursued the matter. The only issue, so far, was that she was thought to have been the last person to see Marie on the island and that, she decided, did not prove anything. Her car, purportedly abandoned at the railway station in Perth, was a puzzle.

The shock of being detained had not receded, although her head was sufficiently clear to conclude that, should anyone from the legal profession be required to act in her defence, it should be someone of her choice.

Anna was shaking as she dialled her mother's number. What could she say? Although desperate to speak to someone – to reveal her plight – she almost hoped there would be no response. Her prayer was half answered. The person who picked up the telephone was her Aunt Rosa, her mother's sister. Breathing a sigh of relief, she relayed the situation, believing that her beloved aunt would be less ruffled. A deathly silence at the other end of the line indicated otherwise. "Are you still there?" Anna queried.

"Y-y-yes, I'm still here. I'm just trying to take it all in. Where exactly did you say you were being held?"

"I'm at the police headquarters in Glasgow," Anna confirmed. Rosa sounded perplexed. So much so that Anna had to reiterate most of her story.

"I'm on my way," Rosa affirmed. "You'll need a lift home."

"B-b-but, Aunt Rosa, they might not release me."

"Oh, won't they now. Well, we'll see about that. You don't think we're going to let you languish in a police cell, do you? If necessary, I'll call your Uncle Bernard."

This sounded more like the Aunt Rosa she knew: confident, self-assured. And, of course Bernard, her husband, was a barrister. For the first time since the trauma of being stopped at the airport, Anna felt some comfort. Aunt Rosa would sort it out.

How was Anna to know that there was something else on Rosa's mind? Something equally disturbing…

CHAPTER 4
Marie

Until the age of twelve, Marie McInnes was brought up in Glasgow where her father was a teacher. From there the family moved to Fort William. For the next four years Marie attended Lochaber High School. After sitting her standard grade examinations the family relocated once more – this time to the Isle of Bute. It was a place where Marie had spent many happy times during the long summer holidays when they lived in Glasgow: she loved it. The idea of living on the island was like a dream come true. Marie McInnes craved the outdoor life and hoped to find employment working on a farm. At sixteen, she was not academically inclined and had no intention of being confined to a classroom any longer than she was forced to.

It was at the High School in Fort William that Marie met Anna Milne. The two girls were assigned to the same class. For the next four years they were close friends, drifting slightly during Marie's final year when Anna, who had opted to remain at school for a further two years, formed friendships with other students who were looking towards going on to further study. Nevertheless, the two girls were sorry to say good-bye when the last day of the school term came around. They promised to keep in touch.

Marie had always known that she was adopted. Her adoptive parents never made any attempt to conceal that fact. However, they had failed to divulge that, although they were not her mother and father, they *were* her aunt and uncle. Shortly after leaving Fort William when, relieved of the pressures of school and exams, Marie became curious about her real identity. It was only then that it was revealed to her that the mother she knew was the sister of her biological father. On discovering this much Marie, quite naturally, became more interested than ever. *Where is this man?*

"My brother – your father – died before you were born," her mother explained, looking sadly into Marie's eyes – the same grey eyes, her brother's eyes. She hoped that Marie's curiosity might be satisfied, at least for a while, for the next question would be more difficult to answer.

"And, what about my mother, *my real mother?* Is she dead too?"

"I don't know," her adoptive mother answered, truthfully. "There has been no communication since we adopted you. We thought it best that way."

"S-s-so, you've no idea," Marie responded, incredulously. "You haven't a clue where my mother is; whether she's dead or alive. How can you care so little about your own sister-in-law, your brother's wife – the woman who, apparently, gave birth to me?" Marie's voice rose in response to the anger within. "I hate you," she blurted out, as she rushed from the room.

Chrissie McInnes, the woman who had cared so much about the baby she had adopted sixteen years ago, was distraught. Here was the child she had nurtured from birth, the girl she loved dearly. Marie's reference to her *real mother* hurt deeply. She had expected her daughter – her niece – might be upset, but she had not been prepared for such an outburst. Her immediate thought was to follow the girl upstairs to her room, to console her, but she then realised Marie needed time to calm down, to come to terms with the information that had just been disclosed.

Marie was never a child to sulk. After almost half an hour lying on her bed she began to regret her reaction. Mum – Aunt Chrissie – whoever she was, did not deserve that. She had been a good mother to her. Slowly Marie rose from the bed and crept downstairs to the living room where Chrissie sat in an armchair, head in hands.

"I'm sorry Mum," Marie whispered. "I didn't mean what I said – I was upset discovering that you have known, all along, who my parents were. I'm still upset."

Chrissie sat up. She drew the girl towards her. "I'm so sorry Marie, nobody ever meant to hurt you. We just did what we thought was right at the time."

"Are you going to tell me about it?"

Although reluctant, Chrissie knew she had little choice. Her daughter would not let go until the whole truth was revealed. So she began to relay the circumstances surrounding Marie's birth and adoption. The circumstances as far as she, herself, was aware…

"Your parents were young when they met – very young. They were both still at school, but they were serious: they were very much in love. My brother – your father – left school when he was sixteen. He started work in a local garage, training as a mechanic. He was anxious to earn money so that he could save up for a future with his girlfriend, his prospective wife. Even at that age, the two considered they were destined to be together. Ellie, your mother, was a year younger than Paul. At sixteen, she too left school. She went to work in a café. Within a year she was pregnant. Despite being so young, the couple married. It was decided that, initially, they would stay with Ellie's mother, a widow, and Ellie's older sister, Rosa, who was living at home at the time: it was not intended to be a long-term arrangement. For two months the pair were happy. They settled well, looking forward to the arrival of their first child. Then, sadly, tragedy struck. Paul was killed in an accident at work. Ellie was distraught. With barely four months until her baby was due, she was in shock – inconsolable.

At the time of the accident, I had been married for several years. I was twenty-eight, ten years older than my brother. I had always adored him, often caring for him when I lived at home. When I heard the news of Paul's death, I was hysterical. How could my little brother be dead?

A few weeks later, as I emerged from the initial trauma, it occurred to me that we – your father and I – might adopt the baby. Ellie was so young. Losing her husband had all but destroyed her: she was beside herself with grief. We were unable to have a family of our own. Perhaps we could ease the situation, give our niece or nephew a ready-made home – a stable environment. I shared my thoughts with my husband, Colin, who agreed.

I contacted Rosa, Ellie's sister, to put forward my idea. She hesitated. Clearly worried about her sister, wondering how she would cope, the idea of adoption had already been considered as an option. "I'll talk to Ellie," she offered. "I don't think she knows what she wants."

For a while, we heard nothing. The last thing I wanted to do was pester the family – they had been through enough. Eventually, towards the end of November, with only a few weeks to go before the birth, Rosa turned up at our house. Ellie, she maintained, was prepared to go ahead with the arrangement. Now that her husband was dead, she felt she couldn't cope with a child. Her baby, she agreed, would be much better off in a secure home. However, if we adopted the child, your mother was determined she would have to let go completely. Rosa faltered, admitting that there could be no guarantees until the birth. There was always a chance that on seeing her baby, Ellie would change her mind.

The next month was tense. We had to be completely ready to take charge of the baby from the time of its birth, yet there was a question mark over whether things would work out. "I lived in hope," Chrissie emphasised, "I wanted you so much. The loss of my brother weighed heavily on my mind. The thought of bringing up his child gave me a sense of optimism. The whole idea put a little sparkle back in my life."

Marie was intent. Her eyes glazed over with emotion as she listened to her mother's story. "So, what happened then?" she questioned – although, of course, the outcome was obvious.

"We received a 'phone call on New Year's Eve to say that Ellie was in labour. If all went according to plan, we must be ready to take the baby as soon as it was born. The call came shortly after midnight on New Year's Day. We went to Ellie's home. Rosa came out with you in her arms and handed you over to me. Rosa registered your birth a few days later, once everything had returned to normal after the Hogmanay celebrations. We arranged for legal adoption."

"Wow," Maria voiced in response. "That sounds like quite a night! I'm glad you've told me."

Thankfully, Marie did not pursue the matter further that day. It was understandable that she wanted to know about her biological parents, especially since it was revealed that her birth mother was possibly still alive. Nonetheless, the whole incident, all the questions, had left Chrissie exhausted. Further, she doubted that the subject would be laid to rest. Her daughter may be satisfied for the time being, but Chrissie suspected there would be a time when she would want to delve deeper. For her part, Chrissie had told the girl all she knew; yet even she had a niggling feeling that there was more to it than she was aware. Despite accepting Rosa's reasoning, that Ellie wanted nothing more to do with her baby, she found it difficult to understand. If *she* had reservations, it was no wonder that her adopted daughter was troubled.

***

Marie settled well to life on the island, as she'd had no doubt she would. Being enthusiastic, young, and fit, she gained employment at a local farm, initially on a temporary basis, until she proved her worth. In some ways, it was a strange life for a young girl, yet it was all that Marie desired. She enjoyed the out-door life, made friends with other farm workers and re-established friendships she had made as a young child during the school summer holidays. As a teenager, she readily joined in with the youth of the island: sometimes enjoying the company of a boyfriend for a short while, but never entering into a serious relationship. Young lads, she concluded, were all immature.

When she eventually passed her driving test and gained more freedom, she was able to drive around the island at will. Occasionally she would venture onto the mainland, crossing at the north end of Bute, although never straying too far away: she was nervous at the thought of driving on busy roads. Cities were out of the question.

Her greatest joy was finding a small cottage to rent. At twenty-three, she considered herself too old to be staying with her mum and dad. Aside from that, she relished her own company, her own space.

Relaxing one evening in her cosy living room, her mind turned once again to her real parentage. On a few occasions since settling on Bute she had broached the subject with her mother but all to no avail. It was always the same story. Her birth mother was young and, on giving up her daughter, she didn't want to be constantly reminded of the past. But how did Chrissie know that?

The short answer was... she didn't. It was the story that Rosa had given. It was the story she wanted to believe.

Marie was of the opinion that, at seventeen, Ellie couldn't know her own mind. She had found herself in tragic circumstances. Influenced by those around her, she had agreed to give up her baby. After all, given the situation she found herself in, she would have to rely on the support of her family, especially her older sister, in order to raise a child. Oddly, Marie never felt anger towards her birth mother for giving her up. However, she was annoyed with her adoptive parents, especially Chrissie, for not making any attempt to inquire after her sister-in-law. Surely, she could at least have been in touch with Rosa. So, although grateful that she'd had a secure upbringing, it irked Marie that she was deprived of half her family... all her real mother's relatives. Hard as she tried to forgive, part of the trust she'd had in Chrissie as a mother had been lost forever the day she discovered the truth. One day she would search for her biological mother: one day soon.

Not long after she had made the decision to find her real mother, something, or rather someone, came along causing her to shelve her plan for the time being. His name was Jack. As she was rounding up sheep, a gentleman, probably in his mid-thirties, observed her from the roadside. He stopped, mesmerised by her obvious skill, notably, her control of the sheep dog to gather the flock. Once safely in their pen, the swarthy stranger opened the gate into the field and made his way over to the young woman who had attracted his attention.

46

Looking towards him as he approached, Marie's heart leapt: she felt heat rising from her chest up towards her neck, culminating in a deep flush to her cheeks. Seeing her embarrassment, Jack Todd slowed his pace, keen not to ruin the moment. Their eyes locked. A short silence ensued, broken by the stranger as he made his introduction. "My apologies ma'am. I don't mean to intrude, but I couldn't help admiring your aptitude in bringing in the sheep. You're a very talented young lady."

Marie was flattered by his kind words, spoken in a distinctive Australian accent, but they did nothing to alleviate her discomfort. "Th-th-thank you", she responded, scarcely audibly.

"I'm Jack, Jack Todd," he stated as he moved forward offering her his hand. His touch sent waves through her body. Never before had she experienced such a reaction. For several minutes the two chatted, sharing their love of the outdoors – their interest in the countryside in general, and farming in particular. That Marie enjoyed life on the farm was obvious to Jack who revealed that he too worked on a farm – a sheep farm in Australia. It was a family business, which he would one day take over from his father.

A quick glance at her watch prompted Marie to end their talk. "I must get back to work," she declared, "There's a lot more to be done this afternoon."

Jack was about to offer his assistance when a call from the farmer, hastening Marie to get back to work, stopped him. Perhaps now was not the time to be so bold.

47

Besides, he had other ideas. "Can we meet later for a drink?" he ventured.

"Yes," Marie replied. "Seven-thirty, in the centre of the town: by the bus stop opposite the ferry terminal," she called, as she turned towards the sheep pen. Almost straight away she regretted her hasty response, wondering if she'd sounded too forward.

Jack retraced his steps through the gate to the road, and continued on his way. He marvelled at the small island he had heard so much about. It had been home to his ancestors more than a hundred years ago. He had come to Britain to see for himself the way that farms operated in this country so far from his home. Arrangements had been made for him to attend various agricultural colleges – to exchange ideas, to lecture, to talk to students as well as experts. He would also take time to visit a selection of farms in order to observe, first hand, the methods and machinery used. In addition to his work schedule, he anticipated having some time to enjoy a holiday. On arrival in the UK his first port of call was, understandably, the place from where his family originated – this tranquil island on the west coast of Scotland. He was not disappointed. In fact, the events of the last half hour had presented a whole new dimension to this mammoth trip to the other side of the world. *Maybe, just maybe*, he mused as he almost skipped along the road. There was something about this girl – this young woman – that struck a chord… And yet, he did not even know her name. Romance could not have been further from his mind as he had boarded the plane to Heathrow. In a matter of moments, all that had changed.

CHAPTER 5
Marie and Jack

Bute was never a place for dressing up, but Marie wanted to look her best for this stranger who had invited her out. Having flung off her working gear, she soaked in a hot bath, dreaming how her life might change forever as a result of the afternoon's encounter. Or was that just wishful thinking? She raked through her limited wardrobe, pulled out a pair of black trousers that she had never worn, selected a plain grey T-sheet, a lightweight grey jacket, and added a pink silk scarf to soften the outfit. "Not too bad," she voiced out loud as she gazed into the tall mirror in her bedroom, holding a hairbrush in her hand. *Now, what to do with this unwieldy mop!*

Her mousey brown hair was not a notable feature – quite ordinary – she thought. But perhaps that was her fault. Hanging below her shoulders she would simply 'wash and go' as the advert for some shampoo or other suggested – except she didn't use that shampoo. So, invariably, she let her hair dry naturally in the wind: a tangled mass of waves. If it got in the way she would tie it back with an elastic band. As she brushed it, with more care than usual, she smiled at the result. *That's better*, she decided. Observing her reflection more critically than she would normally, she gave a murmur of approval. Her attire enhanced her pale grey eyes – an attribute of which she had always been pleased.

Marie found she had little appetite, which was unusual for her. She forced herself to eat a sandwich and have a cup of coffee before setting off towards the town. As it was a fine evening, she decided to walk: it was just over a mile. When she arrived at Guildford Square in the centre of Rothesay, Jack was already there. He greeted her with a broad grin. "You look lovely," he commented, causing her to blush. "It's a beautiful evening," he added, "Perhaps we could stroll along the seafront for a while, before we find somewhere to have a drink?"

"I'd like that," she answered, turning away from his gaze. As when they had met that morning, she found it impossible to hide her embarrassment. *What is the matter with me? What is it about this man? Pull yourself together girl,* she admonished herself.

"This way," she encouraged, in an attempt to disguise her awkwardness. "We can amble along for a while and return part of the way through the woods at the back of the houses."

Marie had hastened a few yards ahead, indicating to Jack to follow. He caught up, grabbing her hand. "Hey," he protested, though in a friendly tone, "I thought this was meant to be a stroll."

Marie slowed, "I'm sorry."

"Don't be," he jested, with a glint in his eye. "But before we go any further, I need to ask you something."

"Oh," she responded, nonplussed.

"What's your name?"

There was a moment's hesitation as Marie returned his gaze and smiled.

52

"It's Marie," she responded.

"Well, Marie, it's lovely to meet you. Now, let's enjoy our evening together, there's no hurry."

Relaxed at last, Marie walked beside this stranger from Down Under, gaining confidence with every step. As they turned into the woods, he gently took her hand: her whole body tingled at his touch. Despite scarcely knowing one another, there was a warm feeling between them – a natural bond.

As the air began to turn a little cooler, and the dreaded midges encircled them, they emerged from the woodland path onto the road. They found a pub where they were able to enjoy a quiet drink. Marie was cautious, limiting her intake to a pint of lager, determined not to make a fool of herself on their first date. She wished she had eaten a proper meal before setting out for the evening.

The time passed quickly as the couple endeavoured to get to know one another. Noticing the darkness descending, Jack asked Marie if she was driving home.

"Oh, no," she answered, "I walked. My cottage is just over a mile from here."

"In that case, I'll walk you home," he offered.

Marie queried, "But what about you? Where are you staying?"

"I'm booked into Bed and Breakfast accommodation just along the road from here. Really, walking you home is no problem."

Although he was willing to accompany Marie to her home, he refused her invitation to go in for a coffee. He had learned, to his cost, that moving too quickly in a relationship could end badly. Before parting, they arranged to meet on Saturday, the day after tomorrow. She would drive into the town to pick him up. From there, she would take him on a guided tour around the island.

During the following week while Marie was at work, Jack continued to explore the island, mainly on foot. Occasionally he used the local bus service to attend prearranged visits to some of the farms, as well as the local dairy. In the evenings the two met up to spend a couple of hours together. The next week was Jack's last on the island. Marie was on holiday so they were able to spend more time together. They enjoyed a day on the mainland, crossing over at the north end of Bute, a day trip on the Waverley – the famous paddle steamer that cruises around the Clyde Estuary – and the rest of the time on the island. One of the highlights was The Highland Games and another, a traditional Ceilidh. All too soon Jack's sojourn on Bute came to an end.

It was Sunday evening, towards the end of August, when Marie waved farewell to Jack as he boarded the ferry to the mainland. "I'll keep in touch," he promised. For the next two weeks he was visiting Orkney and Shetland. On his return to the mainland he hoped to manage a couple of nights on Bute before continuing with his busy schedule: a month, visiting farms throughout Scotland. Thereafter, he was assigned to a college in Edinburgh to join the staff over the winter.

True to his word, Jack rang Marie regularly from the northern isles. When he arrived on Bute a fortnight later, Marie was waiting at the ferry in Rothesay to welcome him. With open arms, he greeted her: a more intense physical response than had occurred at any time so far in their relationship. Jack was booked into the same Bed and Breakfast accommodation as before: his determination to take things at a steady pace remained, although it was becoming increasingly difficult. Arriving on the last boat of the day, once Jack had deposited his luggage in his room, the two of them were anxious to make the most of what remained of the evening. Marie had reserved a table in one of the hotel restaurants so that they could relax in each other's company, while enjoying a meal of typically Scottish fare. Jack would have to leave the island at midday on Sunday, so the weekend was short. For the foreseeable future, the situation would be much the same. It would be a rush for Jack to catch the last ferry across to the island on a Friday evening: there was no guarantee that he would manage to do so every week. Nevertheless he hoped at least to be able to stay until after lunch on a Sunday.

Marie said nothing to her parents about her new friend, preferring to savour the relationship without interference. She was sure that her mother would disapprove, given that Jack was from the opposite side of the planet. *Don't get too attached; it won't work; you'll end up getting hurt.* The words echoed in Marie's mind.

But were they really what she imagined Chrissie would say or were they her own misgivings? Marie shrugged off her doubts and kept quiet about the relationship. There was no point in stirring things up – not yet!

Within a few weeks, as summer turned to autumn, Marie and Jack's weekends became a regular routine: their relationship blossomed. One Friday evening when they met at the ferry terminal Marie announced, coyly, that there was a change of plan. Instead of going out for dinner, she had prepared a meal at home. Much to her relief, he was delighted. Her car was parked on the main street so, within a few minutes, they were inside her cottage – a secure haven for the young couple, away from prying eyes. The atmosphere: the glow of a log burner, the candles, the carefully prepared meal and the wine, all combined for an ideal setting. Marie directed Jack to the two-seater settee by the fire to wait until the meal was ready. Just as she was about to dish up there was a knock on the door. *Oh no*, Marie thought, *not now. Who can be calling at this time on a Friday evening?*

On opening the front door she came face-to-face with her parents. Before she had chance to utter a word, Chrissie stepped into the small entrance porch followed by Colin. The door into the living cum dining area was ajar.

"So it is true," Chrissie remarked, as she peered into the dimly lit room. There could be no doubt that everything had been organised for a romantic evening. Undeterred, the unwelcome visitors ventured inside forcing Marie to introduce them to a mystified Jack, who politely stood up to greet the intruders. He understood that Marie's parents had not arrived by invitation and, from the look of dismay on Marie's face, he would need to use all his powers of diplomacy to get through the next few minutes.

"I'm pleased to meet you," he stated in his unmistakable Australian accent, immediately revealing that he was a stranger to these parts. Marie coughed nervously. Neither she nor Jack made any attempt to make way for Chrissie and Colin to sit down: they remained resolutely standing where they were.

"Jack's a farmer from Australia," she explained, "He's spending a year in Scotland observing our farming methods and lecturing at the college in Edinburgh."

"I see," Chrissie acknowledged. "Yesterday, I was chatting with my neighbour, Mrs Nicholson. She said she had seen you in the town with a young man. We are on our way home from having tea with our good friends in Ettrick Bay so, thinking our neighbour must be mistaken, we decided to call in. Why didn't you mention that you had met such a charming gentleman?"

Marie read the sarcasm in her mother's tone. "I'm just about to serve dinner," she announced. "Jack has had a long day."

Colin, who was feeling rather more uncomfortable than his wife, took the hint.

"I think we should leave these young people to themselves."

"O-oh, yes of course," Chrissie concurred. "Perhaps you would like to come round for a coffee sometime tomorrow? I expect Jack will be staying here for the night."

"I will be returning to my bed and breakfast accommodation in Rothesay later this evening." Jack responded with a smile.

"O-oh, I see," Chrissie murmured, clearly embarrassed.

"I'll give you a ring in the morning," Marie said, as she escorted them to the door.

"Sorry about that," Marie apologised to Jack, who had resumed his seat in front of the fire.

"Not at all," he responded. "I was going to ask why you had not introduced me to your parents but having met them, I understand."

"I just wanted a little more time to ourselves before making any announcement."

"It's okay, really. Although perhaps we should accept their invitation to go round for a coffee tomorrow."

"Yes, I suppose you're right." Marie was, understandably, reluctant given that they had precious little time to be together.

"Cheer up," Jack cajoled, "don't let it spoil the rest of the evening. Now, is there anything I can do to help?"

"Just take a seat at the table. The meal's ready. I'll be through in a minute or two."

The rest of the evening went smoothly, as Marie had planned. The atmosphere was exactly right, setting the tone for their relationship to move forward naturally.

With the food, the wine, and the warmth, their desire could no longer be confined to a simple goodnight kiss on the cheek. However, both remained relatively controlled in their passion: there would be other times. As Jack left that night, it was as if an inner spark had been ignited; a mutual acceptance that they were meant for each other.

The next morning dawned bright and sunny. Marie had arranged to drive into the town to meet Jack. The visit to her parents was an interruption she could gladly have done without, but Jack was right: it would be most impolite to ignore Chrissie's request. They would stay only as long as was necessary to be courteous, Marie decided: she would agree to see them sometime during the week when her mother would no doubt quiz her for the full details of her new friend.

Surprisingly, the morning went rather well. No more assumptions were made about the depth of their friendship. Of course, her parents were interested to know where Jack was from, what he was doing in Bute and how the two had met. Jack, in turn, had questions to ask them, thus taking some of the pressure off himself. It seemed that their connections with the island were more tenuous than his own – a detail that he found quite amusing.

After scarcely an hour, the pair excused themselves without appearing disrespectful. They had planned a walk over the Moor Road, followed by lunch in a hotel at the south end of the island. "Will you be round to see us on Monday evening?" Chrissie asked Marie as they were leaving.

"Yes Mum," Marie responded, happily. In retrospect, she was glad that this meeting had occurred, admitting to herself that she had been feeling a little guilty at keeping her association with Jack from them.

The rest of the weekend passed all too quickly. "It won't always be like this," Jack promised, although just how they were going to manage the future, he could not contemplate. *It'll all work out*, he told himself, *something will turn up – it always does.*

When Marie called to see her parents on Monday evening, things were not quite as pleasant as they had been on Saturday morning. Many more answers were sought. Chrissie commented on how embarrassed she had felt to be told of her daughter's relationship second-hand, via a neighbour. Marie apologised. However, the barrage of questions that ensued caused her to feel less sorry as the evening progressed. "What are you thinking? Nothing can come of the relationship; Jack will return to Australia and forget about you; you're foolish to get involved." Her mother's warnings were relentless and demeaning, yet Marie refrained from defending her position. The warm feeling she'd had at the weekend, as Jack held her in his arms, outweighed all the jibes her mother tossed in her direction.

Her dad said little: he simply nodded in agreement at his wife's warnings. As he accompanied Marie out to her car, he patted her on the shoulder and whispered, "Your mother means well, she doesn't want you to get hurt, that's all."

It was her father's words that unsettled her more than all Chrissie's protestations. Nevertheless, the negative thoughts were dispelled when Jack telephoned just as she was ready to get into bed. He'd anticipated she might have a rough time.

"I'm okay," Marie assured him, "We'll talk about it at the weekend. There are things about my family that I'd like to share with you."

The following Friday, as they chatted over dinner in a restaurant, Marie disclosed to Jack as much as she knew of her family background. Previously all she had revealed was that she was adopted. He was as curious as Marie about the incidents surrounding her birth, especially the knowledge that Chrissie was her aunt – her father's older sister. Like Marie, he wondered that her adoptive parents had not kept in touch with her birth mother. A link, however tenuous, would surely have made sense. He understood Marie's frustration at being denied all contact with the family of her birth mother.

"I was seriously thinking about seeking answers myself when you came along and disrupted my life," she grinned.

Spontaneously, he added, "And, you've disrupted mine."

The next day, they walked over the hills at the north end of the island, arriving back at Marie's cottage late in the afternoon. She had invited Jack for a meal, which she had prepared before setting out in the morning. Within an hour, the log burner glowed in the hearth; a candle was set in the centre of the table; soft music played in the background. After the meal, as they snuggled down on the comfy sofa, talk of Marie's family was forgotten. The atmosphere was perfect. Jack placed his arm around her: they kissed; they embraced. The time was right. Jack did not return to the Bed and Breakfast accommodation that night.

Before leaving on Sunday, Jack cancelled his weekly booking with the landlady of the Bed and Breakfast. From now on he would stay with Marie. He also agreed to help her in her quest for her real family.

***

Although she could go straight to her adoptive parents to ask about her original birth certificate (she already had her adoption certificate), Marie decided that she would make her own enquiries. There was no point in upsetting her mother and father – or causing more grief for herself than was necessary. During the week she discovered that, in order to do so, she needed to contact the National Records of Adoption Unit in Edinburgh.

When she discussed things with Jack at the weekend, he suggested that she travel to Edinburgh on Friday and go into the office in person on Monday. It would be a chance for them to have a couple of days together in the capital providing, of course, she could have the time off work. Marie was delighted with the idea: meeting Jack away from the island appealed to her. She'd never been to Edinburgh.

The weekend went well and, with the original birth certificate in her possession, she had a renewed sense of her own existence, as well as the proof to go along with the search for her birth mother. Since the day she had confronted Chrissie, she knew that her surname was Milne, the same as her aunt's maiden name. However, she was surprised that her Christian name was Laura. She could live with that!

Although already aware of most of the details on her birth certificate, now that she owned a copy she was confident about accessing other documents – her parents' marriage certificate and their birth certificates, should she need to trace her ancestry further back. More importantly, perhaps, she might ascertain whether her mother had remarried. The more evidence she had to hand, the greater the chance of finding her maternal relatives.

Laura, Laura, she whispered softly to herself as she sat on the train on the journey from Edinburgh to Glasgow: she was intrigued. Other information included on the birth certificate was the place of her birth, the town of Fort William, and her mother's maiden name – Roberts. The person who registered the birth was not Ellie, but Rosa Roberts who, she concluded, had also resided in Fort William. From what Chrissie had said, she remembered that it was Rosa who had handed the baby over. In fact, it was Rosa who had done all the negotiating regarding the adoption. This was not surprising, given the state of Ellie's mind at the time of the birth. So, maybe she was further forward in her search than she first thought.

During the week, Marie toyed with her next steps in finding her mother. When she saw Chrissie and Colin on Wednesday she mentioned nothing of her discovery, although she did talk about her weekend in Edinburgh. Colin listened with interest. Chrissie was tight-lipped, indicating disapproval. Marie was sad that she was unable to be more open about her affairs – she would have liked to share things with her parents. If only they could be happy about her relationship with Jack, and her quest to find Ellie.

It was a relief to talk to Jack at the weekend. He was genuinely interested in helping her find her family, a circumstance that drew them even closer together. Equally, Marie was eager to learn about Jack's family in Australia, although that brought up the inevitable question: when would he have to return. "Don't think about it yet," Jack urged, "We have several months ahead. Let's cross that barrier when we come to it." But Marie was concerned.

The winter festive season was drawing close. They would have some time to spend together but it was hardly the time of year to be roaming around the country in search of Marie's past. Worryingly, Marie's parents would be expecting her to join them for some of the festivities. She hoped they would include Jack, as her partner, without a fuss. "Let's compromise," Jack suggested. "We could spend Christmas on Bute and Hogmanay in Edinburgh." That sounded fair enough to Marie, although she doubted that Chrissie would be of the same opinion. Rather than ask her parents Marie, emboldened by Jack, took a forthright approach.

"Jack's staying with me for Christmas," she announced. A statement that clarified the situation – Jack was no longer spending his time on Bute in a boarding house. "Would you like to come round to us on Christmas Day?"

Chrissie was taken aback by the invitation. Realising that Marie's tiny cottage was hardly suitable to accommodate four adults for dinner, she hesitated for a few moments before responding: "That's very kind of you my dear, but I think we should keep to our normal routine. You come to us as usual and bring Jack with you."

Before her mother had time to change her mind, Marie accepted. It was exactly the response she had hoped for. Chrissie could have been a little more gracious and added that Jack was welcome but perhaps that was too much to ask.

It wasn't the best Christmas Day that Marie had ever had, not that anything went badly wrong; more because she was on tenterhooks wondering if Chrissie would say something offensive. Thankfully, nothing awkward passed between them until, that is, around ten o'clock at night, just as they were leaving. "We'll be seeing you on Hogmanay," her mother, affirmed.

"Well, actually…" Marie began.

"We're celebrating the New Year in Edinburgh," Jack intercepted, coming to the rescue. He could see that Marie was feeling uncomfortable, wanting to avoid an unpleasant end to the evening.

"O-o-oh, I see," Chrissie failed to hide her annoyance.

"Goodnight Mum. Goodnight Dad," Marie kissed both her parents on the cheek.

Jack shook hands with them, "Thank you for a lovely day," he acknowledged politely.

Chrissie and Colin stayed by the open door as they watched their daughter and her Australian boyfriend make their way to the end of the road in the direction of Marie's country home. Colin smiled, "What will be will be," he muttered softly, turning to his wife. Chrissie said nothing – the tear in her eye reflected her disappointment.

Before leaving for the ferry, two days after Christmas, Marie and Jack called to say cheerio to her parents and wish them a good New Year. Hogmanay had always been a family affair, especially as it was Marie's birthday on the first of January. She understood her mother would be upset.

The rest of the holiday was a delight. Edinburgh was vibrant with almost 400,000 people turning up for the street party on Hogmanay – rather too many according to subsequent media coverage. Seeing the fireworks with the Castle in the background was spectacular. "A Happy New Year," they shouted in unison as the bells on the nearby church chimed in 1996. "And a very happy birthday to you!" Jack added.

The year was busy as well as emotional for the couple as their relationship deepened, making the separation every Sunday increasingly difficult. Most weekends Jack made the journey from Edinburgh to the

66

island. Now and again, Marie went through to Edinburgh. On one occasion, she again stayed over until Monday, visiting the Registrars and the National Records of Adoption, where she requested various family certificates and viewed her adoption records. She considered going to Fort William at Easter in the hope of tracing her birth mother, until Jack suggested they fly to Paris for a few days – to enjoy a real break. Paris in the springtime appealed to Marie. Searching for her family was put on hold until the summer.

When Marie returned from what had been an idyllic holiday in France's capital, she was alarmed to discover that her mother was in hospital following an angina attack. Colin had left a message on her answer phone, relaying the news. Marie returned his call immediately. "It's all right," he affirmed on hearing the distress in his daughter's voice. "Hopefully, your mother will be home tomorrow. It was a shock – a warning: she'll need to take things steady."

"Can I see her?" Marie asked.

"I'll give you a ring as soon as she's home," her father replied.

Marie had to be content with that, but she didn't settle until she'd visited Chrissie at home the following evening.

"I'll be fine," her mother assured her, "Really, it's nothing to worry about. I just need to rest, take things easy. I've been given medicine to help prevent any further attacks."

For the next few weeks Marie did worry but, as time passed, and Chrissie suffered no further attacks, her daughter began to relax.

CHAPTER 6
The Disappearance of Marie McInnes

The date was set for 5th July. Marie would travel to the Crieff Hydro where she would meet Jack and spend the night. Thereafter, they would travel to Fort William together to begin their search. Marie had rarely driven on roads off the island but by avoiding big cities and busy motorways she was prepared to tackle this relatively long journey.

Having made this arrangement, she received a letter from her old school friend, Anna Milne, asking if she might stay overnight on the 4th July and leave her car while she was away on holiday with her boyfriend. They were flying from Glasgow airport to the Costa Del Sol on 5th July returning on Friday 19th July.

Marie was tempted to say no, except that she'd put Anna off before and it seemed churlish to do so yet again. Besides, she would be leaving work early on the Thursday, so maybe it was as good a time as any. It was ten years since the two, who had been good friends at high school, had seen each other.

By the time Anna arrived, around mid-afternoon, Marie had prepared an evening meal. Her case, which had been packed several days earlier, was already in the boot of her car. She intended to have an early start in the morning. Not that there was any great hurry but, with her lack of confidence behind the wheel, she wanted to give herself plenty of time. The last few days she had been feeling queasy – worried about the journey, she was sure. Also, wondering whether or not she might meet her birth mother and, if she did, would her mother be pleased to see her? Maybe Ellie would not want to know.

The afternoon and evening spent with her friend was pleasant enough. Because Marie had moved to Bute the day after the end of the school term it had been a rushed good-bye. This was an ideal opportunity to catch up on the intervening years. Anna's life sounded exciting: living in Edinburgh for so many years, going to university, having several boyfriends. Anna was so refined, so neat, so well dressed – but then she always had been. Her cropped chestnut hair, though short, was not severe, sitting in natural waves, framing her unblemished features – Marie, by contrast, was casual, with her unruly mop of hair and weather-beaten looks. She felt a little inferior beside her sophisticated friend, lacking confidence. Her current circumstances unnerved her. She said nothing about Jack nor of her imminent quest to find her birth mother. She rambled on about her life on Bute, her hobbies. In retrospect, Anna must have thought her a complete bore. Maybe she would be feeling livelier when her friend returned in a fortnight. Then she could explain herself. Today, she really wasn't feeling well.

At around six o'clock in the morning the 'phone rang. Marie was already awake. She pulled on her dressing gown and dashed through to the living room. It was Jack. "Just checking to see if you're okay. I guessed you'd be up," came the friendly voice on the other end of the line.

"I'm fine," Marie lied. She felt terrible.

"I'm so looking forward to seeing you in Crieff. I should be there around seven o'clock. Drive carefully."

"Love you," she whispered.

"I love you too," he answered.

Marie replaced the receiver. Her stomach heaved: she rushed to the bathroom. It was a long time since she had been so sick. After a quick shower, she washed, dressed and made for the back door: she needed fresh air. Noises, like someone moving around, were coming from the guest room. *Anna,* she thought. *I can't cope with Anna.* She closed the door behind her and headed across the fields.

I'm pregnant – the idea hit her like a train. *No, no, I can't be,* she reasoned, *this is not happening.* Blackness crept across her as she slumped down beside some gorse bushes. How long she lay there she could not be sure. The nausea, the dizziness she had felt before she fainted, had receded, though she felt far from well. How was she going to drive all the way to Crieff? What would she say to Jack?

Recovering from her stupor, she remembered her friend. *Anna... I have to get back to take Anna down to the ferry terminal.* She hurried across the fields to the cottage in time to see Anna trudging down the road, lugging her suitcase. The nausea returned. She watched her friend disappear into the distance: helpless; petrified; unable to move from the spot, she let her go. *I'm a coward, a lousy coward*, she berated herself as she stepped into the house, collapsing onto the sofa. For ten minutes she stared out of the window. Her thoughts turned to Jack. *I have to get to Crieff. I promised to make an early start, to leave plenty of time.*

With renewed energy Marie stood up, went purposefully into her bedroom, tidied herself up, collected her bag and strode out to her car. The key turned easily in the lock. The engine sighed... and died. After several attempts, without success, Marie got out of her car intending to ring the local garage. On passing Anna's car, which was parked by the side of the house, she peered inside. The car keys were lying on the passenger seat. On impulse, she walked round to the driver's side, opened the door and slid onto the seat. She inserted the keys into the ignition. The car purred beautifully as the engine started up.

Without another thought, Marie retrieved her case from her own car, placed it in the boot of Anna's and set off to the small ferry at the north end of the island. She was across to the mainland, and well on her way towards Loch Lomond, before the seriousness of what she was doing struck her. Still, Anna wouldn't need her car for the next two weeks – maybe she wouldn't mind! It was hardly a justifiable excuse but it was enough for Marie to put the crime to the back of her mind and focus on more pressing problems. Was she really pregnant? Would she find Ellie Milne? Would she make it to Crieff? That thought prompted her to check the fuel gauge – it was hovering on empty. Her stomach churned. She was not

72

familiar with the road. Where was the next filling station? In sheer panic she pressed firmly on the clutch and coasted down the hill by the side of Loch Long to Arrochar. She was relieved to see a petrol sign on the left hand side of the road.

Noticing the range of snacks and drinks in the shop when she went into to pay for the fuel, it occurred to her that she had skipped breakfast. Now she was feeling hungry and thirsty. She grabbed a bottle of spring water, a packet of crisps and some chocolate. As she was getting into the car, another thought struck her – she had left her map, on which she had scribbled directions, in her own car. She made a quick search of Anna's car. In a pocket behind the front passenger seat she found an up-to-date AA Road Atlas of Great Britain. Breathing a sigh of relief, she drove the car away from the petrol pump, bringing it to rest on the grassy verge away from the tarmac area. She devoured the water and snacks, and studied the map for the next stage of the journey. *That's easy enough, – Loch Lomond to Crianlarich.* She would stop there to check the map again. The bendy road by the side of Loch Lomond was already busy with holiday traffic. Reaching the village of Crianlarich, about six miles north of the head of the loch, Marie noticed a car park and public toilets on the right hand side. She drew in: it was somewhere to freshen up and study the map for the last leg of the journey. Gazing in the mirror, she gasped at the sight of her ashen face – far from her usual healthy-looking complexion.

Maybe once I get to the hotel I'll feel better, she reasoned. So far, the journey had gone well but her nerves were on edge – she had never driven this distance before. *Just get on with it,* she admonished, as she made her way back to the car... Anna's car!

The sense of relief she felt on driving into the car park at the Crieff Hydro was palpable. *Thank goodness*, she sighed as she switched off the engine. Checking her watch, she was surprised to see that it was barely midday.

It was too early to check into the hotel so she decided to go for a walk. She needed some fresh air – seven hours was too long to hang around waiting, especially on such a beautiful summer's day. Grabbing her shoulder bag, she left the hotel grounds and strolled along the road in the direction of the town. As she was passing a bus stop, a bus marked 'Perth' drew up. She called to the driver, "How long to Perth?"

"Less than an hour," he answered.

Without further thought she boarded, requesting a return ticket. Lunch in Perth and a wander around the city seemed like a good way to pass the time. It was a luxury to admire the beautiful scenery without having to drive. However, all too soon her thoughts returned to reality. Was she pregnant? How could she justify taking her friend's car? What was she thinking?

By the time the bus reached Perth, she was so overcome with anxiety, she failed to notice that every one else was leaving the bus. "This is as far as we go," the driver called.

Jerked out of her reverie, Marie stood up and made her way to the open door at the front. She looked around, bewildered, as she stepped off the bus onto the pavement. Slowly, she began to walk towards what appeared to be the main street, making a conscious effort to move forward. A few minutes later, as earlier that morning, blackness encompassed her: she rocked backwards to the ground. But this time there was no grass to soften her fall – instead, she landed on hard concrete hitting the back of her head on a step. Her bag slid from her shoulder, scattering the contents across the path. She knew no more of that day…

CHAPTER 7
In Search of Marie McInnes

Jack Todd was excited. Although he had enjoyed his year at the agricultural college in Edinburgh, he looked forward to a break and, especially the next two weeks, which he would spend with the delightful young woman he had met on the Isle of Bute. She was a natural country girl who shared his love of the outdoors. He admired her aptitude on the farm, especially her skills working the sheep dogs. But, most of all... he loved her.

Despite the students having left, Jack's last day at the college was busy. By the time he made his escape, it was a rush to get to the station in time for the train he had intended to catch. Much to his frustration, the train was delayed along the way resulting in a late arrival into Perth. He missed a bus to Crieff by a matter of seconds. "That's it!" he sighed in exasperation turning to a nearby taxi rank. He wasn't waiting for the next bus. Even by taxi he would barely make it to the hotel by seven o'clock.

When he arrived at the Crieff Hydro, he was surprised to discover that Marie had not yet booked in. He had given her all the details, yet there was no sign of her. The staff at the reception desk assured him that no one by the name of Marie McInnes had checked in. He scoured the car park in search of her car. Finding no sign of it, he became anxious. *Wherever can she be? Surely she should be here by this time*. He returned to their room, where he remained for the next hour, hoping she would appear at any moment. Back at the hotel entrance hall, he expressed his concern at the reception desk. A member of staff offered to assist him in looking around the car park for her red Ford Fiesta. Jack could not recall the registration number. However, there was no car of that make and colour.

Worried, and at a loss as what to do, Jack decided to call Marie's home number. Unsurprisingly, there was no response. In desperation, he called her parents. Sounding as casual as possible, he asked if Marie was there. "Marie's friend from Fort William is staying with her," came the reply. "Maybe they have gone out for the evening."

"Her friend was leaving this morning," Jack stated. "Marie was meeting me at the Crieff Hydro this evening. She hasn't turned up."

"O-oh, I see. Well, she didn't mention that to us," Chrissie was baffled. "Are you sure?"

"I'm certain," Jack confirmed. "I rang early this morning. Look, if you hear from her can you let me know?"

Jack gave the telephone number of the hotel along with his room number.

Later that evening, once the significance of Jack's 'phone call registered and there was no response when they rang their daughter, Chrissie and Colin drove to her cottage. There was no one at home. Marie's car was on the driveway. They assumed that she would have travelled by train and bus to Crieff: Jack had said nothing about her driving. Had they thought she had gone by car, they would have had more cause to be worried. They decided to wait until the next day before contacting Jack.

It was Colin who returned Jack's call at around nine o'clock the following morning. "There's no sign of Marie here," he affirmed, "Her car is on the drive where she normally leaves it."

There was a brief silence on the other end of the line before Jack responded. "You say her car is still there. Are you sure?"

"Of course I'm sure," came the blunt response.

"She was supposed to be driving here," Jack answered. A longer silence followed.

"We'll check her cottage again. I'll get back to you if there's any news."

Now it was the turn of Chrissie and Colin to be worried. Why hadn't Marie told them of her intentions? "Too much nonsense in her head about this Australian guy," Chrissie voiced, "I warned her that no good would come of it... silly girl!"

"That's enough Chrissie," her husband interjected, "Marie isn't a child any more, she's a young woman."

When her parents visited Marie's cottage that morning they took a thorough look around. A calendar on the kitchen wall showed various events. Anna's name appeared on Thursday – the day before yesterday. Yesterday's date was marked 'Crieff' and on Friday, two weeks ahead, 'Anna returning from Spain', was scribbled in pencil. Chrissie knew that Anna was a friend from Fort

William. Apparently, she was staying with Marie on her way to the airport.

A few unwashed dishes were in the sink: some unused crockery and cutlery was on the table, along with a packet of cornflakes, sugar, milk and a pot, half-full of cold tea. The bed in the spare bedroom was neatly made up. Marie's bed was unmade, and several items of clothing were strewn around. *Nothing unusual there*, Chrissie said to herself. Marie's car was unlocked. A map, with the route from Bute to Crieff marked in red pen, lay on the front passenger seat. So, as Jack said, she was intending to drive to Crieff.

Colin 'phoned Jack again. He confirmed that they had visited Marie's cottage. It appeared that she was ready to travel by car but, since there was no luggage either in the house or in the car, maybe she had changed her mind and decided to go by train instead. It was a mystery.

"I'm worried," Jack declared. "I think it's time to inform the police and ring round some hospitals."

"I'll contact the police here, and get in touch with the infirmary in Glasgow," Colin offered.

"Thanks, I'll make enquiries here," Jack confirmed.

Jack spoke with the hotel receptionist, explaining the problem and requesting he stay at least one more night.

"I'll book you in for tonight and keep the room available for as long as required. You can use the hotel 'phone to ring round the hospitals and contact the police.

It will save the expense of dialling out from your room."
The receptionist directed Jack to a telephone in an office
behind the reception desk. Voicing her concern, she
added, "Please let us know if you need any help. If your
partner has been involved in an accident she would
probably have been taken to the hospital in Dundee.
Perhaps you should try there first."

Jack nodded in thanks. There was a directory next
to the office telephone. He phoned Ninewells Hospital in
Dundee, as the receptionist had suggested. No one by the
name of Marie McInnes had been admitted. Instead of
ringing the police, Jack decided to visit the police station
in Crieff to report Marie as missing. The officer in charge
took the details. He agreed to make enquiries, suggesting
that Jack call in again later in the day. Leaving the police
station, Jack wandered around Crieff. Never in his life
had he felt so helpless – so alone. He bought a local
newspaper and went into a café where he found a seat at
the only vacant table. It was by the window, looking
directly out onto the street. He'd have preferred to hide
away in a corner at the back where he could wallow in his
misery. Here, he was exposed to the world, or so it
seemed. A waitress approached to take his order. "Are
you all right, sir?" she enquired.

"Y-y-yes," he stuttered, "I'm just a bit tired. Can
you get me a black coffee please?"

Jack stared out of the window, sipping the hot
bitter liquid. He glanced at the headlines in the
newspaper, but couldn't concentrate to read any further.
When he left the café, he tucked the paper under his arm

thinking he would look at it later. Back at the hotel, there was still no sign of Marie. He paced his room… agitated, despairing. *Where is she? What has happened to her? Somebody must know?*

It was mid-afternoon when Jack returned to the police station, desperate for news. There wasn't any. The officer explained that the matter had been referred to the headquarters in Glasgow, since that was closer to her home on Bute. As far as could be ascertained, it was from there that she had disappeared.

"What about her friend, Anna?" Jack asked.

"They are checking that out," the officer responded. "It is understood that she intended to fly to Spain from Glasgow airport on Friday. There's no more news."

Later in the afternoon Jack 'phoned Marie's parents. As well as contacting the infirmary in Glasgow, Colin went to the Victoria Hospital on the island. Neither had any information on Marie. The police in Glasgow were back in touch with Colin before he'd got around to ringing them. Officers would be sent to the island the following day, Sunday, to check out Marie's cottage and her car. Colin arranged to meet them at the property.

"I'll stay here for the next day or two," Jack confirmed, "just in case she turns up."

On Tuesday, when there was still no sign of Marie at Crieff, Jack went back to his apartment in Edinburgh, giving Marie's parents his contact telephone number. Colin promised to keep him abreast of any developments; Chrissie was so shaken, she had taken to her bed. The police had turned up on Sunday to make a thorough search of Marie's cottage. They had also interviewed several neighbours, as well as the manager of the farm where she worked. He had confirmed that Marie was on a fortnight's leave, but had not mentioned anything about going away. One couple, living in a cottage half a mile away, had seen a silver estate car parked by the side of the building on Friday afternoon. Nobody knew anything of Marie's movements over the last few days, nor was anyone aware of her plans for a holiday. After all their checks, the police concluded that her friend, Anna Milne, was the last person on the island to have had any contact with her.

Jack decided to visit the police headquarters in Glasgow. Although they were unable to reveal much more than he already knew, they were keen to interview him. The police wanted to know everything about Jack's relationship with Marie, from the time they first met until the arrangements they had made to meet at the hotel in Crieff. At the close of the interview, the officer in charge thanked him for his cooperation, before adding, "Please let us know if you think of anything else, Mr Todd. We will question Anna Milne as soon as she returns from Spain. Until then, there isn't much more we can do."

Jack sighed as he left the interview room. With more than a week to go, he wondered how he would cope. As he sat on the train on his way back to Edinburgh, pondering over the meeting, something occurred him. The police had referred to Anna Milne: the name sounded familiar. He puzzled over it, trying to think where he had heard it before. It wasn't until he was back in his flat that he remembered. It was the name on Marie's original birth certificate. Her birth name was Laura Milne. Was there any significance in that or was it merely a coincidence?

CHAPTER 8
Freddie

Saturday 13th July 1996

Freddie was nineteen years old. He was a lively lad, a bit of a chancer. Currently, he assisted in the kitchen at the Crieff Hydro – chopping vegetables, clearing up, washing pots and pans – all the menial tasks that typically befall a potential trainee; he was hoping for better things in the future. It was a Saturday, supposedly his day off, since young students were often available to work at weekends. However, he had been cajoled into covering until lunchtime. That was before he had learned that there was a gig on at a club in Stirling where his friend, Duncan, was playing and singing in a folk group. Duncan had offered to give Freddie a lift from Perth in the afternoon, and back to his home, between Perth and Crieff, after the event. Freddie didn't have a car, although he had recently passed his driving test.

During the last week, Freddie had noticed a silver Nissan Sunny parked under some trees in a corner of the hotel car park. It was now covered in bird droppings. *Maybe it's abandoned*, he thought. On his way into the hotel that morning he had a snoop around. He tried the car door, which to his surprise was unlocked. "Mmm," he murmured, "I don't even need to break in." He made a decision. *If the car is still here in the afternoon when my shift ends, I'll 'borrow' it and drive to Perth.*

As he had predicted the car, looking dirtier than ever, was in the same place. He opened the door and slid into the driving seat. Before attempting to start the engine with a piece of wire, he rooted around, just in case the owner had left the key inside. No luck, but no problem. He started the car, reversed, and headed for the exit. As he drove along the A85 to Perth he whistled a lively tune, thoroughly pleased with himself. He'd done a bit of shoplifting in his youth, but never anything as ambitious as this. It gave him a thrill. *Well, at least I'm partially legal*, he argued smugly. *I do have a driving licence.*

Not wishing to advertise his criminal activity to his friend, he parked the car at the railway station. It wasn't far to Duncan's home.

The gig was a great success. The group was much more proficient since Freddie had last heard them play. He was glad that he had made the effort to be there. Despite not leaving until almost midnight, Duncan was happy to take Freddie home, as promised. It had crossed Freddie's mind that he could save his friend the trouble by telling him about the car, but that would have left him with a lot of explaining to do. So, the car was left abandoned at Perth railway station.

CHAPTER 9
Detective Sergeant Boyle

Friday 5th July 1996

The emergency team at Ninewells Hospital was on alert as the ambulance came to a halt outside the main entrance. A young woman had been found lying on the pavement in the centre of Perth. She was unconscious. A passerby had picked up her bag and collected some of the contents that were scattered across the pavement and the road. She handed the bag, complete with the items gathered, to a paramedic. According to an onlooker, who had seen the woman topple backwards, she had hit her head on a step as she fell. On examination at the hospital, the patient was found to be suffering from concussion as a result of a bang to the back of her head. Since the injury matched up with the evidence from this witness, no one else appeared to have been involved.

Searching the woman's handbag for some form of identification, the only relevant documentation was a birth certificate, tucked safely into an inner zipped pocket. It was assumed, therefore, that the victim of the mishap was Laura Milne. After the examination, the patient was moved into intensive care where her condition would be carefully monitored.

By Monday, Marie McInnes, or Laura Milne as she was known at the hospital, remained in a coma. Nobody had made any enquiries concerning a Miss Milne, so the details, as far as they were known, were passed onto the police in Perth. A fax of the birth certificate was sent directly from the hospital. Nobody bearing that name had been reported as missing. A police investigator used the information from the document in an endeavour to trace the woman's mother. An enquiry to locate a Mrs Ellie Milne in or around Fort William proved unsuccessful. Maybe Ellie Milne had re-married. Indeed that was more likely than not as Laura's birth certificate showed that her father had died before she was born. Before following that up, the investigator searched the telephone directory and the electoral role for 'Roberts'. Roberts, according to the birth certificate was Ellie's maiden name. An Audrey Roberts was found to be living close to the town centre. Could this person be Ellie Milne's mother? He picked up the receiver to dial her number.

"Hello, Audrey Roberts speaking," came the refined tone of an elderly lady.

"I'm so sorry to bother you Mrs Roberts. This is Detective Sergeant Boyle. I'm trying to locate Ellie Milne."

"Oh, I see," Audrey Roberts, replied, "Ellie is my daughter."

"It's all right, Mrs Roberts," the investigator responded, sensing the concern in her voice, "I'm sure it's nothing to worry about but we do need to speak with your daughter."

"If you give me your number I will ask Ellie to return your call as soon as possible." There was no chance that Audrey Roberts would provide any details about her daughter to a stranger, especially over the telephone. In addition, she failed to enlighten him that her daughter was no longer Ellie Milne, but Ellie Scott.

Although slightly disappointed that he did not, as yet, have any knowledge of Ellie's whereabouts – he must rely on *her* contacting him – the investigator had, at least, found Laura Milne's family, or so he believed.

It was not until the middle of the afternoon that Detective Boyle received the call he was waiting for. On answering the 'phone, an anxious woman responded hesitatingly. "My mother said you needed to speak to me."

"Yes, Mrs… Milne?" he questioned.

"It's Scott, Ellie Scott," she corrected, "Can I help you?"

"It's your daughter, Laura, Mrs Scott. Last Friday she fell. She is in hospital in Dundee."

"Who did you say?"

"Laura, your daughter, Laura Milne," the investigator emphasised.

"My daughter is Anna, I don't know of a Laura. You must be mistaken."

"B-b-but I have evidence," Detective Boyle insisted.

"Have you spoken to this woman, this Laura Milne," Ellie asked.

"N-n-no, she's still unconscious from the fall."

"I'm sorry. I can't help you, Mr Boyle." The 'phone went dead.

Detective Sergeant Boyle was dumbfounded. He took another look at the birth certificate – a close look. There could be no mistake. The name on the certificate was Laura Milne, the mother Ellie Milne, nee Roberts. How could Ellie Scott, as she was now known, not be Laura's mother? He shook his head. He consulted his colleagues – maybe he was missing something. There was another person named on the certificate, a Rosa Roberts. She had registered the birth. Surely she must be a relative. But how could he contact her without going back to Ellie? The afternoon was drawing to a close: he would reconsider the matter in the morning.

Meanwhile, still in the intensive care unit at Ninewells Hospital, Marie McInnes remained in a coma, oblivious to the misunderstanding surrounding her identity. "Poor lass," the sister in charge commented to her fellow nurses. "It seems that no one has missed her."

"Or, maybe they are looking in the wrong places," a colleague countered.

"It seems rather odd that there was no bankcard, driving licence or money in her bag," the sister remarked, "Surely she would have carried a wallet and the keys to her home."

Of course, the nurse was correct in her assumption. Marie did have other items in her bag before it slipped from her shoulder as she fell. Unfortunately, she wasn't having a good day – her keys skidded a few feet along the road and into a drain. The supposedly thoughtful lady, who gathered most of the contents and replaced them in the bag before handing it to the paramedic, was not quite so generous after all. While others stopped to assist the injured woman, she dropped the victim's wallet into her own open shopping bag.

The following morning, having come to terms with the problem of the birth certificate, Detective Boyle considered his next move. Plucking up courage, he telephoned Ellie Scott. This, he decided, would be the quickest way to locate Rosa Roberts, provided Mrs Scott was amenable.

"It's Detective Boyle here. I'm so sorry to bother you again, Mrs Scott," he began. "I'm trying to locate Rosa Roberts. I wondered if you would be able to help."

Having reflected on the conversation of the previous afternoon, Ellie was somewhat ashamed of her abrupt response to the detective. It had crossed her mind that he was simply trying to find the family of this unfortunate woman lying unconscious in hospital. The least she could do was cooperate. How would she feel if it was her daughter?

"Rosa is my sister," she responded. "Her married name is Marshall. I'm sure she wouldn't mind you contacting her."

The detective took down the telephone number for Rosa Marshall, thanked Ellie Scott, and replaced the receiver. He sighed. Maybe now he was getting somewhere.

Rosa was not at home when the detective 'phoned, so he left a message on her answer machine. Unfortunately, when she responded, he was not available. The receptionist apologised saying the detective was out of the office: he would be back at his desk in the morning.

In the meantime, Rosa had a call from Ellie who told her about the enquiries concerning a Laura Milne. "He thought that I might be her mother."

"So, what does that have to do with me?" Rosa asked, trying to sound casual.

"I've no idea," Ellie replied. "I told him he was mistaken, that my daughter was Anna Milne. "I suppose he's just doing his job." She paused before adding, "Should I have told him anything else?" Rosa said nothing.

Rosa Marshall was unsettled. She decided to avoid any communication with this detective. After all, she had returned his call so she could not be accused of ignoring him. It wasn't her fault that he was out of his office. During the next few days, Detective Boyle made several unsuccessful attempts to talk to Rosa, never getting beyond the answer 'phone. Towards the end of the week, frustrated at his failed efforts to make contact, he decided to visit her at home. Ascertaining her address near Fort William was not a problem. He left Perth around mid-day on Friday, determined to talk to this woman. There was something very strange about this whole affair.

He was not too surprised that no one was at home when he arrived. However, if Rosa and her husband were at work they would, no doubt, return by late afternoon. He settled in his car with a newspaper, prepared to wait for as long as it took. An hour later a BMW turned into the driveway. A smartly dressed gentleman, probably in his sixties, emerged from the vehicle and entered the house. The detective remained in his car for a further fifteen minutes to allow Mr Marshall, assuming that was who he was, a little time before interrupting him.

As he walked purposefully towards the front door, he was hopeful of a positive outcome. He introduced himself with an apology for calling at this hour on a Friday afternoon. "I would like to speak with Mrs Marshall, you're erm…" he hesitated, " her husband?" he enquired.

"Yes, that's right. I'm Bernard Marshall. Do come in. Can I get you a cup of tea? I take it you've travelled quite a distance?"

"Yes please, Mr Marshall. That would be much appreciated. I've come over from Perth."

"Oh, please call me Bernard. And you are?"

"Henry, Henry Boyle."

"Please have a seat," Bernard invited, indicating an armchair in the corner of the lounge. "I'll be with you in a few minutes."

Detective Boyle was bemused. It was as if this gentleman was expecting him. As he waited, he gazed around the room, admiring the exquisite décor, the elegant furnishings and exotic paintings: this was an affluent home.

Once Bernard Marshall returned with the tea, along with some refreshments, the two gentlemen settled down to business. "I really need to see your wife," the detective began. "We were hoping that she might be able to help us with our investigations regarding her niece."

"I'm not long home. Rosa left a message on the answer phone. Apparently, Anna contacted her from the police headquarters in Glasgow. I don't know the full story, Henry, but her niece is very upset. Since her car was found abandoned and is currently impounded, Rosa offered to drive down to bring her home. I'm not sure when she will be back.

"You say her niece's name is Anna?"

"Yes, that's right."

"She doesn't have a niece called Laura."

Bernard looked puzzled. "No," he responded, "just Anna."

Henry sighed. "It seems there has been a misunderstanding. I am searching for the relatives of a young woman by the name of Laura Milne, who is currently lying unconscious in hospital in Dundee. I am so sorry to have taken up your time." He shuffled in his seat, ready to make a move.

"Please don't apologise, Henry. I'm sorry you've had a wasted journey, but there is no need to rush away."

For the next twenty minutes or so the two men chatted casually. Bernard, it transpired, was a retired barrister, although his services were called upon now and again. His wife Rosa, a midwife, was also retired. The couple married quite late in life and had no family of their own. Rosa doted on her only niece. Henry revealed little of his family life but spoke of his hobbies: he was a keen golfer and fisherman.

Driving home to Perth, Henry Boyle remained puzzled: none of this seemed to make sense. Why had Rosa Roberts registered the birth of Laura Milne who, according to the certificate, along with his enquiries, appeared to be her niece? Yet, those he had spoken to denied any knowledge of this woman. By the time he reached his home near Perth he was tired. He ordered a takeaway from the local Chinese restaurant and had an early night. It was the weekend – he would relax, forget about this confusing case, and come back refreshed on Monday morning. However, that was not to be…

His weekend was interrupted by a 'phone call from the hospital in Dundee, which cut short his leisure time. The young woman, assumed to be Laura Milne, had emerged from her coma late on Friday evening. His presence was required. Two minutes later, and he would have missed the call. He was already on his way out when the telephone rang.

As soon as he reported to the reception desk at Ninewells Hospital, he was escorted to a private room where Marie McInnes was sitting up in bed, looking pale and considerably weakened by her ordeal. Understandably, she was alarmed to wake up in the unfamiliar surroundings of a hospital ward and even more perturbed to be told she had been there for two weeks. Dazed at first, the patient was encouraged to rest as she recovered consciousness. By the time the detective arrived at her bedside on Sunday morning, she had recalled the day of the accident. Her mind was now focused on escaping from her hospital bed and seeing Jack, but no one was listening.

"Good morning Laura," Henry greeted her with a friendly smile as he entered the room. Seeing her puzzled look, he hesitated… "It is Laura, isn't it?"

"No, it isn't," she countered. "Why does everyone in here insist on calling me Laura? I'm Marie, Marie McInnes."

"Do forgive me," Henry apologised.

"I want my Jack," Marie retorted. "Where is he?"

Henry sat back, looking sadly at this young woman who was obviously very confused. "Perhaps you could tell me what you remember before you found yourself in here. I will do everything I can to help. I'm a detective. I've been trying to find your relatives."

Marie emphasised her name was Marie McInnes – she lived on the Isle of Bute. Her parents, Colin and Chrissie McInnes, also lived on the Island: they were the only relatives she had ever known. The detective jotted the address down in his notebook. After establishing these facts, Marie proceeded to relay her movements on the day she had left her home and headed for the Crieff Hydro to meet up with her boyfriend, Jack Todd. The last thing she remembered was stepping off the bus in Perth and feeling dizzy.

Although Marie was quite specific about her movements, there were important details that she failed to disclose in her narrative. She made no mention of abandoning her friend, 'borrowing' her friend's car, or the real purpose of her journey – in pursuit of her birth

96

family. Neither did she refer to her presumed pregnancy. Why should she? After all, she didn't know this detective – this stranger. She desperately wanted the man she loved… and her parents. She was feeling guilty that she had not informed them of her intentions, but she had expected to be home within a fortnight. She needed to return Anna's car. *Anna,* she thought. *Anna was due back on Friday, the day before yesterday.*

Marie ended her tale and asked abruptly, "Where are my belongings? I had a shoulder bag when I fell."

Henry stood up immediately, "I'll ask," he stated decisively. A few minutes later he returned with a nurse who retrieved the bag from the bottom of the locker beside the bed.

Marie rummaged through before tipping the entire contents onto the bed. "Things are missing," she affirmed, glaring at Henry and failing to disguise her anger.

"As far as I know, your bag was handed to a paramedic at the scene of the accident. It must have slipped from your shoulder when you fell."

Marie was barely listening. "My keys are not here, and neither is my wallet!" she exclaimed. It was then that she remembered her birth certificate. She'd placed it safely in the zipped compartment inside the bag. It was still there.

"That explains it!" she breathed a sigh of relief, but said nothing more.

"Explains what?" the detective queried.

"Oh nothing," she replied. "It's just a birth certificate. I am interested in family history."

Henry decided not to pursue the matter further. Marie was not a suspect: she was simply the victim of an unfortunate mishap. "Would you like me to ask for a telephone to be brought to your room? I realise you are anxious to ring your boyfriend and your parents. Do you know their numbers?"

"Yes please," Marie smiled. "And yes, I know the numbers."

Henry located a nurse to request a telephone for Marie to make a couple of calls. "The nurse will bring a telephone to you in a few minutes," he assured her when he returned to her room. "I've notified the staff that you are Marie McInnes, so there'll be no more confusion. Please do not hesitate to call if you have any further problems." He handed her his card as he said 'goodbye', wishing her well.

Detective Henry Boyle stood outside the hospital entrance pondering his next move. Marie McInnes was on the missing person's list: he would have to inform the headquarters in Glasgow that she was in Ninewells Hospital in Dundee. Henry's mission was to locate the relatives of the young woman thought to be Laura Milne. He had endeavoured to do that, and failed… or had he? He was perplexed. Now, it was irrelevant since the woman in question had regained consciousness, and claimed not to be the person he thought she was. Further, it was not his job to investigate the disappearance of Laura Milne – although it was obvious that there was a connection. This morning was not the time for him to hassle the recovering patient with problems of mistaken identity. He decided to drive home to Perth before contacting Glasgow, thereby giving Marie time to get in touch with her boyfriend and her parents before being confronted with more investigators.

Marie rang Jack Todd first. The relief on hearing her voice was palpable. "I'll be on the next train to Dundee," he promised. He asked no questions – there would be time for that later.

As soon as she put the telephone down, she picked it up again to 'phone her parents. She was surprised that her father answered the call. "Where are you? We've been so worried. You're mother is ill thinking about what might have happened to you. It's been almost a fortnight."

"I'm fine, Dad," Marie assured him. "I fell and knocked myself out. I was taken to hospital. I've only just woken up."

The questions kept coming. Her father wanted to know everything. Where was she? Why had she not told them she was going away? How did she get there? They would come to Dundee and bring her home.

"No, no," Marie objected, "Jack's already on his way here. I will come home as soon as they release me from hospital."

Her father insisted she get in touch with them again later in the day to speak to her mother. Marie sighed as she replaced the receiver. Her father was normally quite calm about things – it was her mother who made a fuss. Now she knew why she didn't tell her parents everything that was going on in her life!

It seemed an eternity to Marie, lying in her hospital bed, waiting for Jack. At last he appeared at the door, looking thinner and scruffier than she remembered: he was unshaven. She regarded him warily as he approached her bed, trying to read his thoughts. Was he angry? Then, he smiled – a warm, broad smile. She relaxed, opening her arms to welcome him.

After a long hug and a kiss, he released his grip. "You could do with a shave," Marie commented, with a grin.

Jack looked down at himself. "I'm so sorry, I left the flat in a hurry as soon as you called. I grabbed my bag, which was by the door, already packed. I'll tidy myself up later."

For more than an hour the two of them chatted, sharing the events of the last two weeks. Marie spoke of the anxiety she had felt on the morning she left her home, deserting her friend, then taking her car. "Anna!" she exclaimed. "I left her car in the hotel car park in Crieff, I must get in touch with her. I'm so sorry – I shouldn't have taken her car." Marie shuffled uncomfortably in her bed, sitting up straight. "I have to get out of here. I felt so ill that morning, so anxious about everything. Then, when I threw up, I thought I must be pregnant… but I'm not pregnant. I was desperate to see you."

"Anna's car was found at the railway station in Perth," Jack informed her. "You didn't drive it there?" he questioned.

"No, no, I told you. I took the bus to Perth. When I stepped off the bus, I felt terrible – really dizzy and sick – I don't remember anything after that, until I woke up last night," she confirmed.

Jack decided he should tell Marie about Anna. He knew that she had been stopped at the airport in Glasgow on her way home from Spain.

Marie's face turned even paler on hearing this news, "What have I done?"

"Calm down," Jack consoled, "Anna was the last person to see you on Bute before you disappeared. Naturally, the police wanted to question her."

Marie flopped back on her pillow. She wanted to disappear, to hide away until all this was sorted.

"I'm going to find a washroom," Jack announced. "I won't be long. I need to tidy up; to have a shave."

He also needed to find a 'phone. Talk of Anna reminded him that he must contact the police headquarters in Glasgow to let them know he had found the missing Marie McInnes. However, by the time he rang, they were already aware of the situation. Detective Boyle had reached them first.

When Jack returned to Marie's room, she was looking a bit brighter. "I'm not staying here a moment longer than I have to," she announced.

"You're not going anywhere until the doctor sees you tomorrow morning," Jack retorted. "I want to be sure that you're okay. We've all been so worried about you."

"You've been in touch with my parents?" she eyed him suspiciously.

"Of course I have. When there was no sign of you at the Crieff Hydro, and you weren't at home, I had to 'phone them."

"They don't like you," Marie stated defiantly.

"They think I'm going to whisk you off to Australia," Jack answered.

"And are you?" Marie gazed helplessly into his eyes.

"We'll talk about that later. Let's get you better first."

On Monday morning, after seeing the doctor, Marie was discharged from hospital. Jack accompanied her to the Isle of Bute where, he insisted, their first priority was to visit her parents. Marie was reluctant. However, it was not quite the ordeal she had anticipated. Chrissie was so relieved that her daughter was safe and well, she was just pleased to see her. Colin asked no more questions about Marie's disappearance: more questions seemed irrelevant now that she was home. Further, both parents showed a respect for Jack that had not been evident previously. There was no longer tension in the air. Nevertheless, Marie was thankful to be back in her own cottage. With Jack by her side, she was able to relax and enjoy the fresh air. For a few days, they were on holiday on this idyllic island that, at least for the time being, was her home.

CHAPTER 10
Rosa to the Rescue

Friday 19th July

As Anna stared at the walls of the cell in the police station, waiting for her aunt, she contemplated the events of the last fortnight. When she had arrived on Bute, Marie was welcoming. It seemed to her that they enjoyed each other's company, recollecting their schooldays and catching up on the ten years that had passed since. Yet there were moments when Marie appeared distant. Was something bothering her? Was she preoccupied? And why was there little reference to relationships? Surely she must have friends on the island. Most puzzling of all, where did she go the next morning? Her concern for Marie had turned to annoyance, as she struggled into Rothesay with her luggage. But by the time she boarded the ferry, her uneasiness had returned. Surely her friend would not have abandoned her deliberately?

Her thoughts then turned to William. The holiday in Spain was pleasant enough, but from the start she was beginning to have her doubts. There were times when he came across as loving and caring, behaving as the perfect gentleman. But there were other times when he seemed to dismiss her. During the entire fortnight, she was never able to communicate her concerns about her old school friend. Ultimately, she concluded that he didn't want to know. She did her best to engage when he talked endlessly about his daughter whom she had yet to meet.

He insisted he wanted to keep that part of his life separate, yet why did he obsess so much about the girl in her presence? Her greatest concern was his lack of support right now when she needed him most. Why had he left her at the airport? She understood that he was looking after his daughter over the weekend, yet surely he could have contacted his ex-wife to let her know he had been delayed. *He has no consideration for me*, she concluded. *Why was I so foolish as to get involved?*

By mid-afternoon, Anna was becoming increasingly anxious. Then, around four o'clock, her Aunt Rosa arrived, entering the room accompanied by a police officer. She strode towards her niece, who stood up to greet her. "Thank goodness you're here!" Anna exclaimed, as Rosa hugged her tightly.

Rosa turned to the officer, "Is my niece under arrest?" she asked.

"W-w-well, yes," he replied.

"You don't sound too sure. Was my niece questioned in the presence of a witness?"

"N-n-no,"

"In that case, please leave us alone." Rosa sounded so officious, Anna almost jumped to attention. Left alone, Rosa very gently coaxed Anna to explain exactly what had happened.

"Mmm," she mused, "they don't have much evidence. All they know – or think they know – is that you were the last person to see Marie on the island. They imagine you drove from Bute to Perth, got rid of your friend on route, left your car at the railway station, and took the train from Perth to Glasgow airport."

"I suppose so"

"And what do they think you did with Marie?"

"They didn't say."

"Of course they didn't say," Rosa was cross. "They've no idea what happened to Marie and they don't have sufficient evidence to detain you." Anna was weakening. Tears welled up in her eyes. "Don't worry lass, I'll have you out of here in no time."

Rosa exited the cell into the corridor where the police officer was standing on guard. "Take me to your superior," Rosa demanded, "I'm taking Anna out of here."

Within fifteen minutes Rosa was back. "You were detained for questioning, you are not under arrest. We're going to collect your things. I'm taking you home."

Anna sighed deeply, attempted a smile through her tears, and left with her aunt, asking no questions. She was just grateful that Rosa had come to her rescue. At the moment, nothing else mattered.

They were well away from the city before either of them spoke, both relieved and deep in thought. "I expect you're feeling hungry," Rosa commented, "I don't suppose you've had much to eat since you landed at the airport."

"No, I haven't. They did bring me some food, but I was too upset to eat. You're right, I am feeling a little peckish."

"We'll stop for a meal. I know a nice little restaurant not far from here." Within ten minutes, Rosa pulled into a car park outside a hotel. A notice at the entrance indicated that meals were being served. "This is perfect," she remarked.

At last the two women were able to relax, free from the constraints of a police cell. It had been a traumatic day for them both. Now, for the first time, Anna was able to relay her tale in a calm manner, beginning with the day she had left her home in Fort William more than two weeks ago. Rosa made little comment about Anna's short stay with Marie, except to agree that her friend's disappearance the following morning seemed odd. However, she did have plenty to say about William West. Despite not having been introduced to the man, she had long had her suspicions about her niece's latest boyfriend. From the way Anna spoke of him, she doubted that he was serious about the relationship. Listening to her recall his behaviour on holiday convinced her that her reservations were well founded. Nevertheless, she refrained from expressing her opinion – at least, that is, until hearing that he had deserted the poor girl at the airport without so much as a good-bye.

"Are you telling me he just walked away and left you!" her aunt exclaimed.

"Yes, that sums it up," Anna replied.

"It sums him up!" Aunt Rosa gasped in horror.

Anna looked away, her eyes once again filled with tears. Her aunt was right, of course.

106

It was dark before they arrived in Fort William. Bernard would be anxious to see his wife safely back from her mission. Anna declined Rosa's invitation to stay with them overnight, insisting that she wanted to get back to her own home. She needed time to herself to recover from her ordeal. Rosa understood.

Anna felt strangely deflated on entering her apartment – a sense of loneliness crept over her. There were no messages on her answer 'phone. Not that she imagined there would be any. Her mother hadn't been expecting her to return for a few days and maybe Rosa hadn't told her about her call from the police station. It was too much for Anna to hope that William would have tried to contact her. As she lay in bed contemplating her first holiday abroad, she decided it hadn't matched up to her expectations. *What a disaster!* Yet, to her surprise, despite the events of the last twelve hours whizzing around in her head, she soon fell asleep.

The next day, Saturday, she busied herself: unpacking; washing and ironing; generally pottering around. Shortly after mid-day on Sunday the telephone rang. It was a police officer from the headquarters in Glasgow, an official call informing her that Marie McInnes had been found safe and well, followed by a brief apology for any inconvenience caused.

"What about my car?" Anna asked.

"Erm… I don't know about that."

"Well, perhaps you could put me through to someone who does?"

"One moment please…"

One moment turned into several minutes, when a gruff voice reeled out a reference number indicating that her car would be available for collection in Perth as of nine o'clock the next morning. Having had time to recover from the trauma of her arrest, Anna was cross. The phone call further angered her: it was glib to the point of rudeness. Although she fully expected having to make her own way to Perth to pick up her car, the reality brought tears to her eyes: tears of frustration. She decided to ring Aunt Rosa – she would understand. Unfortunately, Rosa was not at home.

***

The journey from Fort William to Perth on Tuesday morning was tedious, having to travel via Glasgow. By the time Anna reached the police station it was mid-afternoon. When she enquired about her car, she was told to take a seat in the waiting area: someone would be with her shortly. Fifteen minutes later, a gentleman arrived, introducing himself as Detective Sergeant Boyle.

"I have come to collect my car: I understand that it was found abandoned at the railway station," Anna stated.

"Ah, so you would be Miss Milne?"

"Yes, that's right," Anna replied.

"Please, Miss Milne, follow me through to my office."

Anna hesitated… "I have been travelling since early this morning. I hope this won't take long."

"I'll not keep you any longer than is necessary. I promise."

No sooner had she sat down than a young officer arrived with tea and biscuits. "I'm sure you must be in need of some refreshment after your journey," the detective commented.

Anna resigned herself to a lengthy delay. At least this man was courteous, which was more than could be said of whoever had spoken to her from the Glasgow office.

"I'm so sorry about all this, Miss Milne," the detective apologised. "Your abandoned car caused some confusion. It appears that it was stolen twice. Firstly, as I'm sure you are aware, by your friend, Marie McInnes, who drove it to the Crieff Hydro.

Anna shook her head – "Why would Marie take my car when she had her own car?"

"Erm, well," the detective stuttered, "Marie took your car from outside her house and drove it to the Crieff Hydro. However, Miss McInnes insists she did not drive it to Perth. It seems that it was taken from the hotel car park and driven to the railway station here by someone else. Since three sets of fingerprints were found in the car, we assume your friend is telling the truth."

"Where was she? What happened to her?" Anna asked.

"You haven't been in touch with her?"

"Sergeant Boyle," Anna addressed him boldly, "I was arrested, suspected of being involved in her disappearance. Now you tell me she took my car. I've no idea what has been going on. I received a telephone call from Glasgow on Sunday to say Marie had been found safe and well. That is all I know."

"On the day you left Bute, Miss McInnes was found unconscious in the main street here in Perth. She was taken to hospital in Dundee, where she remained in intensive care, suffering with concussion. She regained consciousness on Friday night. It seems that she collapsed, hitting her head as she fell. As far as I know, she was discharged from hospital yesterday."

So much was swirling around in Anna's head. Nothing that the detective revealed about her friend answered the question as to why Marie had disappeared that Friday morning more than two weeks ago. Neither did it explain why she had taken the car. Anna just needed to retrieve her vehicle and get back to Fort William. Maybe someday everything would be clear: for the time being she'd had enough.

Before leaving home, Anna had placed her spare car key in her bag. Once the detective had completed the paperwork, he offered to escort her to the compound to locate her vehicle. He insisted on waiting until she did a quick check. On discovering a case in the boot, she looked questioningly at the detective. "Everything, including the case, has been thoroughly inspected," he assured her.

"But it isn't mine," Anna stressed.

"Ah," Detective Sergeant Boyle concurred, as he lifted the luggage out of the boot, "I'll see that this is returned to its rightful owner."

"Thank you," Anna smiled, as she drove the car onto the street and headed out of the city.

On passing through Crieff it occurred to her that this was the place where Marie had left her car. Feeling rather tired, she decided to stop for a break… at the Crieff Hydro. The break turned into an evening meal and an overnight stay. It had been a long day. It really was not sensible to continue driving for another ninety miles.

Safely home on Wednesday, Anna again tried to get in touch with her aunt. Again there was no reply. She was anxious to thank her for coming to her rescue, and also to let her know that her friend had been found safe and well. *I'll try tonight, she'll be at home then*, she thought.

Now that she was cleared of abducting her friend, or whatever the police imagined she was supposed to have done, she could go round to see her mother. Ellie would be expecting her daughter home about this time. She would want to know all about her holiday in Spain, and the elusive William. Her mother, she realised, was no more enamoured by this latest boyfriend than was her Aunt Rosa. Anna had to admit that they were both right.

Her mother greeted her with open arms. "I'm so pleased to see you. How was the holiday?"

Such was the reaction of her mother to her homecoming Anna thought, at first, that Rosa must have told her about her ordeal in Glasgow. However, that was not the case, as she would soon discover. Ellie listened as she relayed the events of the reunion with Marie and her holiday in Spain. She mentioned that she had been

111

questioned about her friend's disappearance on her return but assured her mother that the situation had been resolved.

"So," her mother asked, "Will you be seeing William again?"

"I don't think so," Anna replied, "I guess he doesn't really care that much about me." Changing the subject, she continued, "I've been trying to get in touch with Aunt Rosa."

"Rosa has gone away for a while," her mother announced.

Anna was totally floored. Why would her aunt go away without letting her know? Where had she gone? Had Uncle Bernard gone away too? The questions came thick and fast, but Ellie could tell her very little. Bernard had said that Rosa needed time to herself – time to think things over. Ellie was as shocked as her daughter. As far as she was aware Rosa and Bernard had an ideal relationship. Having met quite late in life, they had no family. So what had happened?

***

When Rosa arrived home on Friday night after dropping Anna off, her husband was curious to know what was going on. He waited until his wife had finished her story, before mentioning the visit from Detective Sergeant Henry Boyle. He explained that the detective had initially asked for her; he was trying to trace the family of a Miss Laura Milne. Apparently, the poor woman was lying unconscious in hospital in Dundee.

112

"I have to say I was confused," Bernard commented. "When the detective appeared on our doorstep, without prior warning, I assumed it was related to Anna's detention in Glasgow. I invited the man in, offered him tea and made him welcome. Of course, I soon realised that his call had nothing to do with Anna. I knew nothing of a Laura Milne." Bernard looked quizzically at Rosa who appeared decidedly uncomfortable. "Is something wrong?"

"No, no," Rosa answered, "I'm just tired, that's all. It's been a long day."

For the moment, Bernard did not pursue the matter, although he had his suspicions. Rosa understood that, sooner or later, she would have to tell him the truth.

When the telephone rang on Sunday afternoon, it was Bernard who answered.

"That was Henry Boyle," Bernard announced as he joined Rosa in the sitting room.

"Who?" Rosa queried.

"Detective Sergeant Boyle – the man who came here on Friday enquiring about Laura Milne."

"Oh," his wife responded, with concern. She had tried to put the issue to the back of her mind but obviously it wasn't going to go away. "What did he have to say?"

"I think it was just a courtesy call," Bernard replied. "It seems that there has been a mix up. The woman in hospital, thought to be Laura Milne, regained consciousness late on Friday night. Her name is Marie McInnes. That's rather odd, don't you think?

Rosa squirmed in her seat. She could no longer keep up the pretence. "We need to talk," she declared, guiltily. Her husband was the best... loving, kind, caring. There was little came between them, but he was no fool. What she was about to confess occurred many years ago, long before they had met. This was going to be difficult!

"YOU DID WHAT!" he shouted, as her tale unfolded. "Now what do you propose to do?"

PART 2

ROSA

CHAPTER 11
Rosa

Rosa Roberts was born in 1941, the elder daughter of Audrey and Geoffrey Roberts. The couple, both from wealthy families, had been married for several years before the arrival of their firstborn. Originally from London, Geoffrey met his future wife in her hometown of Inverness, where they married and set up home. However, just before the outbreak of war in 1939, they purchased a rather grand residence on the outskirts of Fort William. Geoffrey, already a second officer in the Merchant Navy, was doing rather well, moving through the ranks. The downside to his occupation was the amount of time he had to be away from home. Yet, secretly, this arrangement suited Audrey. To others, rattling around in a large house might have seemed an extravagance: to Audrey, it was idyllic. She loved her home with its magnificent views of Ben Nevis and the surrounding countryside. Further, she enjoyed her own company, and the freedom that came with it. If ever she felt like a change, she could be in Inverness in half a day, where she could stay with her parents, and go over to the Black Isle to visit her aunt who lived in a small village beside the Moray Firth. Aunt Clara's home was close to a quiet sandy beach, with a backdrop of woods and rolling hills… another idyllic place where Audrey could relax. In the winter months Audrey was often absorbed in a book, or designing and creating beautiful pieces of embroidery.

Then came the war. Geoffrey being away in peacetime was one thing but his absence when the country was in conflict was another. The dangers facing those in the armed forces were immense. Audrey wanted her husband close to her or at least to know where he was but in wartime that was impossible. When, towards the end of 1940 he joined a ship bound for India, Audrey was distraught. No longer content in her own company, she was unsettled, bereft; like so many others, grieving for the life and security she had, until recently, enjoyed.

Just when she believed that things could not get worse, Audrey discovered that she was pregnant. It should have been a happy time; a time for celebration. She wrote to Geoffrey, as she did every week, to relay the news, trying her best not to convey her distress. Of course, there was no guarantee when he would receive the letter, if at all.

In a state of anguish, she arrived unannounced at her parents' home in Inverness. Such was her pallor, her mother, on opening the door, feared the worst. Something must have happened to Geoffrey.

"No, no," Audrey assured her, "It isn't about Geoffrey... I-I-I'm pregnant," she stuttered. Having blurted out the words she fell into her mother's arms, sobbing uncontrollably. This was far from normal for Audrey, who was usually self-assured and rarely prone to tears.

"Come now," her mother consoled, "that's wonderful news. Maybe it's not the best timing, but you'll manage – we'll help you. Don't be upset, Geoffrey wouldn't want that. Now," she ordered, "take off your coat, sit down, and I'll make you a cup of tea."

Once settled by the fireside, Audrey calmed down.

"When is the baby due?" her mother asked, although she was fairly sure of the answer: Geoffrey had been home on leave at the end of November before his departure to India.

"Late summer," Audrey replied.

"So, you've six months to prepare. You can stay here for a few days until you're feeling better. After that, you must return to Fort William, settle down, and make your beautiful home ready for a family. Geoffrey could be back at any time."

Audrey accepted that her mother was right. Besides, she had a duty to her husband, as well as their unborn child. Oh, how she hated this war.

Despite her misgivings Audrey became reconciled to her condition. During the summer months she made a point of going out to meet up with other women, mostly involved in voluntary work to support the war effort. Through time she achieved a sense of satisfaction, a feeling that she was of some use. When her confinement drew near, her mother arrived from Inverness to help: Audrey had opted for a home birth. Since all appeared to be well, there was no objection from the midwife.

Towards the end of August 1941 Rosa Roberts was born, a healthy baby girl weighing just over seven pounds. Her grandmother was delighted, her mother less so. After a few days Audrey became depressed. She yearned for her husband, becoming alternately angry that he wasn't there and anxious for his safety. She struggled to feed her baby and, after two weeks, she gave up, pushing the child away. Her mother, normally a no-nonsense person who dealt efficiently under any circumstances, was disturbed by Audrey's behaviour. Nevertheless she persevered, taking care of her daughter as well as her granddaughter. Her husband, a businessman running an established family firm, joined them each weekend to support his wife with their depressed offspring.

After several weeks, with a great deal of patience on the part of her mother, Audrey began to come to terms with her situation. Day by day she paid a little more attention to baby Rosa. Eventually, mother and baby could be left alone: the crisis had passed. Only when her mother was certain that Audrey was fully recovered and capable of caring for the child herself, did she return to Inverness. Even then, she visited regularly. Having grown close to her young granddaughter over the weeks she was anxious to maintain the bond. For Audrey, the whole episode had been traumatic yet thankfully, now that she had to take responsibility, she rose to the challenge, adapting to a new routine.

For the next four years, Audrey settled to motherhood, caring for her delightful little girl. Although her life was somewhat restricted, she was content and fortunate. There was never a problem with money, unlike with so many young mothers. She could visit her parents in Inverness whenever she wished and, in turn, since her mother was always willing to look after Rosa, she was able to spend time with her old school friends. In Fort William, she shied away from friendships, losing contact with those she had met when involved in voluntary work before Rosa's birth. Considering her husband was away and the country was at war, Audrey and Rosa could not have fared better. Aside from the few weeks after Rosa's birth, Audrey continued to write to Geoffrey regularly. There were times when she did not hear from him for weeks, or even months at a time but, eventually, letters arrived. Perhaps the most anxious time was waiting for his homecoming in 1945, after the war in Europe ended. With no news throughout May and June, she began to fret. Surely nothing could have happened to him at this stage – not now.

Late one evening in mid-July, heralded only by a knock on the door, Geoffrey arrived. Pale and thin, a shadow of the man she remembered, he stood on the threshold awaiting a reaction. For a moment, she too stood still, not recognising the figure before her. Gradually, realisation struck, her eyes widened. She reached up, stretching her arms around his neck. "Audrey, oh Audrey," he whispered, as he grasped her round the waist, struggling to lift her off her feet, "How I've missed you." It was several minutes before another word passed between them as they hugged and kissed – still on the doorstep.

"May I come in?" he asked, with a twinkle in his eye. Audrey stepped back as he picked up his bag and made his way into the hall. "Can I see my wonderful little daughter?"

"She's fast asleep," Audrey responded, "But you can go upstairs and peep into her room; the door is open."

Geoffrey crept up the stairs and quietly sneaked into Rosa's room. She looked so peaceful, tucked up neatly in the single bed with her arms around a golden coloured teddy. He gazed down at the sleeping child, as the tears welled up in his eyes, trickling down his sunken cheeks. He had missed so much. Almost four years of her life had passed. He hoped, how he hoped, that he could make it up to her.

Downstairs with his wife, he could not avoid the look of concern in her eyes. "I know what you're thinking Audrey," he commented, "It's been hard, very hard, I'm weary – but it's over." With that familiar gleam in his eye he added, "I need feeding up, porridge in the morning and some good hearty stews."

"I'll see what I can do," she responded.

Rosa was, at first, a little tentative about this strange man in the home she had, so far, shared only with her mother. Although Audrey had spoken often to her about her estranged father, the child was bewildered. However, as the weeks passed, she warmed to him and, by the time of her fourth birthday in August, Rosa and her parents had become a solid family unit. Geoffrey was looking much better, his cheeks no longer hollow, his face no longer pale. In physique, at least, he was beginning to return to his former self. Unfortunately, this was not the whole story for, deep down, Geoffrey had

122

suffered, escaping with his life on more than one occasion.

As Rosa adjusted to the presence of her father, the day arrived when he had to return to his post in the Merchant Navy. Again she was bewildered. But this was the way her life would continue, sometimes only the two of them, at others three. Over the years she became accustomed to the changes. She grew into a sturdy, resilient child, helping her mother at home, enjoying friendships at school. During the holidays they would stay with her grandparents in Inverness and her great aunt on the Black Isle. She made more friends as she played on the beach by the Moray Firth or up in the woods behind Aunt Clara's house.

Sadly the good life didn't last. When Rosa was ten years old her mother was ill. Well, not exactly ill – she was pregnant, although she did not reveal that to Rosa. Nor did she reveal it to anyone else, including Geoffrey, who had been away for two months when she realised her fate. *This is not happening*, she told herself. *I'm nearly forty: I can't have another baby.*

In the summer holidays she took her daughter north as usual, staying a short time in Inverness but mostly with Aunt Clara, where she could relax and Rosa was free to play with her friends. Even at the end of the holidays, when she was six months into the pregnancy her condition was not obvious. She did not see a doctor: that would confirm what she didn't want to know.

Two weeks later Rosa turned eleven. A few of her friends came to the house for a party. Audrey made a real effort to entertain the children with games and a treasure hunt in the garden, followed by a party tea. That was the last celebration that Rosa enjoyed for a long time to come. Two days after her birthday, while Rosa was at school, a young boy on a bicycle rode up to the house. He hopped off his cycle and proceeded up the garden path on foot to the front door. Audrey, who was becoming more lethargic by the day, answered the bell on the third ring. The boy handed her the telegram without a word: he knew he must be cautious about such deliveries. As he reached his bicycle, which he'd left propped up against the garden wall, he heard the piercing scream coming from within the house.

Rosa, carefree as ever, swung her satchel from side to side as she made her way up the lane towards her home. Opening the garden gate to continue up the path she experienced a most odd sensation: something was not right. She made her way around the side of the house to the back door, which was always left unlocked during the day. "Mum," she called, as she entered the kitchen. There was no reply.

CHAPTER 12
Geoffrey Roberts

Geoffrey Roberts, like so many others, had suffered greatly during the war years. In his case, half his crew was lost when his ship was targeted in the Pacific Ocean. As the last off, he was lucky to escape with his life, and even more fortunate to be rescued. Despite doing everything he could to save his men, as any captain must, he was distraught at the enormous loss. As well as the battles of war, Geoffrey suffered from various illnesses – dysentery, cholera, and malaria, of which he had three bouts. So, when he arrived home at the end of the war, it was little wonder that he looked so pale. Audrey did her best to help: encouraging him to eat well and go for long walks over the hills. However, it was his daughter who provided the real cure, distracting him from thoughts of the tragedies he had endured, delighting him with her smiles, her laughter and her constant chatter. How he missed her when he was away.

When the war ended, Geoffrey had considered retiring from the navy. *But,* he asked himself, *what else would I do?* It was the only life he had known. Besides, in the post-war years he had the command of a ship as well as the respect of his crew. He couldn't abandon that. Every time he waved good-bye to his family he felt guilty. Every time he came home on leave he was ashamed that he had left them. Yet he was unsure that he would be able to cope with the alternative.

In March 1952, as he set off to join his ship after several weeks on leave, he was determined to make it his last trip. He hinted as much to Audrey before he left, understanding that once he had made his decision known to his wife, he would have to keep his promise. Audrey kept the information to herself. She was afraid to reveal the news to Rosa fearing that, if it did not happen, the disappointment would be too great.

Geoffrey had made up his mind. The next time he returned home it would be for good. He adjusted to the idea. He looked forward to a new life, when he could be a real husband and father. Thoughts of a new job, a different lifestyle began to excite him – all would be well. But all was not well with Geoffrey Roberts. It was August. He'd been away for five months when he fell ill – constantly tired, often feverish: he was losing weight. At Cape Town, where the ship was berthed for a week, he went on shore in search of a doctor. He was diagnosed with leukaemia. It was a death sentence. With blood transfusions he might survive for a few weeks: that was the best he could hope.

Feeling much better after a transfusion in the city's hospital he returned to his ship declaring that he was fine, hoping that the boost he felt would last, at least for a few days. He needed time to think, to decide what to do for the best. As far as possible, he must get his affairs in order.

Although he might dupe the lower ranks, he could not fool his chief officer, the man who would have to take over from him in an emergency... an emergency that would occur sooner rather than later. Within a matter of days Geoffrey's health deteriorated visibly. He retired to his quarters where he put everything in order before writing two letters – one to his wife and one to his daughter. He gave the letters to his chief officer asking that he deliver them personally if that was possible. "Surely you will be all right until we get home," the man argued.

"Maybe," Geoffrey replied. He did not reveal the nature of his illness, not wishing to alarm him further. But the officer was no fool: he knew that something was seriously wrong.

It was a dull, moonless night; the ship was in mid-ocean. Putting on a brave face, Geoffrey made his presence known throughout the ship, carrying out checks as usual and chatting with officers and several members of the crew. Returning to his quarters, he completed his paperwork for the day. He placed the logbook on his desk along with the letter from the doctor bearing the details of his illness, his prognosis and the treatment he had received in the hospital in Cape Town. Gazing around the room, his eyes rested on the photograph of his wife and daughter taken during his last leave. Tears filled his eyes as he whispered, "I'm so sorry, please forgive me but this way is best for all of us." He lay on his bed, quietly reminiscing, until well after midnight. Aware that most of the crew would be in their cabins, he left his quarters, ascended the stairs to the top deck, and stepped cautiously to the side of the ship.

***

The next day dawned bleak and chilly. There was no sign of the Ship's Master. Guessing his health must have deteriorated the Chief Officer went to his superior's cabin. After knocking several times he opened the door to peer inside, fearing the worst. Discovering, to his surprise, that the Master was not there, he alerted the crew, ordering a thorough search of the ship. Only after he was sure that he was not on board, did he return to the Shipmaster's quarters. Seeing the hospital letter sitting beside the logbook he read it through, digesting the content. It was clear that Geoffrey Roberts was terminally ill. Given that his colleague had already handed him letters addressed to the two most important people in his life, there was only one conclusion that could be drawn.

The Chief Officer was faced with a dilemma. The letters that were addressed to Geoffrey Robert's wife and daughter were undoubtedly suicide notes. They would surely clarify his intention thus ascertaining, without doubt, the cause of death. However, Geoffrey had given the missives to the officer on trust. His moral obligation to his missing colleague outweighed his temptation to open them, or notify anyone of their existence. Nevertheless, he did show the medical report to the other senior officers on board, who came to the same conclusion as himself. The entire crew was called together in an effort to determine whether anyone had seen the Shipmaster in the late evening or early hours of the morning prior to his disappearance. Those who had been on duty overnight were approached individually to ascertain whether they had observed or heard anything suspicious. During the investigation, several comments were made regarding the health of the Master, which led the First Officer to reveal to them that the man was terminally ill. Of course, the news soon spread to the entire crew. For several days rumours were rife on board but there were no formal announcements. Shipmaster Geoffrey Roberts was missing, presumed dead.

CHAPTER 13
Tragedy Strikes

"Mum," Rosa called again when she failed to get a response from her mother. She dropped her satchel by the kitchen table and cautiously stepped into the hall, stopping abruptly at the sight of the motionless figure of her mother lying on the floor. For a moment she stood frozen to the spot, not daring to move forward. Her hand jerked up involuntarily to cover her open mouth as she inhaled deeply averting a scream. Then, with a sudden lurch, she was kneeling beside her mother, shaking her and calling out in desperation, "Mum, Mum, wake up, wake up," as the tears streamed down her now colourless cheeks. Audrey's body twitched. "Mum," Rosa called again. This time her mother opened her eyes – just for a second. Rosa knelt up, breathing deeply. Casting her eyes around the limp form she noticed the telegram a few inches from her mother's right hand.

Audrey stirred as her daughter reached out to grasp the ominous message. Turning to a sitting position, Rosa scanned the grim content, before collapsing on top of her mother, utterly devastated. How long the two lay like that, Rosa could never be sure, but she was the first to move. As she made the effort to heave herself up, she was aware of her mother's arm around her. "Mum," she whispered, "I am so sorry, I'll make us some tea."

Slowly Rosa stood up and, as she did so, Audrey turned around, gradually raising herself until she was sitting upright. Assured that her mother would be all right Rosa proceeded to the kitchen. She prepared tea and toast – the easiest items to produce in a few minutes. Mother and daughter sat in silence, sipping their tea, nibbling their toast. It was more than an hour before either of them spoke.

"Thank you," Audrey murmured at last, "Whatever would I do without you?"

Rosa did not attend school for the rest of the week, remaining at home to support her mother. Little conversation passed between them: they were merely there for one another.

"What does 'missing presumed dead' mean?" Rosa asked, as the two of them sat hunched over breakfast on Saturday morning. Although Rosa was well aware of what the words meant, she could not fathom the link to her beloved father.

"I don't know darling," Audrey replied. "It's a common term during wartime but we're no longer at war. I don't understand how your father could possibly be missing from his ship in peacetime, or why anyone would assume that he was dead. I wonder whether we will ever know."

Rosa went back to school on Monday morning. Audrey considered going along with her daughter to explain to the head teacher what had happened. Ultimately, she decided against the idea. After all, she didn't know what had happened so how *could* she explain? She'd just get upset and make a fool of herself. And what if Geoffrey turned up on the doorstep? So far she had no proof that he was dead. Further, although she was still trying to ignore her pregnancy, she was aware that it was beginning to show. She could not face the questions or, worse still, the stares: she didn't want sympathy. In the end she waved Rosa off, returned to bed, and wept.

It was a strange grief that Audrey suffered. How could Geoffrey desert her again, leaving her to suffer the birth of a second child without him? She mourned more for herself than for her husband. What should she do? How would she cope? The unborn baby rolled over, enhancing her sorrow. "This is not happening," she moaned.

Rosa dashed home from school. She was worried about her mother who was normally so practical, so poised. Even before her father's supposed death Audrey was acting oddly, often in a world of her own, lacking concentration. Something else was bothering her – of that, Rosa was sure. Despite having not quite reached womanhood, she was aware of changes in her own body and, at the same time, noticed the changing shape of her mother's figure. Surely her mother would tell her if she was expecting a baby, more so now that her father was unlikely to return. Rosa dared not ask. Instead, she turned to her best friend at school.

Morag was from a large family. She already had five siblings and had told Rosa that her mother was pregnant again. "My mother's not too happy this time," Morag disclosed to her friend, "She says she is too old to be having more babies. William was supposed to be the last – he's six." Rosa thought about this family – so different from her own. Audrey had said they were Catholics and Catholics often had lots of children. Rosa was intrigued. There was Michael – the eldest – he was seventeen. Then there were three girls: Maggie, Megan and Morag and finally, George and William. That was a lot of people in one house. It was a little house, not a grand, stately home like Rosa's. *Wherever did they all sleep?*

Rosa confided in her friend. If they were both going to have a new baby in their family, that would be exciting – or so she thought! "Why don't you just ask your mother?" Morag remarked.

"I can't do that," Rosa argued. "Mum doesn't talk about things like that."

"Things like what?" Morag questioned.

"Just things," Rosa shrugged. "I don't know, but I think there are lots of things about being grown up that I don't know. If my mum is having a baby, how did it happen?"

"You must know that," Morag cajoled.

As Rosa's eyes filled with tears, it occurred to Morag that her friend really didn't know.

"I can tell you everything," Morag boasted, "But we need somewhere private to meet. There's never any peace at my house."

Rosa also realised that was not an option. "How about Saturday at mine," she suggested. "My mother won't bother us."

So, as planned, Morag made her way to Rosa's house on Saturday morning. Wearing a loose fitting housecoat, Audrey answered the door. She always welcomed her daughter's friends and particularly, Morag who, despite her seemingly chaotic background, was always so polite. "Rosa's in her room, Audrey informed her, "Just go up – you know where it is."

"Thank you, Mrs Roberts," Morag responded.

Rosa was at once excited, yet scared, at what her friend would tell her and, indeed, she had cause to be. She'd no idea about the implications of what was happening to her own body let alone what was to follow. Why had her mother not told her? On the other hand Morag, with brothers and sisters, was well aware of the gender differences. She may not know everything, as she had bragged, but she knew a great deal. Rosa was shocked. It took several days for it all to register, during which time she constantly plagued her friend for answers.

"What about my mum?" Rosa ventured, around two weeks later. "She's definitely getting bigger around her tummy."

"I think you're probably right, she must be having a baby," Morag declared, knowledgeably. "What are you going to do about it? Does she have a midwife?"

"Midwife!" Rosa exclaimed.

"Yes, a midwife," Morag repeated. "A lady who helps to deliver the baby."

"I know that," Rosa was indignant. Of course she knew what a midwife was, but the reference in connection to her mother emphasised the reality of the

135

situation. As far as she knew her mother had never attended a clinic, as Morag's mother did. Whatever was she thinking?

The problem was… Audrey wasn't thinking. She was living her own nightmare, hoping her husband would return, denying that she was pregnant. Each night she prayed she would wake up in the morning and all would be well.

***

One evening, a month after the telegram had arrived, there was a knock at the door. "Whoever can that be?" Audrey murmured, "You answer it," she urged, turning to her daughter.

Recently Rosa had noticed her mother's reluctance to be seen out and about or to respond to callers. She was also aware of her swelling stomach.

"Okay Mum," she obeyed, getting up to answer the door. A few minutes later she called out, "It's a gentleman asking for you."

Grudgingly, Audrey moved from the comfort of her armchair to come face to face with a smartly dressed stranger standing uneasily on the threshold. "Y-y-yes?" she questioned.

"Mrs Roberts," he asked, checking that he had come to the right house.

"Yes, I'm Audrey Roberts," she replied, staring curiously at the visitor.

"George Ellis, Ma'am, I was the chief officer on your husband's ship," he stated slowly, introducing

136

himself: his task made more difficult seeing her current state. It took a moment or two for the significance of his words to register, followed by a deathly silence.

"Perhaps you'd better come inside," Audrey offered although having an outsider – or anybody for that matter – enter her domain at this particular time, was the last thing she wanted.

"Thank you," George Ellis acknowledged, as he followed her into the lounge. "And this must be Rosa," he added, with a nod to the young girl who had answered the door.

"What's happened to my husband?" Audrey demanded. "Is he dead? Is he? Tell me. I want to know. I want to know now," her voice had risen to a crescendo in her frenzy.

"Yes... he's dead," the officer responded.

"Where is he? I want to know where he is."

Witnessing the anger consuming her mother, Rosa came to her aid, "Sit down Mum, sit down," she pleaded.

Silenced by her daughter, Audrey slumped down into her armchair. Rosa indicated to the stranger to be seated and she too sat down.

"What happened to my dad?" Rosa asked simply.

Looking alternately at mother and daughter, George Ellis began to relay the sad news. From the inside pocket of his coat he withdrew the medical report from the hospital in Cape Town. "Your husband was taken ill with Leukaemia," he explained, handing the document to Audrey. "He left this on the top of his desk before he disappeared from the ship – mid-ocean." Reaching into his pocket again, George continued. "Two days earlier Geoffrey handed me these letters, one for each of you. He asked me to deliver them to you personally, if it was possible... that request is the reason for this visit." Handing the letters over, he fidgeted in his seat, wondering if this would be an appropriate moment to depart, leaving this family to grieve.

"Do you know what's in these letters?" Audrey asked.

"Your husband gave no indication of their content, simply entrusting them to me. No one else knows of their existence." I'll leave you in peace now," he added, getting out of his chair.

"Please stay," Audrey offered, "At least until we have read these."

Much as he wanted to accept the invitation to remain, he declined. "I'm staying in a hotel about a mile from here. I can call back in the morning and perhaps answer any questions you may have."

His response satisfied Audrey. She was sure she would have more to ask this gentleman. As she escorted him to the door it occurred to her that she had been less than hospitable yet, under the circumstances, he would hardly have expected otherwise.

Left alone once more, mother and daughter opened their letters. Tears filled Rosa's eyes as she absorbed the loving message, together with the devastating news, incorporated in her father's missive. She kissed her mother gently on the cheek before escaping to her bedroom. Flopping onto her bed, she wept as if her heart would break. During the last few weeks, since her mother had received the telegram, Rosa had remained hopeful that her father would return. Now that she knew he would not, the finality hit hard: she would never see her dad again. How could she go on living?

Audrey reacted in an entirely different way. Realising deep down that the telegram spelt the end, she had shed her tears. She had experienced the mixed emotions of anger and despair that accompanied bereavement. In her case, the letter brought the closure she needed. Geoffrey was dead. The sadness would remain for a long time to come; the trauma had passed.

When George arrived the following morning, Rosa was still in her room. She had no desire to see the visitor again, leaving her mother to discuss all the implications of the situation… and there were many. Audrey took on the responsibility with more courage than she had shown in the preceding weeks. She allowed the officer to peruse the letters written by her husband. They clarified, without doubt, his imminent intention to end his life. In order for the death to be certified the information therein, together with the medical report, would be required. The officer acknowledged that the process might take some time. Audrey, in turn, disclosed the name and address of her husband's solicitor, the man who would ultimately deal with the legalities. Fortunately, Geoffrey had left a will. Following a more general chat over a cup of coffee, George left to return to his home in the north of England.

Rosa spent the whole of Sunday in her room: she cried until no tears were left. Although Audrey managed to persuade her to have some soup at teatime she tried, but failed, to coax her to talk. There was no chance of Rosa attending school on Monday. It was late afternoon before she emerged from her bedroom, puffy-eyed and devoid of her usual sparkle. During the course of the evening she began to brighten slightly. Eventually she asked her mother what the chief officer had said. Relieved, Audrey spoke to her daughter as if to another adult. As she explained the procedure, Rosa listened intently. "Will there be a funeral?" she asked.

"I doubt it," her mother replied, "Your father often said he belonged to the sea. He didn't want to be placed in a box to be lowered into the ground. However, there could be a memorial service in London where he was born and brought up. I'll leave that to his parents to organise. I've written to your grandparents in Inverness to let them know of the visit we've had from the chief officer.

For a while there was silence between mother and daughter. Not a deathly hush, just a quiet time as they both reflected on the last few days. Then, unexpectedly, Audrey announced, "I'm going to have a baby."

"Yes I know," Rosa shrugged.

"Oh!" was all her mother could say.

"I'll go and make us some cocoa," Rosa offered. Having waited so long for her mother to make her condition known, she was at once thankful and annoyed. How could she have avoided telling her for so long?

140

Sitting down with a mug of cocoa and a plate of cheese and biscuits, Rosa endeavoured to stay calm as she sought answers from her mother.

"When is the baby due? Are you going to be in hospital? Do you have a midwife? Do Granny and Grandpa know?"

Apart from the answer to the first question – November – the rest received a negative response. "So," Rosa persisted, "What are you going to do?"

Audrey weakened, "I don't know," she cried, "I don't know."

Seeing her mother's distress, she gave her a hug before announcing that she was tired, she was going to bed, adding that she would go to school in the morning.

At school Rosa experienced the security that during recent weeks had been lacking in her home life. At least her mother had written a note for her to take to her teacher explaining her absence the previous day. Sympathy came with a lowering of expectations – "Don't worry if you can't manage this today, dear." Although Rosa understood the concern, she did not want to be patronised in that way. Being a bright, diligent pupil, she worked as hard as ever. She needed to focus to take her mind off the loss of her father, as well as her mother's attitude towards the unborn child. At playtime and dinnertime, Rosa confided in Morag.

"She's told me at last," she disclosed to her friend.

"That's great," Morag enthused, "We'll each have a baby to fuss over."

"Mmm," Rosa pondered – she had not quite thought of it in that way.

"Your mum will need you to help her. Has she got a midwife?"

"No," Rosa answered, sadly "She doesn't seem to have done anything about it. All she told me was the baby is due in November."

Morag shook her head. No wonder Rosa appeared so upset.

CHAPTER 14
The Birth

Frustratingly, Audrey continued to ignore her current condition. Now and again, Rosa asked her what would happen when the baby came: her mother didn't want to discuss it. "Your father's dead, and I'm too old to be having a baby," was as much of a response that was forthcoming. Rosa gave up.

It was October, and with it came two weeks holiday from school. Audrey, her pregnancy now obvious, would not go out at all. She sent her daughter for the groceries; she left the fortnightly laundry of bedding and towels in the porch at the front door to be collected.

Aside from the shopping, Rosa was free to do more or less as she pleased. She spent most days with Morag and her family, coming home for the evening meal before dark. Rosa enjoyed being at her friend's home where things were so different from her own. There, the birth of the new baby was thought to be imminent and preparations for the arrival had been made. Baby clothes, nappies, and a cradle were all ready as was some formula milk and a bottle, in case Morag's mum had problems with breastfeeding. Arrangements were in place to contact the midwife. It seemed everything was in order. Rosa was alarmed. "My mum's having a baby," she voiced to Morag's mother one afternoon when they happened to be alone together in the kitchen.

"Yes, so Morag was telling me."

"I'm worried," Rosa continued, "Mum has made no plans at all. There's no nappies or baby clothes, and she doesn't even have a midwife."

Mrs Jamieson tried to hide her concern. She knew that Rosa had just lost her father and guessed, from what Morag had told her, that Mrs Roberts was refusing to accept the pregnancy. "Do you know how to make a call from a telephone box?" she asked.

"Yes," Rosa answered, confidently. "My granny and grandpa in Inverness have a telephone. I've been to the kiosk with mum and spoken to them myself."

Morag's mother wrote down some numbers on a notepad, tore out the page and handed it to Rosa. "Keep this safe," she advised, "I've written down some numbers that might help – the doctor, a midwife and 999 in case you can't contact either of them. You'll need coins so be sure to have some handy." Then, to offer some reassurance, she drew the girl towards her and said, "I'm sure your mother will have things ready before she goes into labour. After all, she's already had one baby," she smiled, "And, remember, if you need any help, you can call round any time."

"Thank you so much, Mrs Jamieson," Rosa responded.

Once the school reopened after the October break, it was barely a week before the clocks were turned back, heralding the dark nights and the onset of winter. The next Friday was Halloween. Rosa knew not to ask her mother about a party – it was definitely not an option this year. Although Audrey was never a great socialiser, she had welcomed her daughter's friends, usually just one or two at a time but, when it came to Rosa's birthday or to this annual event on the last day of October, she had always made an effort. Several of Rosa's friends would be invited. At Halloween, fancy dress was encouraged. There would be party games, ducking for apples, a fine spread for tea and goodies to take home. The children were delighted to go up to the 'big house' on these special occasions.

As Rosa made her way home from school on this normally joyful day, she thought about the good times they'd had in previous years. Now the cold, dark nights ahead, cast a shadow over her. When she had left home that morning, her mother looked pale. Rosa detected the pain from the look on her face, yet her mother insisted that all was well: she seemed anxious to wave her daughter off to school.

Rosa went round to the back door, entering the house through the kitchen, into the hall. It was then that she heard it – a low whimpering sound. She took off her coat and hung it on the hallstand before going into the lounge, expecting to find her mother sitting in her favourite armchair by the fire. Audrey was not there. The room felt cold: the fire had not been lit… Rosa shuddered. Returning to the hall, she was again aware of the whining: it was coming from upstairs. "Mum," she called out, "Mum, where are you?" There followed an agonising scream.

Rosa rushed up the stairs. The bathroom door was wide open: another shriek emanated from within. "Mum, Mum," Rosa called again, stopping abruptly at the scene that presented itself. Her mother was sitting, propped up against the bathroom wall, her nightdress ridden up round her thighs and the head of a baby visible between her legs.

"Help me," Audrey pleaded, seeing Rosa at the door.

***

How Rosa coped during the next half-hour she would never be sure yet, somehow, she helped her mother deliver a healthy baby girl.

"What about feeding her?" she asked, when her mother was in bed. The child, wrapped up in sheets and shawls, was lying in an empty drawer pulled out from her mother's chest of drawers.

"I'm not feeding her," Audrey answered, defiantly, "I'm exhausted."

"You'll have to," Rosa retorted, "We don't have any formula milk; you can't let her starve."

"I can't feed her, I just can't," her mother persisted.

"I'm going out to get help," Rosa announced as she hurried out of the room, ignoring the demands from her mother to stop.

Satisfied that her mother was too weak to pursue her, she retrieved the note that Mrs Jamieson had given her, donned her coat and headed for the nearest telephone box.

The kiosk was occupied so Rosa had to wait. Only then was she aware that she was shaking. A few minutes later, a middle-aged lady joined the queue. "Are you all right my dear?" she asked, kindly.

Normally Rosa would have merely nodded and replied that she was fine but, at this moment, her head was spinning – she needed help.

"My mum's just had a baby," she blurted out, "I need a midwife or a doctor or somebody… there's no clothes, no nappies, nothing, and Mum can't feed her, and I don't know what to do."

For a moment the woman was too taken aback to respond. "Okay," she spoke slowly, at last. "Why are you here at the 'phone box?"

"I have the number of a midwife."

"So… you do know what to do."

Rosa sniffled, wiped away the tears that had sprung to her eyes and answered, "W-w-well, I s'pose so."

"Are you the girl from the big house over there?" the woman queried, pointing in the direction of Rosa's home.

"Yes," Rosa answered.

"I'm Mrs Marshall, I live just along the road from here. You pass my house on your way to school – it's Rosa, isn't it?"

"Yes, that's right. I'm Rosa Roberts."

"Well, Rosa Roberts, would you like me to stay with you until you get the help you need?"

"Yes, please," Rosa sighed with relief.

A gentleman stepped out of the kiosk, holding the door open for Rosa and Mrs Marshall, who had offered to assist Rosa in making the call to the midwife.

Rosa was glad of this woman's assistance in accessing the operator, who put the call through to the number she had been given for the midwife. In fact, the number was a direct line to the maternity unit at the hospital. With the neighbour by her side, Rosa relayed the details giving her name and address, her mother's name and the time of the baby's birth. "We'll send an ambulance right away," the midwife affirmed.

"O-o-h, I don't think Mum wanted to go to hospital," Rosa stuttered, somewhat alarmed.

"I'll be in the ambulance," the midwife assured her, "I'll examine your mum and decide what's best."

Stepping out of the kiosk, Rosa turned to Mrs Marshall, "I'd best get back home as quickly as possible," she said, "I don't suppose the ambulance will be long."

Mrs Marshall accompanied Rosa so that she could help her after a decision was made regarding her mother and the baby. She was sure that the midwife would insist on having them admitted to hospital. Not wishing to cause further stress for the household, she waited in the lounge until, as she suspected, the mother and the newly born infant were taken away in the ambulance.

"I can't leave Rosa," her mother cried, in a last desperate attempt to avoid the inevitable.

"I've called Granny and Grandpa," Rosa lied, to placate her mother, "They're on their way." To the midwife, she revealed that she was not in the house alone – a neighbour was staying with her. A quick glance into the lounge confirmed Rosa's story. Confidant that the elder daughter was being cared for, the midwife was happy to leave.

When the medical team had departed, Rosa informed Mrs Marshall of the outcome: her mother and the baby were being admitted to the maternity unit at the Belford Hospital. "I must ring my grandparents in Inverness," she added.

"I'll come with you," Mrs Marshall offered.

"I'll be all right now," Rosa assured her, "I don't want to cause you any more trouble."

"It's no trouble, you've had quite a shock."

This time, after the operator had connected the call, Mrs Marshall stepped out of the 'phone box, giving the girl some privacy to talk to her grandparents. Rosa was grateful. She did not want the neighbour to know that the couple in Inverness had no idea that their daughter was having a baby. The conversation might be difficult.

When Rosa revealed that her mother had given birth to a baby girl at half-past four that afternoon Granny, without hesitation, said they would come straight away. "I'll be all right tonight," Rosa protested.

"We're on our way," her grandmother insisted, "It'll be late when we arrive, but we'll be with you as soon as we can." The phone went dead.

Rosa's Grandpa drove a Vauxhall: it was his pride and joy. When the two of them came to visit, normally for long weekends in the summertime, they would arrive by car. They would take Rosa and her mother for days out during their stay. More often, however, Granny would come by herself, travelling by bus.

"They're on their way," Rosa announced, as she emerged from the kiosk."

Mrs Marshall smiled, "That's good," she said. "Now then lassie, have you had anything to eat?" She realised that Rosa's grandparents would not be arriving for a while.

Rosa had to think for a moment – when *had* she last eaten? "Well, no," she answered, aware that her stomach was rumbling.

"Come along to my house, I'll make you something. You must be hungry."

It was only half-past six. So much had occurred in the last two hours Rosa was unsure what to do. Nevertheless, the idea of going home to an empty house to prepare a meal for herself did not appeal. This woman had been so kind – surely it could do no harm to accept her hospitality. She was, after all, a close neighbour. So despite what her mother had always maintained about being wary of strangers, Rosa accepted Mrs Marshall's invitation. She felt comfortable in the neighbour's living room, where she sat beside the fire while her host was in

150

the scullery preparing a meal. The house, though small, was clean and tidy, and so cosy. Within ten minutes, Mrs Marshall appeared with a tray on which she had placed a plate of beans on toast for Rosa and a cup of tea. "I've already eaten," she stated, almost apologetically, "but I'll join you with a cup of tea." She disappeared once more into the next room, returning with tea for herself.

"It's strange that I've never met your mother," the neighbour remarked, "considering that we live so close."

"Not really," Rosa volunteered, "Mum doesn't go out much. She has friends in Inverness and she lets me have friends round whenever I want. Having a big house keeps her occupied. In her spare time she likes to read and sew. Usually, on Halloween, we invite some girls in my class at school for a party." A sad look on her face did not escape the attention of the neighbour.

"What happened today?" Mrs Marshall ventured. Rosa relayed how she had arrived home from school to find her mother on the bathroom floor already in the throes of giving birth. She explained how she had helped deliver the baby. "She's beautiful," Rosa enthused. "I washed her, wrapped her up warm and cuddled her. She gurgled at me. I'm glad I've got a little sister." For the first time since they'd met at the telephone box, Rosa was relaxed. Mrs Marshall could see a glimmer of happiness – a twinkle in the girl's eyes. She wondered that the child could have coped.

Rosa changed the subject. "Weren't you supposed to be making a 'phone call?" she asked, remembering that the women had been in the queue behind her.

"Oh, it's all right. I was going to ring my sister-in-law, but it was just for a chat. I can 'phone her tomorrow."

"Do you live on your own?" Rosa was curious.

"Yes," she replied. "My boys are grown up and my husband was killed in the war."

"Oh," Rosa, sympathised. "My dad died in September. He survived the war, then got leukaemia while he was away on another trip at sea. So there's just me and my mum… and now my sister.

For more than an hour, the two strangers chatted. Rosa was pleased to talk with this woman. In turn, Mrs Marshall was glad of the company: mesmerised by this brave, intelligent young girl. Noticing the time on the carriage clock on the mantelpiece, Rosa realised that she must get back home. Although it was unlikely that her grandparents would be arriving for some time, she needed to tidy around and warm the place up a bit. She should probably clean out the grate and set it ready to light the fire in the morning.

"I'll walk along the road with you," Mrs Marshall insisted. "I really don't like the thought of you being alone – you've had a lot to cope with today."

Independent as she was, Rosa wanted company tonight: she didn't want to be alone in the house waiting for her grandparents. Of course, her mother would have misgivings about her association with a stranger but it was her mother who had created this mess… she should have made proper arrangements for her confinement. Nevertheless, secretly Rosa was proud to have helped with the birth of the baby – it had been exciting, even if it was a bit scary.

As soon as they arrived at the house Rosa set to with the chores, directing her visitor to a pile of magazines on the coffee table. For almost an hour she worked diligently, refusing any assistance from her guest. After turning on electric fires in the living room, hall and the bedrooms that would be used, she swept floors, dusted, polished, cleaned the bathrooms and laid the fire ready for the next day.

"Would you like a cup of tea," she asked Mrs Marshall, when she'd finished.

However, the doorbell interrupted her offer. "That'll be Granny and Grandpa."

"I'll be going," Mrs Marshall stated, immediately standing up and putting on her coat. She followed Rosa into the hall.

Rosa's granny entered in a flurry, grabbing her granddaughter in a hug, "Are you all right, my dear. I've been so worried about you? Whatever's going on?" Only after releasing her grip did she catch sight of Mrs Marshall.

"I'm okay Granny," Rosa responded, "really I am," and, turning to the neighbour, she announced, "This is Mrs Marshall, she's been with me all evening."

"Pleased to meet you," Mrs Marshall uttered, with a smile directed towards the elderly couple, "I didn't want to leave Rosa on her own. You can be proud of her; she's done well today."

Both grandparents thanked the neighbour who had obviously taken care of their granddaughter until they arrived. As she turned to leave, Mrs Marshall invited Rosa to call on her anytime, and requested that she must let her know how things were going with her mother and her baby sister. Rosa assured the neighbour that she would be in touch and thanked her for staying with her.

"Now then," Granny demanded, before she'd even taken off her coat, "What's all this about your mother having a baby?"

Undeterred by her granny's authoritative tone, Rosa offered to make some tea, before relaying the events of the day. Grandpa, as usual, sat calmly listening to the whole tale. Granny, on the other hand, was appalled at what her granddaughter had endured and made no effort to keep her thoughts to herself. "Silly girl," she declared with reference to Audrey, on more than one occasion. Rosa was rather amused at her granny's comments. She'd never viewed her mother as a 'silly girl' but had to acknowledge that her behaviour in recent months had been bizarre.

"She misses Dad," Rosa stated, in her mother's defence.

"Of course she does. And I'm sure you do too. But this isn't just to do with your father's death. She has obviously been denying this pregnancy since well before Geoffrey died. This explains why she dissuaded us from coming at the time. I should have come anyway, it might have saved you from being in this situation – I'm sorry Rosa."

"It all right Granny. I'm glad I was with Mum when my sister was born."

"Maybe so, but it shouldn't have happened like that. When did your mother tell you she was pregnant?"

"Erm," Rosa shrugged, "Just a few weeks ago – after we knew that Dad had died. But I guessed a long time before that."

"How did you manage to persuade your mother to go into hospital?"

"I didn't," Rosa confessed. "When she said she wouldn't feed the baby herself, and there was no formula milk in the house, I went down to the telephone box without telling her. My friend's mum had given me the telephone numbers for a midwife, and the doctor – in case of emergency. Well, I wasn't going to let my little sister starve to death."

Granny was astonished at her granddaughter's competence in these unwarranted circumstances. How could her daughter be so foolish? Hopefully, having given birth, what followed would not be a repetition of her behaviour when Rosa was born. Disturbingly, judging by her total lack of preparation, the next few months were looking grim.

It was grandpa who interrupted the silence that ensued. "Come on," he urged, "I think it's time for bed, there's been more than enough excitement for one day."

Grandpa was up at seven o'clock in the morning as he was every day. Granny had not slept well. As down to earth as she usually was, yesterday's drama had upset her. When, by half-past eight, there was no sound from

155

Rosa, her grandmother tapped gently on her bedroom door. There was no response. Quietly, she opened the door and peeped inside. Her granddaughter was sleeping peacefully: there was no point in disturbing her.

It was nearly ten o'clock before Rosa eventually emerged. The first thing that came into her head... she had a sister! By the time she went downstairs, the fire in the lounge was already ablaze, there was tea and toast in the kitchen and Grandpa had gone into the town in the car to buy provisions for the next few days.

"Good morning Granny," she declared joyfully, giving her grandmother a hug.

"You're cheerful, this morning," her grandmother replied, "I take it you slept well.

"Yes I did. I'm so pleased to see you and I'm glad I have a sister... Mum will be all right, won't she Granny?" A hint of doubt threatened to cast a shadow over her otherwise joyful state.

"I'm sure she will darling, but it might take a while." Her grandmother didn't want to dampen her mood, yet neither did she want to raise her hopes too much.

"The midwife said we can go to the hospital this afternoon," Rosa stated.

It was a fine day for early November so the three of them walked to the hospital. Audrey was in a single room, the baby in a cot by the side of the bed. Rosa went over to the bed to give her mum a kiss, before turning her attention to her sister. "What are you going to call her," Rosa asked.

"You can choose a name," her mother answered.

"Ellie," Rosa said, without a second thought, "I want to call her Ellie."

"Okay," her Mum shrugged, "We'll call her Ellie."

Rosa was delighted that she was allowed to pick the name but worried at the sad look on her mother's face.

"She's beautiful Mum, she's really beautiful."

Audrey shrugged again. Rosa bent over the cot, staring in wonder at the tiny form she had helped bring into the world. Grandpa pulled a chair up to the bed, took hold of his daughter's hand and squeezed it lightly. "Are you all right sweetheart?" he whispered, "I hear you've been having a tough time."

A faint smile crossed Audrey's lips, although it was betrayed by the forlorn look in her eyes. Her father leaned over and kissed her on the cheek. "It'll all work out in the end," he promised. Audrey leaned back on her pillow – the tears were not far away. Maybe her father was right. After all, she'd felt the same when Rosa was born, and now her elder daughter was her closest companion – she was a gem. Nevertheless, she couldn't help the way she felt, or so she reasoned. Half an hour passed before Granny appeared in the room. Grandpa was still sitting beside his daughter, holding her hand. Ellie was awake. Rosa had picked her up. She held the child close to her and chatted to her, oblivious to the others in the room. It was obvious that she adored this new addition to the family.

Despite wanting to stay, Granny insisted that they leave Audrey to rest. Both mother and baby were being well looked after in the hospital and, for the next ten days at least, that is where they would remain. "Come on, Rosa," she coaxed, "We have lots to do. We must have everything ready for your Mum when she comes home with Ellie. This afternoon we'll go shopping for a pram and some baby clothes."

Like her grandmother, Rosa was practical. Choosing outfits for her little sister was a joy. For Granny, after the visit to the hospital, the afternoon came as a relief. Her discussion with the matron had been troubling. Audrey was proving difficult. Aside from refusing to feed the infant herself, she would not entertain bottle-feeding her either. As for changing her nappy – that was out of the question. The matron had hinted that Audrey might benefit from being moved into a psychiatric hospital, where she would receive specialist help. Granny was horrified, and voiced her opinion. "We will take care of her and the baby," she insisted.

Audrey was almost two weeks in the maternity hospital where everything was done to help her come to terms with being a new mother. She was encouraged to lift Ellie out of her cot when she cried but, after a few minutes, she would claim she was tired and hand the baby over to the nurse, "You'll have to deal with it," she would cry, "I can't do this."

"She won't be able to manage on her own," the matron commented, when the time came for Audrey to be discharged from the maternity hospital. "We can offer regular visits from a midwife and hope that, with time, the situation improves."

Any attempt to protect Rosa from her mother's problems was not an option. The girl was well aware that things were not right – just as they had not been right from the beginning of the pregnancy. "We'll be here for as long as it takes," Granny assured her.

Having helped deliver her baby sister on Friday afternoon, Rosa was back at school on Monday morning. Granny occupied her time getting ready for Audrey and Ellie coming home. Grandpa returned to Inverness for two days to retrieve the clothes and other items he and his wife would need for a long-term stay in Fort William. He also made arrangements for being absent from home, although he intended to go back each week to collect the mail.

Rosa was excited to tell Morag all about the new baby. "Gosh Rosa," she remarked, "You must have been scared."

"Not really, there wasn't time."

"So, where's your mum now?"

"She's in the maternity hospital. I rang for the midwife like your mum said. How is your mother?" Rosa queried.

"She's fine. She reckons it'll be another week but she's prepared. Everything's ready."

In fact, Mrs Jamieson went into labour early on Friday morning that week. Mary was born late in the evening, just a week after Ellie.

"It's a pity it's winter," Rosa remarked, "I don't suppose we'll be allowed to take the babies out – not unless we get a good weekend.

When Audrey and Ellie were discharged from hospital the family adapted to a routine. The care of the baby rested with the grandparents and Rosa – Audrey would have little to do with her offspring, except when the midwife came. She didn't want this stranger, this woman, interfering in her house but concluded that the best way to be rid of her was to persuade her that all was well. Aside from ignoring her child, Audrey continued with her usual routine, generally taking charge of the household – she cooked, she cleaned, she shopped. Granny, and even Rosa, knew better than to foist Ellie on the unwilling parent. Instead, gradually they coaxed her to watch at bath time, to observe as they amused the baby and, now and again, encouraged her to pick up the child. Only after six months, did Audrey begin to accept Ellie.

In springtime Rosa took her sister out in the pram. She knocked on Mrs Marshall's door. "I've brought my sister Ellie to see you," she announced.

"Come in, come in," the neighbour responded, "Bring your sister in. You can leave the pram by the front door, it'll be safe enough there."

Rosa was delighted to show off her sister to someone outside the household – she'd been desperate to get out all winter. Mrs Marshall was equally thrilled to see the young girl, so obviously fond of her sibling. They chatted for half an hour before Rosa said she must get

160

back home. "You come round any time," Mrs Marshall invited.

"I will," Rosa promised.

From the onset of the spring, through the summer, things improved for the family. Two weeks before the end of the school year Rosa's grandparents went back to Inverness, confident that Audrey and the girls were settled. Rosa, with Ellie, was entrusted to meet with her friend Morag and her baby sister, Mary: they had already enjoyed several afternoons together. Rosa had also persuaded her mother to come out for short walks with Ellie, although Audrey seemed happier to stay in the garden. Since Rosa came home from school for lunch each day, her mother was never on her own with the baby for too long.

Most of the summer vacation was spent in Inverness with Granny and Grandpa or with Aunt Clara on the Black Isle. At the end of the holidays Granny came to Fort William for the first fortnight of the term until a new routine was re-established. By the time Ellie was a year old, everything was more or less back to normal. Rosa was overjoyed that her mother was, once again, hosting a traditional Halloween Party for her school friends.

CHAPTER 15
The Midwife

Time slipped by as year upon year Ellie and, of course, Rosa grew. Despite the setbacks, during and after both her pregnancies, Audrey proved to be a good mother. In time, she became friends with Mrs Marshall, to whom she was introduced by Rosa. However, there was never any reference made to the night the neighbour had first met the girl, trembling outside the telephone box on that dismal October afternoon.

Always practical and confident like her granny, Rosa fared well at school. She was an intelligent young girl and, from the day that she had helped deliver her sister, her future was defined – she would be a midwife. "You want to work with babies!" her mother exclaimed in disbelief when Rosa first revealed her intention.

"Yes," she declared, "And that's what I'll do." Her mind was made up long before the idea became a reality. At sixteen, Rosa began her training.

Ellie was five years old at the time. She missed Rosa, who was often away from home but like her sister before her, she and her mother became close, creating their own world in the big house. Rosa never had any regrets about her chosen career path. Although many of the births she attended were more complicated than her mother's, she always delighted at bringing a new life into the world. Being a mid-wife, she was responsible for visiting new mothers and their babies at home, so became involved with families. As well as happiness, she came across much hardship, sadness and grief. There were days when things were particularly hard – stillbirths, miscarriages, and women who suffered serious complications. It was a cruel world out there, making Rosa ever grateful for her own close family. Growing up, for the most part without a father, struggling with a mother who seemed to have an aversion to newly born babies had not been easy; but she appreciated the family she had and their fortunate circumstances: they never had to worry about money and where the next meal was coming from.

Following her initial training, Rosa stayed in Fort William for a while but eventually, in a bid to widen her experience, she moved to Glasgow, where she was employed as a district nurse, working in some of the poorest areas of the city.

On her first day she arrived at the nursing home early in the morning. Feeling nervous and bewildered she climbed a few steps up to the front door of the establishment. As she leaned forward to ring the bell, she noticed a cardboard box set against the door. At first she ignored it, assuming it to be a delivery. A moment later, as her finger rested on the bell she was aware of a slight movement followed by a distinct noise – a cry. She stooped down, pushed aside some newspaper on the top of the box revealing, to her horror, a tiny baby.

The sound of footsteps from within signalled the approach of a respondent to her ring. Rosa stood, frozen to the spot. The middle-aged matron who opened the door looked questioningly at the terrified young woman standing on the threshold. Rosa stared down at the box, unable to speak. The matron blinked as she cast her eyes down towards the object of the girl's attention. Another cry caused her to take a step forward. She bent down, peered into the package and, sliding her hands inside, scooped up the tiny form, wrapped in a filthy pink blanket.

"Come in," she welcomed Rosa, "I take it you're the new midwife. We're expecting you."

"I'm sorry," Rosa apologised, "It wasn't quite w-w-wh…"

"The welcome you anticipated," the matron intercepted. "Come this way, let's have a look at this wee mite – see what we can do."

Once Rosa had recovered from the shock of finding a newly born baby abandoned outside the building, she removed her outer garments and set about her first task in her new job. The baby, probably only a few hours old, was cleaned, clothed and fed. The police were called to investigate. The nurses in the home named the little girl April, since that was the month.

It was a rude awakening to life in the back streets of this city. Although initially alarmed, Rosa was not fazed for long. Part of her reaction that morning was perhaps due to her anxiety in facing a new position in a strange place. She would soon adapt to the challenges, supported by an incredible team of colleagues, but it would never be easy. Despite the problems, Rosa enjoyed her work as a district nurse, meeting expectant and new mothers in their homes, running clinics, and attending emergency cases in the maternity hospital. Pregnant women were encouraged to have their babies, especially their first, in the nursing home but many preferred home births.

Rosa shared accommodation with another midwife. Her name was Irene – a Catholic from Clydebank. Like Rosa, she was dedicated to the job yet there was one aspect that Rosa found troubling. Many women, particular those of the Catholic faith, endured pregnancies year on year, despite the risks to their health. Post-natal clinics offered advice on family planning. The emergence of the pill as a much more reliable option against unwanted pregnancies marked a significant advance in contraception. Rosa, like many of her colleagues, was willing to advise women on the merits of its use, and direct them to a clinic for further information. Irene was totally at odds with this notion. Her beliefs, in tune with that of her religious persuasion, rendered her against contraception. Marital relations were meant for procreation. Preventing conception was not acceptable; it was a sin, no matter the suffering. There was no point in pursuing the argument.

Many situations facing midwives were challenging, especially home births when a midwife might be unassisted with no reliable means of calling for help. Many houses were unsuitable for home births – unhygienic, no running water, inadequate or, in some cases, no heating. Explaining this to the families was impossible – it was their home; how dare anyone suggest it was not fit for a birth?

***

It was a particularly busy day in the delivery room, with several births imminent. Rosa was in charge of two women for whom there were no available beds in the main ward. Instead, they were placed in a side room with a screen between them. One was a woman approaching forty – considered far too old for child bearing, especially a first child. This prospective mother had already endured several miscarriages. Now, she was full-term and, so far, everything seemed to be going well. The other was a young girl, just sixteen. She was unmarried and distressed to be in this situation. On the instructions of her parents, the baby was to be removed at birth, giving the girl no opportunity to become attached. The girl herself agreed. She did not want the child. Within minutes of each other, the two women were in the throes of giving birth. Rosa called for assistance, but no one was available. The older woman gave birth first. The child was lifeless; the woman was desperate, "Do something, do something," she cried, before flopping back in despair. Rosa, rocking the child in her arms, went round to the teenager at the other side of the screen. She placed the dead child in the cot beside the bed. Within seconds, the cry of a healthy, new born baby pierced the atmosphere. The young girl dropped her head back onto the pillow. Rosa washed the healthy baby, wrapped her in a blanket and took her round to the other side of the screen, placing her gently into the arms of the older woman, who smiled with relief. No questions were ever asked: the delighted new mother called her baby 'Rosa', after the midwife who had saved her!

Rosa sometimes contemplated this reckless act, conducted out of pity. It had been an automatic reaction taken in unprecedented circumstances: it just happened. She hoped little Rosa would thrive in the care of such deserving parents. Yet a tinge of guilt would always remain with her.

***

It was a miserable morning on the day that Rosa completed her final shift as a midwife in Glasgow. She had spent more than three years in Scotland's largest city. Although it had been a challenge, she had enjoyed the experience, the camaraderie and the independence it brought. Nevertheless, she was not sorry to be making her way back to her hometown. It was 1967. Now twenty-six years old, there would be different challenges to face. The position she had accepted in Fort William came with added responsibilities: taking charge of young nurses yet to complete their midwifery training. Also, she was returning to live at home, looking forward to spending a little more time with her sister Ellie, who was now fifteen.

Ellie had grown into an attractive young woman. Elegantly dressed, with the same deep chestnut hair as her older sister, she was not short of admirers. But to Ellie, there was no competition – she had found her beau.

168

Paul was a year older and ready to leave school in the summer. His ambition: to work hard so that he and Ellie could marry and settle down in their own home. Accepting an apprenticeship at a garage in the town set him on the right path. Young as they were, the couple were serious about their future together.

There was no point in Rosa attempting to caution her adorable sibling; to encourage her to enjoy her teenage years before thinking of settling down, for Ellie's mind was made up. On a positive note, Paul appeared to be a fine young man. His devotion to Ellie was indisputable.

Now approaching sixty Audrey, as fond of her home as ever, kept the house pristine. Twice a year professionals arrived to give the place a thorough clean and, despite purchasing an automatic washing machine, she continued to send the bedding and towels to the laundry every fortnight. A gardener was employed during the summer months.

The following year, Ellie left school. Having little ambition other than to marry and bring up a family, Ellie found work in a café. With visitors most of the year, the small business thrived. The relationship between Paul and Ellie continued to blossom, although their romance was restricted. Living at home allowed them to save but it had its drawbacks. Nevertheless, there were opportunities for secret rendezvous, especially during the summertime. They thought they were careful but, in the spring of 1969, Ellie was pregnant.

It may have been premature but the couple accepted the situation with joy. The problem was announcing it to their parents – a daunting prospect. Paul accompanied Ellie as she confronted her mother. Audrey stood as the pair entered the lounge, immediately sensing something ominous was about to be revealed – something for which she was not prepared. As the news unfolded, her face drained of colour. The change in her demeanour was not lost on Ellie who, for the first time, felt regret. Deep down, as soon as she suspected she was pregnant, she knew she had let her family down. Nevertheless, she was happy: it was what she wanted; it was what Paul wanted. She squeezed Paul's hand tightly as he stated simply but politely that he intended to marry Ellie. Audrey, clearly in a state of shock, turned away from the couple. "Perhaps we should leave this for a day or two. I need some time to think."

Clutching onto Paul's arm as they left the house, Ellie intimated, "It's all right, she'll come round. It's just been a bit of a shock."

Facing Paul's parents was not so traumatic. They were proud that their son had chosen such a delightful girl and that he was working hard in order to provide for her. However, they did have concerns for the immediate future. Their small three-bedroom home was not big enough to accommodate Ellie and a new baby: Paul already shared a room with his younger brother and there were two daughters still living at home. "We'll sort something out," his mother offered, smiling kindly at her prospective daughter-in-law.

When Rosa arrived home to find her distraught mother pacing the living room, she knew that a serious crisis had arisen. "What is it, Mum?" she asked, taking her mother's hand and leading her through to the large dining kitchen. "I'll make us a pot of tea."

For several minutes Audrey said nothing. She was numb with shock. Then, as the warm sweet liquid crossed her lips, the colour began to return to her cheeks. "It's Ellie… she's pregnant."

It was Rosa who now turned pale. Knowing her sister was serious in her relationship with Paul, she had spoken to her at length about taking precautions. Why had she not listened? Coming from her sister, rather than her mother, Rosa thought she might take heed. "Oh Ellie, you stupid girl," she whispered under her breath.

"They're getting married," Audrey declared. "The baby's due in January."

Rosa sat down at the table beside her mother, silently contemplating the news. If what her mum told her was correct, Ellie would be eighteen and married by the time of the delivery. Rosa had attended girls as young as twelve; she'd seen many a pregnant teenager abandoned by the father of the child, and rejected by their own family and friends. Ellie was not in that situation.

The couple were married in July: a small family affair with a service in the local church, followed by a reception lunch at the big house. It was agreed that they would stay at Ellie's childhood home until they could afford a place of their own. With plenty of privacy, together with the novelty of being newly married, Ellie

171

and Paul were happy. For the time being Ellie kept her job at the café. She attended the ante-natal clinic for check-ups. Paul continued to work hard. Together they made preparations for the arrival of their offspring. Then, in September, tragedy struck...

CHAPTER 16
Another Tragedy

It was a warm, sunny day in mid-September; Ellie's day off. Mother and daughter sat in the garden, relishing the late summer sunshine. Audrey was reading a novel; Ellie, knitting a shawl for the baby. The screech of tyres on the road disturbed the peaceful atmosphere. A van came to a halt outside their property. Unseen from the back garden a middle-aged man leapt out of the vehicle. He stopped abruptly at the gate, looking up at the imposing building. With a deep intake of breath, he braced himself for his mission: the bearer of bad news. When he reached the front door he hesitated momentarily before pressing the doorbell. There was no response. He tried again. Instead of footsteps from within, the voice of young Ellie Milne turned his attention away from the door. The grim look on his face betrayed his fear, alerting the young woman to call out frantically. "What is it, Kenny? What's happened? Is it Paul?"

"I'm sorry," was all he managed, before feeling the full force of Ellie's attack as she gripped his shoulders and shook him with all her strength.

"Where's Paul?" she shouted. "I want my husband."

Kenny, unable to restrain his tears, uttered the words she didn't want to hear… "He's dead."

The piercing scream that followed as she released her grip and fell to the ground brought her mother to the scene. Unlike her daughter, Audrey did not recognise the man from the garage, but she did know that something terrible had taken place. "What's happened?" she asked quietly, looking to the shattered figure who stood on her doorstep.

"Paul's dead," he answered, "An accident at work."

"Go," she ordered, although not raising her voice, "I'll look after my daughter."

Kenny disappeared back down the path and out to his van. He sat for several minutes without starting the engine: his eyes were so blurred with tears, he couldn't see out through the windscreen.

Audrey sat on the doorstep and wept. As she gazed at Ellie, her limp body strewn awkwardly on the concrete path, her own memories of eighteen years ago flooded her mind. On that occasion, it was she who had collapsed, unable to move on receiving the telegram recording the information that Geoffrey was 'missing presumed dead'. It was Rosa who had come to her rescue but, as the weeks passed and she had given birth to another baby girl, she had sunk to the depths of despair. Now, here was her baby, her beautiful, adorable younger daughter: the girl she had, at first, rejected in her despair. How would Ellie cope?

How long she sat staring at the girl she had come to love so dearly, she did not know. A dark shadow fell across the path as a cloud blotted out the sun. Audrey shivered. Rising from her position on the step, she bent over her daughter, caressing her gently, until finally she coaxed her to her feet.

**

The next few months were difficult for the family. Ellie disappeared into her room, the room she had shared with Paul, and refused to come out. It was fortunate that Rosa, to whom she had always been close, was a midwife, for she would not attend ante-natal clinics or see the doctor. The thought of going through with the pregnancy without her husband by her side was cruel: this was not how things were supposed to be.

Audrey was afraid, not just for her daughter but also for herself. She too had endured the heartache of losing her husband, the father of her unborn child. She had not fared well. The circumstances surrounding both her pregnancies had induced panic, not abating until several months after the births. On both occasions her mother had stepped in to help. She doubted she was capable of fulfilling such a role for Ellie. At least Rosa would be there; yet that did not seem fair. Her elder daughter had taken on such responsibility when Ellie was born. Audrey shuddered – remembering the scene as she gave birth on the bathroom floor. Whatever would she have done without Rosa?

In a way, Audrey's prayers were answered. In mid-December, her father was rushed to hospital in Inverness suffering from a massive heart attack. He did not survive. As their only child, Audrey considered it her duty to be by her mother's side during this sad time.

"It's all right," Rosa assured her, "We'll manage. The baby isn't due for another month." Although Rosa made light of persuading her mother to go, something else was troubling her about Ellie's condition – something she was not prepared to share with anyone, least of all her sister: she would deal with it.

Christmas came and went – a miserable affair for the whole family, separated and grieving. In the meantime, Rosa took care of her young sibling as far as she was able; she bought all the clothes, nappies and other items in readiness for the new arrival; she made arrangements for a home birth, despite hoping her sister would change her mind. So far, Ellie insisted she did not want to go into the nursing home or a hospital to have the baby.

"It would be best for you, especially with a first child," her sister cajoled.

"There won't be another one," Ellie retorted. "Besides, you're a midwife, aren't you? Why would I need anyone else when I've got you?"

It was hopeless. Ellie was sullen; she was grieving physically as well as mentally: she was a mess. Her once beautiful chestnut hair hung down to her shoulders, limp and greasy. Her eyes were dull; her face aged and grey. Where was the happy, attractive young woman of a few weeks ago? Rosa couldn't persuade her to come out of her bedroom, let alone get out of her nightclothes. However, she did insist that her sister eat and drink enough, threatening to call the doctor if she refused. She took food up to Ellie's bedroom and, if she was going away to work, she left sandwiches and a flask of tea.

During the weeks following Paul's death, his older, married sister kept in touch with Rosa. There was an age gap of ten years between Chrissie and Paul. When he died, she had already been married for several years but had no children. After a recent examination, their hopes of having a family of their own were dashed.

Ellie's health was of concern to both Rosa and Chrissie and, when Rosa hinted that her sister had spoken of having the baby adopted, Chrissie suggested that she and her husband, Colin, would like to bring up the child. "Please," she urged, "let us have the chance to adopt my nephew or niece."

Rosa knew that Chrissie's offer was sincere and, of all people, she and Colin were in an ideal position to take on the child. She couldn't make any promises since she had no idea how Ellie would feel once the baby was born, but she could confirm that, if her sister wanted her child adopted, they would be the first to be considered. Ellie was aware that Rosa maintained contact with her in-laws, but she was in no condition to entertain anyone: she just wanted to hide away in her own world. Rosa was there to look after her.

It was Hogmanay morning, the last day of 1969, when Ellie went into labour, two weeks earlier than expected, but Rosa was ready. She made a last attempt to persuade her sister to go into the nursing home. Ellie refused. Nevertheless, she alerted the doctor to the situation. "Get in touch if there's a problem," he stated, adding, "You're a competent midwife Miss Roberts – the best we have. I'm sure you'll manage."

Rosa made another 'phone call. *Maybe, just maybe, her plan would work!*

It was ten o'clock in the evening. They should be out celebrating. This wasn't just a new year; it was a new decade. Rosa turned on the television in the bedroom. Ellie did not object. By eleven o'clock the pains were closer together and more severe. Her face contorted, the agony was plain to see yet Ellie did not cry. Though her body writhed, it was not like the pain of death she had so recently endured: this she could stand, it would soon be over.

At five minutes to midnight, Ellie gave birth to a daughter. Rosa cut the cord, gave her a quick clean and laid her in a carrycot beside the bed. Ellie slumped back on the pillow before once again writhing in pain. "What is it, what is it? I'm done," she called.

"It's all right Ellie," her sister reassured her, wiping her brow, "It's just the afterbirth. One more push, and it'll all be over." The bells rang out; Big Ben chimed and a cheer went up. Ellie pushed. The pain gone, she closed her eyes, oblivious to the outside world and the singing of Auld Lang Syne emanating from the television: oblivious to her sister coming and going and the ring of the doorbell. Now, it was over.

CHAPTER 17
A New Challenge

Rosa took some of her annual leave to take care of Ellie and the new baby. Managing her sister was exhausting and, despite her resilience, Rosa was tired. Following the birth Ellie had perked up, giving Rosa some hope that things might improve. After weeks hiding away in her room, Ellie had emerged, tidied herself up and begun to assist her sister with the household chores. But worryingly, she did not acknowledge the baby as hers. "I'll help you now that you have your daughter to look after," she had announced.

"No, no," Rosa countered, "She's not my daughter, she's yours." Ellie smiled sweetly and continued to ignore the child.

"What are you going to name her?" Rosa asked. "We can't keep calling her 'baby', we have to register her birth."

"I don't know, she's your baby," Ellie insisted, "you choose a name."

"Okay," Rosa relented, "let's both think of names we like. We'll start with the letter 'A',"

"Anna," Ellie said, straight away.

"Alice," Rosa suggested.

"Hmm," Ellie pondered, "I think I prefer Anna."

"Okay, we'll call her Anna," Rosa agreed.

Ellie grinned, "Yes, I like that name."

Rosa sighed: she was glad that was settled. She couldn't imagine what was going on inside her sister's head. Apart from denying the little girl was hers, she was confused about other things. Whenever anyone came to the door she was convinced that they were going to take her away. She attached undue significance to letters, maintaining she was going to be prosecuted. Rosa caught her talking to imaginary people in the hallway and on the staircase.

In order to stop lactation Rosa had obtained medication for Ellie, who, despite the discomfort she was suffering, had refused to acknowledge the problem. There were no other physical effects resulting from the birth but mental issues were becoming more evident as each day passed. After two weeks, Rosa had little option but to seek help: her sister was not going to get better at home. Whatever was wrong required more drastic measures. She requested a home visit from the family doctor, who recognised immediately that Ellie was suffering some kind of nervous disorder – maybe post natal depression. He prescribed medication. Another week passed. Ellie's condition deteriorated further. As well as the original symptoms, it appeared that she was experiencing an adverse reaction to the drug she had been given. Rosa was frantic. Competent as she was, looking after the baby and coping with her sister was proving too much. Audrey remained in Inverness where her elderly mother needed her. Rosa was tempted to alert her to the problems at home but decided against it. She arranged another visit from the doctor. This time there was no doubt in his mind that Ellie must be admitted to hospital for psychiatric treatment. He explained that there was a nursery attached to the unit, where Anna could be accommodated so that Ellie could attend to her. Rosa was alarmed, "She doesn't accept the baby is hers. How is she going to look after her?"

"It might take time," the doctor agreed. "Nevertheless, the child needs to be with her mother. With the right treatment Ellie should recover."

"What treatment?" Rosa questioned. She was not sure about all this but she knew that she was helpless to support her sister at home.

Ellie was admitted to hospital. Rosa took Anna the following day. As a nurse, she questioned the matron on everything that was happening. In her mother's absence, she was acting as her sister's next of kin. As such, she would be kept abreast of any procedures that might follow.

Returning home to an empty house, Rosa felt helpless and forlorn. It was as if she had been defeated. Throughout her life she had always tackled problems, fighting against the odds. When Ellie was born she had been there for her mother. Until her sister was five years old, she had taken on much of the responsibility for her sibling's upbringing: young children, especially babies, were of little interest to Audrey Roberts. Rosa suspected her mother's attitude had not changed. On 'phoning her to relay the news that Ellie and the new baby were in hospital, her mother was alarmed, but added that she was confident Rosa would do whatever was best.

Rosa returned to work the following day. Despite the tensions within the job, it was a relief to be back – a relief that Ellie was in the care of others.

A week later, having re-adjusted to her old routine, Rosa began to consider her future. Unexpectedly, a thought crossed her mind… *I'll be thirty years old next year.* True, she was only twenty-eight now, yet suddenly it seemed that this milestone was rushing towards her. It occurred to Rosa that life was passing her by. Although she had spent more than three years away from home, it had been focused entirely on her career. There was no one of any significance with whom to share her thoughts, her ambitions or her problems. And, here she was, back home – her own choice – but caught up in a family drama that she could never have anticipated. It was a drama that had already resulted in taking on responsibilities that she assumed to be her duty. *Now,* she pondered, *is it wrong to have expectations for myself? Would it be selfish to follow my own aspirations?* Rosa wanted to have fun, to travel, to meet the man of her dreams – whoever that might be. She wanted to live, while there was still time.

Though these thoughts occupied what spare moments Rosa had, she knew that, realistically, a complete change of direction was not an option at the moment. With her sister in hospital and her mother in Inverness caring for Granny, there was no one else to manage things in Fort William. Yet she was optimistic that Ellie would recover and, determined that once her sister was better, she would have to take control of her own life and that of little Anna. So, despite the change in her attitude, Rosa continued as before, maintaining the role of housekeeper and carer as well as running a maternity unit. Visiting her sister and young niece every day, while fulfilling her obligations in the workplace, was exhausting.

Thankfully, after two months in hospital, Ellie was showing signs of improvement. The head psychiatrist was pleased with her progress, expressing his belief that she would make a full recovery. To Rosa, her sister was a shadow of the young vibrant teenager she had been. Clothes hung from her thin frame; her face was pale; there was no sparkle. However, she now accepted Anna as hers, taking charge of the child's everyday needs... perhaps the doctor was right.

***

One day, as Rosa hastened down from her house to the local grocer's shop, a familiar voice called out her name. Looking up, she was greeted by the friendly smile of Mrs Marshall who was walking towards her. Startled out of her daydream, Rosa stopped.

"Rosa, my dear, I've missed your company. How are you?" Mrs Marshall enquired.

"I'm so sorry," Rosa replied. "Things have not been going so well recently."

Mrs Marshall, like everyone in Fort William, had heard of the death of Paul Milne, so tragically killed at the garage where he worked as an apprentice: the incident had made headlines in the local newspaper. The friendly neighbour had not seen Audrey or Ellie since the funeral.

From time to time she had observed Rosa dashing along the road – always in a hurry.

"You look tired. Would you like to come in for a cup of tea? There is someone I'd like you to meet."

Rosa was tempted. For a few seconds she hesitated: later in the afternoon she was on shift and, in the meantime, she needed to visit her sister as well as get the messages. *This is ridiculous*, she thought, *the shopping isn't urgent, there's enough food in the house. I'm not superwoman*. "Yes please," she answered. Remembering the day that Ellie was born when Mrs Marshall had been her saviour – the Good Samaritan – she felt ashamed that she had ignored the woman for the last few months, even though it had not been deliberate.

As she followed Mrs Marshall into the hall, a tall, well-built man in his late forties appeared in the doorway to the lounge. "This is my son, Gerald," Mrs Marshall announced, proudly, "He is here from Australia. His wife, Monica, is visiting her parents in Edinburgh, and," she continued, turning to Rosa, "this is my neighbour, Rosa Roberts."

"Pleased to meet, you," Gerald responded, smiling at the young woman standing in the hallway. He had heard about her from his mother who spoke highly of this girl from the big house.

Gerald backed into the lounge, directing the visitor to an armchair by the fireside, while his mother disappeared into the kitchen to make tea. Rosa, who had felt troubled and weary a few moments ago, brightened.

"So," she questioned, "you're over here from Australia? I imagine it must be quite a different lifestyle down under."

"Very different," he concurred, "although Scotland is a much more beautiful country, and it has a history."

"Tell me about Australia," Rosa invited. "So far, I've never ventured from these shores but one day I'd like to travel, to see a bit of the world."

Gerald needed no further encouragement: he loved his life at the other side of the world, never regretting his decision to make the move, despite leaving relatives and friends behind. He had always enjoyed his work in insurance in Edinburgh and, when the opportunity arose to take up a position in Sydney, he did not hesitate.

Thrilled at his enthusiasm, Rosa was more inclined than ever to pursue her dream. One day she would find her own life. When Mrs Marshall emerged from the kitchen carrying a tray with an array of cakes and scones, as well as a pot of tea, she was glad to see her guest looking happier. "Gerald has a good life in Australia," she remarked, entering the conversation. "It's a pity it's so far away. Nevertheless, I've had some wonderful long holidays with Gerald and Monica, and my two delightful grandsons. They've both pursued careers in pharmacy and sometime soon they will each spend a year or two in Britain."

Mrs Marshall had always spoken enthusiastically about Gerald and his family in Australia. She had another son, ten years or so younger than Gerald, who lived in

185

Edinburgh. He wasn't married and, it seemed, had been a bit of a rebel in his youth. Whenever she spoke of him, her words were accompanied with a surreptitious grin. Rosa was never quite sure what to read into her strange look. Did she admire her younger son or was she ashamed of his antics?

"Well Rosa," Mrs Marshall queried, after pouring the tea and offering her home baking, "What has been happening up at the big house? I've not seen your mother or Ellie during the whole winter."

Rosa gave a deep sigh – an ominous introduction to the tale she was about to tell. When she had finished, Mrs Marshall could not withhold her concern, although she refrained from expressing the horror she felt that, once again, it was Rosa who had been left to bear the burden. "Does anyone else visit your sister?" she asked.

"No one," Rosa answered.

"What about Paul's family?" Mrs Marshall persisted.

"Paul's parents moved to Glasgow a few weeks after their son's death. Living in such close proximity to the garage where he died was too upsetting for them." In a low voice, almost inaudible, Rosa added, "Their eldest daughter, Chrissie, and her husband moved away early in the New Year."

"Does your sister not have any school friends or friends from the café where she worked?"

"Nobody that bothers with her," Rosa admitted, sadly. She realised that she was making excuses for Ellie,

186

who had been obsessed with Paul to the exclusion of all other friendships.

Mrs Marshall understood. She smiled sympathetically at Rosa. "How about I visit Ellie in hospital tomorrow," she suggested. "It's time she faced somebody other than her big sister."

"Would you really?" Rosa responded.

"Of course, I'd be delighted. You can tell her when you visit today."

Although Mrs Marshall, who was now in her late sixties, did not want to get too involved, she was keen to help the girls. Ultimately, she would try to persuade Ellie to get in touch with some of her old friends.

When's your next day off?" Mrs Marshall enquired, as Rosa was about to leave.

"Thursday… until Sunday evening," Rosa replied.

"In that case, would you like to join us for a meal on Friday evening? Gerald's wife is due here tomorrow. It'll be a nice little get-together."

Rosa looked questioningly at Gerald, who nodded in agreement with his mother. "Yes, please join us," he stated with such keenness she could hardly refuse. It was the first time in many months that Rosa had had an invitation to go anywhere. She accepted without further hesitation. By the time Rosa arrived home she had barely enough time to get ready to go out again.

Ellie was more talkative than usual, intimating that she hoped to be able to come home soon. Rosa had reservations. Although her sister was improving as each day passed, she was not convinced that she was capable of taking complete charge of herself and her daughter. Much as she wanted Ellie back home, she was not prepared to take any more time off work. Ellie needed to understand that she could not depend on her older sister for round the clock care and attention.

"I'll speak with the matron," Rosa agreed, before proceeding to tell her that Mrs Marshall would visit her the following day.

"You'll come too?" Ellie beseeched, betraying her vulnerability.

Rosa paused. She was filled with anguish for her younger sibling, yet she knew she must be firm. "No," she stated clearly, without explanation.

"Oh," Ellie responded, tearfully.

Rosa gently took hold of her sister's hand. "I love you so much Ellie, and little Anna, but I can't be with you all the time. Mrs Marshall is looking forward to seeing you and the baby. I'm sure you'll have lots to talk about. I'll be back again the day after."

Ellie was not quite as excited when Rosa left as she had been when she arrived. For the first time since Anna was born, Ellie realised that her sister might not always be by her side. She was afraid: afraid of the future and what it might bring. Paul was gone. If Rosa went too, who else was there?

Rosa called at the reception desk on her way out hoping to have a word with the matron. Unfortunately the woman was occupied with another patient and Rosa didn't have time to wait.

An hour after Rosa's visit, a nurse came to escort Ellie to the nursery – it was time to feed Anna. Seeing her small offspring wriggling in her cot, flailing her arms, put an end to her self-pity: she had a daughter. "I'm a mother," she muttered, as if it had just occurred to her, "I have to take care of my baby." As she leant down to pick up the small child, the child in turn stretched her arms up towards her mother. A warm feeling coursed through Ellie's body – this tiny being needed her. She did have someone after all.

When Mrs Marshall arrived the following day, Ellie was prepared for her visitor. Having attended to Anna, she had insisted on keeping her by her side, rather than placing her straight back in her cot in the nursery, and walking away. No longer simply her duty, the baby was a little person – her daughter. She wanted to show her off; she was proud of her; proud, at last, to be her mother.

Despite such short notice, Mrs Marshall came armed with a gift for the baby, a beautiful pink dress edged with lace. "And a little something for you too," she smiled, handing Ellie a box of chocolates.

"It's lovely to see you," Ellie remarked. "So far, Rosa's been the only one to visit me in here. I don't know what I would have done without her."

Mrs Marshall turned her attention towards the baby. "Can I hold her?" she asked. "It's a long time since I held a baby in my arms and," she reminisced, "that was you." Ellie, very carefully, handed Anna over to her visitor who cooed with delight. "She's beautiful, Ellie. I'm sure she'll bring you much joy."

Mrs Marshall continued to make a fuss of the baby and, to avoid dwelling on Ellie's recent tragic circumstances, she focused on the future. Ellie was looking forward to being discharged from the hospital, hoping that it would be soon.

On visiting her sister the next day, Rosa noticed a distinct change in Ellie's attitude. The sister she had known and loved was returning: her depression was lifting; she was no longer confused. Nevertheless, Rosa stopped herself from becoming too excited. Ellie had endured much heartache; she had been seriously ill. It would be a mistake to jeopardise her recovery by being over confident. When she managed to speak with the psychiatrist at the end of her visit, she was pleased by his measured response. "Ellie tells me she is anxious to be discharged," he revealed. "If she continues to improve, I suggest she spend the weekend at home, just to see how she gets on. I want her here, under observation, for a little while longer.

"I'm going out tomorrow evening," Rosa stated bluntly: she was reluctant to cancel her invitation to have dinner with the Marshalls.

"Perhaps you could pick her up on Saturday morning and bring her back on Sunday evening. That's long enough for a start."

"That would be fine," Rosa acknowledged.

"However," the psychiatrist continued, "Ellie must be able to manage at home on her own before she leaves here permanently. You cannot be there for your sister all the time, you have your own life."

The psychiatrist was aware of the situation. As his patient, his first concern was for Ellie but he had sympathy for this young woman who had taken on so much responsibility for her sister. Rosa was grateful for the man's understanding.

Rosa was glad of the day off. It gave her time to shop and prepare for Ellie's brief homecoming the day after, as well as some time to herself to prepare for going out in the evening. As she soaked in a hot bath she began to fret about the evening ahead. It was so long since she had spent time in the company of others, aside from work colleagues, she was at once excited, yet apprehensive. What would Gerald and Monica think of her – still single at nearly thirty? The furthest she had ventured from home was Glasgow, and that was for work. She had never been across the border into England, let alone abroad. And, as for boyfriends, she'd never had one… apart from one date with Jimmy McFee that had not gone well. She'd had a few offers to be escorted home from dances in Glasgow but never accepted, deciding that they were a rough lot with their broad accents and common patter – *aw c'mon hen; tae posh fer the likes o' us are ye? Fer the love o' Christ lass, anither drink ul no dae ye no harm* – they were not her type.

Wrapped in a towel, she padded through to her bedroom wearing a pair of mules that were too big for her. *Now, what to wear?* Opening her wardrobe she flicked through every item, becoming more desperate as,

191

one by one she rejected them all. *I can't wear that; I've had that for five years; I don't have shoes to match!* Catching a glimpse of herself in the mirror she gasped in horror – "I'm a mess; my hair's a mess!" she cried, as she plonked down on the edge of her bed, head in hands. The grandfather clock in the hall below struck five. Forcing herself up, Rosa went through to her mother's bedroom. Audrey may not be a great socialiser but she was always elegantly dressed, even in her leisure time at home. Rosa selected a pair of brown trousers, a plain cream silk blouse and a tweed jacket. It was modest – not too dressy yet slick. She had shoes of her own that went well with the outfit. Standing in front of the tall mirror in her bedroom, she brushed her deep chestnut hair, applied some makeup and gave a sigh of relief. The attire complemented her colouring in a way that none of her own clothes did. *Maybe I should go shopping with mum in future,* she thought.

Rosa walked the short distance down to Mrs Marshall's home. She was feeling more confident – looking forward to the evening. When she arrived the family were ready to set off. Gerald, who had hired a car for the duration of his stay in Scotland, was driving them to a restaurant a few miles south of Fort William, on the banks of Loch Linnhe. It was a family run establishment, catering for residents and visitors alike – an ideal venue for their small group. Rosa was completely relaxed with the Marshalls who welcomed her with such warmth she felt like part of the family. Rarely had she experienced such a pleasant evening in the company of relative strangers.

By the end of the evening Monica, whom she had never met before, was like a friend she had known all her life. Like her husband, Monica was equally enthralled with their life in Australia, a topic they returned to frequently. Rosa was mesmerised by the couple's worldly experiences, listening intently to tales of their travels across the globe as well as their home in Sydney. More than ever, she was determined she would widen her horizons, although perhaps not for good. She couldn't imagine deserting her Scottish homeland forever.

"If you do decide to tour the world sometime in the future, you must come to stay with us for a while," Monica stressed.

"Yes, definitely," Gerald added. "You'd love our country." Mrs Marshall nodded in agreement.

Although the big house was only a few hundred yards from Mrs Marshall's home, Gerald insisted on taking her right to her door. "I hope all goes well with Ellie and Anna tomorrow," Mrs Marshall commented as Rosa stepped out of the car. "Please let me know, and remember I'm always here to help."

"Thank-you," Rosa responded. "And thank-you all for a wonderful evening."

Rosa felt comforted to realise that she had friends outside her family and her work: it occurred to her that it was what she missed, and what she wanted. As she contemplated the evening, she was conscious that the pleasure lay in being transported to another life: escaping her daily routine. Of course, Mrs Marshall had made reference to her visit to see Ellie and Anna, and there were several allusions to past events but these were not dwelt upon.

It was a while before Rosa fell asleep, so much was buzzing around in her head. It seemed that she had just dozed off when she was woken abruptly by her alarm. She stretched over to switch it off and was about to turn over and cosy down for another hour or so when she remembered – Ellie and Anna! Hauling herself out of bed, she stretched to her full height, stumbled through to the bathroom, washed, dressed and had a slice of toast and some coffee. Fortunately, she had everything else prepared for the day.

By car, it was only a few minutes to the hospital. Ellie was already at the entrance waiting for her as she pulled up in front of the main doors. Negotiating the carrycot, pram base and all the baby paraphernalia into the car took a few minutes: Rosa sighed – she would get used to it.

CHAPTER 18
Ellie comes home

Three weeks later Ellie was officially discharged from the hospital, although she was still being weaned off the medication. It was early May, the spring sunshine lit up the countryside around the big house, highlighting the pastel shades of the blossom on the trees and the contrasting colours of the crocuses and daffodils edging the garden. *This is the best time of year*, Rosa thought. With summer ahead, she was optimistic. It had been a dark, miserable winter, bringing so much heartache to the family in the big house; surely the future would be brighter.

Instead of a traditional pram, Rosa had purchased a duel purpose pram-cum-carrycot, which could be transported in the car. Anna, now more than four months old, gurgled away her waking hours, peeping out from the soft, white blanket that Audrey had knitted. But despite the passing of the months, Audrey had not returned to Fort William; she had not yet seen her first grandchild. Although Rosa understood her mother's concern for Granny, she had hoped she might make the effort to return to Fort William for a few days to see Ellie and the baby. Did she have any idea how ill her younger daughter had been? Whenever they spoke on the 'phone her mother reiterated the same message: "Granny needs me here," followed by, "I know you can manage, my dear." At first Rosa was flattered by comments relating to her competence yet, as time passed, she was becoming irritated, especially when Ellie began to ask if their mother was ever coming home.

Ellie had made excellent progress in hospital. The first noticeable change had been her acceptance of Anna as her daughter. The next came with the realisation that the young child needed her. From that time, she took responsibility for Anna's care, making up her bottles, washing and changing her, keeping her by her side. However, in the hospital so much was done for her. She didn't have to buy food, change beds, wash clothes or clean. When she came home, she assumed that things would be the same and, for the first week or so, that was the case: Rosa had been well prepared for her sister's homecoming. Nevertheless, as Rosa had stressed to Ellie, she would not be there for her all the time. Reality struck only when Rosa, clad in her nurse's uniform, announced that she was 'on shift' overnight.

"How am I going to manage?" Ellie questioned, somewhat alarmed.

"I'll be home just after seven o'clock in the morning… if I'm not delayed. You'll be fine."

Ellie grimaced. She was not happy. Rosa turned towards the door, heading out before her sister could object. When she returned the following morning Ellie was having breakfast – she had already attended to Anna. Rosa sighed. Her sister had survived for twelve hours without her. However, the sense of relief was short lived. As she announced that she was going to bed, requesting not to be disturbed until mid-afternoon, Ellie's face registered disappointment.

"B-b-but you can't sleep all day; there's only enough formula milk for today. You need to get some more."

"No," Rosa responded. "*You* need to get some more."

"I can't," Ellie protested, "I can't leave Anna."

"Of course not. You'll have to take her with you."

Ellie squealed with anger. "I can't. I won't. You don't *have* to work."

For the first time in her life, Rosa was angry with her sister. She was not going to give in to her.

"I am not giving up my job to look after you," she retaliated. "You're eighteen years old. You have a baby. Now, get on with it." Rosa stormed out of the room. She was tired after her night shift but it was a long time before sleep came. At three o'clock in the afternoon she was woken by her alarm. She washed, dressed in her uniform ready for another night shift, and had a light meal. She spoke briefly to Ellie, asking if she'd had a good day. The response was a grunt. Rather than stay around until it was time to go to the nursing home, she checked that her sister had bought more milk, before driving down to visit Mrs Marshall. She needed to talk to someone: her neighbour would understand.

In the meantime Ellie sat in the lounge – sulking. It was not her usual behaviour, but she was used to getting her own way. She sat until Anna began to cry. Snapping out of her sullen mood, Ellie scooped her

197

daughter from the carrycot where she had had a longer than usual afternoon sleep. For a few minutes she cuddled the infant, before setting her down on a large beanbag in the corner of the room while she went through to warm the bottle that she had prepared earlier. Anna, already familiar with the routine, knew that the beanbag meant it was nearly teatime.

For the next hour or so, Ellie was occupied feeding and bathing her daughter, getting her ready for bed and singing her to sleep. She sorted out the washing, had her evening meal, and tidied up in the kitchen. Only when she sat in front of the television did it occur to her that she had survived a whole twenty-four hours without her sister. Maybe Rosa was right.

Rosa was still angry when she knocked on Mrs Marshall's door and, for once, she did not hide her frustration. Her neighbour hardly needed to have the problem explained; she had fully expected Rosa to lose patience at some point, and was surprised it hadn't happened sooner. She allowed the young woman to spill out her fury without interruption until eventually she calmed down, apologising for her outburst. "I'm so sorry Mrs Marshall. I just had to tell someone."

"Please don't apologise to me," she responded, while moving over to the settee and placing a reassuring arm around the distraught young woman. "And please, call me Edith." A few minutes passed as Rosa gained control, her mood calming in the presence of the neighbour she had come to trust and love.

For nearly two hours they chatted, mostly about Rosa's current predicament. She loved her sister, she wanted to be there for her but, as Edith pointed out, Ellie had to take responsibility for herself and her daughter; kowtowing to her all the time was not helping. "I can't leave her yet," Rosa admitted. "Not while Anna is so young." In making this statement, Rosa was voicing what had been occupying her mind for sometime, especially since the evening she had joined the Marshalls for dinner. She yearned for the freedom to have her own life but the time was not right.

"Well, don't leave it too late," Edith warned, "Don't let life pass you by."

Rosa nodded in agreement, although how much attention she was paying was another matter. Mrs Marshall insisted on making tea for Rosa before she was due on shift at seven o'clock.

Despite being much less anxious when she left Mrs Marshall, Rosa couldn't help worrying about her sister. Would she be all right? Had she been too hard on her? These doubts, however, were overshadowed as soon as she entered her workplace: it was a night fraught with problems. Not that her job ever left time to contemplate personal troubles, a fact that Rosa realised was one of the benefits of her profession.

There was no comment from Ellie when Rosa went straight to bed after returning from her second night shift. The shock of Rosa's anger was enough for the younger sister to understand that she would have to do her fair share; she could no longer sit back and expect

Rosa, or anyone else, to rush around doing things for her. Besides, she didn't like arguments... neither of them did.

When Ellie and Anna had been home for three weeks, with still no sign of Audrey making an appearance, Rosa decided to take matters into her own hands. The next time she spoke with her mother on the 'phone she insisted she come home for a few days. "You must see your little granddaughter," she urged. "She is beautiful, and Ellie is so much better. "If you come on the bus, I'll take you back to Inverness in the car. I would like to see Granny."

Reluctantly, Audrey gave in to her daughter's pleas. She knew she should have made the journey before, but the idea that she might be expected to take charge of her granddaughter was too much for her to contemplate: she really was not comfortable around babies. Aside from that, she made herself believe that Granny really did need her and, to some extent, that was true; although her elderly mother was not helpless. In preparation for their mother's visit, the two girls made sure that the house was in perfect order as it had been when she left, not that their home was ever neglected.

After so many months away, it was a strange feeling coming back to her own home. Rosa picked her up from the bus station to drive her the short distance to the big house. As they drew nearer, Audrey wondered that she could have stayed away for so long. The onset of summer added to the thrill of the moment; a moment filled with nostalgia – all the memories she had shared with Geoffrey and the happy times spent with her daughters as they grew into young women.

As soon as she heard the front door open, Ellie rushed to greet her mother. Audrey was relieved. Her younger daughter had made a remarkable recovery. Seeing her granddaughter for the first time brought tears to her eyes. She was ashamed that she had stayed away for so long. Inexplicably, she felt closer to this child than she had towards her own when they were infants, perhaps because she didn't have to be responsible. It was clear, after just a few minutes that Ellie was in charge: she doted on her young offspring.

Audrey stayed for a few days until Rosa had some time off and was able to drive her mother through to Inverness, as promised. She stayed overnight, before returning to Fort William. Granny, now in her eighties, was pleased to see Rosa. She hinted that she would have loved to see Ellie and the baby but wasn't happy about travelling. Although she was sprightly for her age she had lost weight and her eyes seemed sad: she was, understandably, missing Grandpa.

"When Anna's a little older I'll bring them here," Rosa promised.

"And I'll visit you more regularly," Audrey affirmed, as she waved goodbye to her daughter.

CHAPTER 19
Ellie and John

The next few years were uneventful. Rosa turned thirty, yet had taken no further action about her future. Despite still clinging to her dream, her commitment to Ellie and Anna was stronger than ever. Audrey made regular trips from Inverness, sometimes staying for as long as a week. Edith Marshall often visited the big house, as did a few of Ellie's friends. There was always someone to babysit if Ellie wanted a night out which, as the years slipped by, became a more regular occurrence. From the age of three, Ellie enrolled Anna at a day nursery for two days a week. She felt that the little girl needed to be in the company of other toddlers in preparation for starting school. It also meant that she could pursue interests of her own, something which her sister encouraged. She liked to walk, to play badminton, and she learnt to drive.

One night, when Anna was almost four years old, Ellie returned from a dance accompanied by a gentleman, possibly in his early thirties. She invited him in to meet her sister, introducing him as her dance partner. It was obvious that the couple had known each other for quite a while. John Scott was sturdy, of medium height, with thick, dark hair that touched his collar, curling round his ears. He was from further north, the only son of a Scottish Laird. Having been brought up on a large estate, he had always enjoyed outdoor pursuits. As a teenager he became involved in mountaineering, which ultimately led him to join a mountain rescue team as a volunteer, initially in the Cairngorms.

With a degree in business studies and experience in retail, he had always been keen to set up his own business. The opportunity came when he noticed an empty property for sale in Fort William – an ideal location to set up a store selling outdoor gear. After just two years, the enterprise was proving successful. As well as supplementing the allowance from his father, it served as a means of meeting others with similar interests. Within a few months he joined a local mountain rescue team.

Encouraged by a fellow bachelor in the team, John was persuaded to go to a dance in the town. "Isn't it time you broadened your social life?" his young colleague had quipped, rather cheekily.

"Okay," John had replied, much to the surprise of his young friend who had expected the request to be met with more of a challenge.

John Scott was not a stranger to social dancing, having attended functions in the castle where his parents were anxious to introduce him to 'suitable' young ladies. However, he was never interested in his parents' idea of a bride: he would make his own choice when the time was right. A widow with a daughter might not have been what they, or indeed he, anticipated but single women, other than young girls, were not in abundance.

As soon as he set eyes on Ellie across the dance floor, he recognised her as the same young woman who had purchased a pair of walking boots from his store a week earlier. He had been drawn to her then: he was even more attracted towards her now. Boldly, he approached her, inviting her to dance.

"I'm n-n-not very good," she stuttered, afraid of disappointing this stocky Scotsman, who had already captured her attention.

"I'm sure you'll be fine," he answered, "Don't look so worried."

After the first few steps Ellie began to relax, comfortable in the arms of this stranger... well, relative stranger, for she too recognised him as the man who had served her in the outdoor clothes store.

Since that first dance, neither of them had eyes for anyone else.

***

Three months after introducing him to her sister, John Scott proposed to Ellie Milne. They had spent more time together during the preceding months, including taking Anna out on day trips, allowing the little girl to get to know her future father – the only father she would ever know. Ellie had visited John's parents, dispelling her fears of his affluent family. Yes, they seemed rather overpowering at first with their well-to-do English accents, unlike their son who had adopted a warm Scottish drawl. But, behind the pretence, there was genuine warmth. They liked the girl.

On the day of the proposal, the couple drove straight to Ellie's home. They wanted Rosa to be the first to know. As they burst excitedly into the big house to break the news, John caught hold of Ellie by the arm, stopping her as she was about to call her sister's name. All was not well: somehow John had a sense of foreboding. The house was deathly quiet.

"What's wrong?" Ellie urged.

"I don't know," he responded. "Just take things easy."

The blood drained from Ellie's face as she too detected the strange, unfamiliar atmosphere. Moving slowly now, in accordance with the mood, Ellie reached the lounge. Gently, she pushed open the door to see her sister, head in hands, curled up in an armchair, her whole body trembling. Rosa had not heard the couple entering.

"Rosa," Ellie whispered, not wishing to frighten her older sibling.

"Rosa," she repeated, "Whatever is wrong?"

"Granny's dead," Rosa stated flatly, retaining her position in the chair.

Ellie said nothing. She placed an arm around her sister, as the tears welled up in her eyes.

John disappeared into the kitchen to make tea, giving the girls some time to themselves.

So, one of the happiest days in Ellie's life was overshadowed by the death of her grandmother. The news of the engagement was delayed until after the funeral, held ten days later in Inverness. Although Granny was an old lady, she had not been ill: her death came as a shock to the family. It took many months to sort out her affairs. Her house was sold and the whole estate passed to the sole benefactor – her only child – Audrey. Within a year, Audrey returned to her home in Fort William. She provided each of her daughters with a generous lump sum – a wedding gift for Ellie; an opportunity for Rosa.

John and Ellie were married in the spring of 1975. Anna was five years old, a delightful bridesmaid. The event took place at the home of John's parents – a castle. The couple bought a house in Fort William, the town where they intended to make their permanent home.

"Well!" Edith Marshall exclaimed when Rosa paid her a visit a few days after the wedding, "Now you have no excuse; there's nothing to keep you here a moment longer."

"I've already handed in my resignation," Rosa declared, much to the delight of her neighbour.

CHAPTER 20
Rosa takes a break

Rosa had indeed tendered her resignation. With Ellie and John married and her mother back in the big house, it was time for Rosa to take a break. She knew she wouldn't stay away forever yet also realised it was now or never. At thirty-three her life had passed in looking after others, both as a midwife – a vocation to which she had been dedicated – and as a support to her mother and sister at home. Although nobody denied her the right to follow her dreams, her family were surprised when she announced she intended to travel abroad for the next two years.

"But so much can happen in two years," her sister protested.

"That's true," Rosa retorted, "But I'm sure you'll manage."

She added nothing further to justify her decision. As Edith Marshall frequently reminded her, she had no need to defend her position – since the day Ellie was born, when she was just eleven years old, she had done her duty by her young sibling. Nevertheless, a feeling of guilt crossed Rosa's mind whenever her friendly neighbour praised her dedication towards her family as she considered, *I'm not the person she thinks I am.* It was during such moments that her need for justification arose. *Still, what else could I have done? As it was, Ellie had barely survived her ordeal.*

Forget it, she admonished as her focus returned to the future. Her departure, so soon after her sister's wedding, was prompted by a colleague who had recently divorced. A free agent, with no family to consider, Josie had made arrangements to emigrate to Perth in South West Australia, where she was assigned to a hospital to continue her nursing career. Australia had always been Rosa's destination of choice – they spoke the same language and drove on the left, she reasoned. Her idea had been further inspired on meeting Gerald and Monica Marshall five years earlier. Edith Marshall reminded her that there was still an open invitation to stay with her son and his wife in Sydney. "They would be delighted to see you," she insisted. Rosa accepted their offer. In addition, she planned to travel by plane, train and maybe hire a camper van, to make the most of her visit to this vast country. The idea of a trip to New Zealand was another consideration.

When Josie revealed that she fancied breaking the journey in India, spending a month visiting the sights in and around Delhi and perhaps a little further afield, Rosa was enamoured, though a little hesitant at the prospect. "I'm not thinking of the Hippie Trail," Josie assured her. "We'll travel in style; we'll stay in hotels."

So, in early May the two young women set off on their adventure. Audrey was comfortable about her daughter going to Australia. However, the idea of her staying in India was another matter. "We'll be fine," Rosa assured her, though perhaps a little more confidently than she felt. "I'll write," she promised. The feeling of dread she'd had whenever Geoffrey had gone to sea, especially during wartime, came back to haunt her. Having no contact for weeks at a time troubled the elderly lady. Over the years she had come to depend on her elder daughter. How would she manage if another crisis should occur? Fortunately, Edith Marshall provided words of comfort and reassurance that helped Audrey through the first weeks of her daughter's absence. The onset of summer also helped raise Audrey's spirits until, that is, Ellie announced she was expecting a baby!

***

Rosa was, at once, both excited and fearful as she boarded the flight to Delhi. It was her first experience of flying as well as the first time she had left Britain. She held tightly onto the edge of her seat as the engine revved for take-off. Josie gripped her arm, telling her everything would be fine, yet her ever-firmer grasp indicated that she too was scared. Both sighed as the wheels left the ground and the plane flew smoothly through the clouds, on into the wide blue yonder. The adventure began.

India was an experience – the people, the colours, the smells and, of course, the amazing sights. British influence was apparent in the capital, with its architecture, its tree-lined streets, and the fact that they drove on the left although, with myriad cyclists, cows, and pedestrians spilling over from the pavements, it was difficult to tell. "I'll not hire a car here," Rosa commented.

The hotel in Delhi was a grand structure, opulent in style with obliging staff who cared for guests like royalty. With assistance from the information desk, they booked a week in Shimla – the summer capital during the British Raj – around 180 miles from Delhi by train. They chose this mode of transport as an experience, rather than a convenience, and experience it certainly was! Everywhere was crowded – the streets, the station, the trains – a real taste of India. Far from the most comfortable journey but worthwhile for the opportunity to visit this renowned city and its beautiful surroundings. They returned to their original hotel in Delhi for a further three nights before visiting Agra, where they booked into a hotel for two nights. The Taj Mahal, close to their accommodation, was the highlight of their tour. They gazed in awe at the splendour of this great wonder of the world.

After Agra, they travelled by bus to Jaipur, the Pink City, relishing the hustle and bustle of this famous location with its magnificent pink buildings – the colour symbolic of hospitality. Instead of returning to Delhi, as they had intended, they decided to go to Bombay to see a little more of the country. From there they flew to Singapore for a very different experience.

The next stage of their journey took them to Cairns on the tropical north-east coast of Queensland, Australia. Here they had a packed week of sightseeing, including the Great Barrier Reef and the Rain Forest, experiencing a taste of Aboriginal Culture.

Their next destination was Sydney, where the friends parted company. Arriving almost a week later than they had anticipated, Josie caught the first available flight to Perth. She would have preferred to stay on in the capital with Rosa, but her new job in Western Australia beckoned. Considering that the two young women barely knew one another before setting out on their epic journey, they had become close, enjoying each other's company. Both were thrilled to have taken time to see a little of the world on the way. India had been a good choice – a wonderful experience – offering a rare glimpse into a totally different culture. Josie gave Rosa her contact address in Perth. Rosa gave Gerald's address in Sydney, although she didn't intend to be there for long.

Not wishing to impose on the Marshall family, Rosa booked into a hotel close to the centre of the city. She would acclimatise, before making her presence known: a city tour, a cruise from the harbour and a shopping expedition. She had no wish to be caught out as she had been five years earlier when Edith Marshall had invited her to join her family for dinner. With some embarrassment, she remembered raking through her mother's wardrobe to find a suitable outfit. *This time I must be prepared*, she decided.

Having relaxed and settled, following almost six weeks filled with more freedom and adventure than she had ever experienced in her life, Rosa was ready to meet the couple who had so enthusiastically invited her to spend time with them in Sydney. Although they were expecting her around about this time, she decided to ring rather than arrive at their door unannounced. After all, she had not seen Gerald and Monica for so many years and, although pleasurable, their acquaintance was short.

It was Friday evening, Gerald answered the 'phone. Sounding pleased to hear Rosa's voice, he straight away offered to pick her up from her hotel the following morning. It was a relief. Yet even so, she was anxious. Going out for dinner with the couple on one evening was quite different from staying with them. Would they get on with each other? What would she say to them? Rosa's stomach churned as she paced her room on Saturday morning, waiting until it was time to meet Gerald in the foyer. Wondering if she would recognise him was her greatest concern in the few minutes pending his arrival. By the time he entered the hotel reception area through the revolving doors she was in a state of agitation. He smiled broadly as he strode over to greet her – a lone figure guarding her luggage. "Don't look so worried," he jested, as he took her hand and gently kissed her on the cheek. "It's lovely to see you."

"It's lovely to see you too," she responded.

"This way," he directed, wasting no time. He picked up her suitcase and beckoned her to follow, her rucksack slung over her shoulder. They exited the hotel, turned left and headed some fifty yards to the spot where he had parked his car. "Our house is a few miles to the north of the Northbridge area; we'll be there in less than half an hour." Rosa relaxed. She was missing her travelling companion. It was good to have company again.

214

"Mother said you were coming to Australia with a friend and breaking the journey for a bit of sightseeing. Where's your friend now?" Gerald asked. "We thought you might bring her to meet us."

"Josie left for Perth as soon as we landed in Sydney three days ago. She was offered a job as a midwife in the hospital there. I'm afraid we were behind schedule; hence she didn't have time to stay here. Her intention is to live in Australia, so she'll no doubt have plenty of opportunities to visit in the future."

"And what about you?" Gerald enquired, "Will you settle here?"

"No, no," Rosa replied, "that was never my intention. I just wanted to travel for a while, to see a bit of the world. Australia seemed like a good idea, especially after the way you and Monica spoke so enthusiastically about it when we met. I would like to visit New Zealand as well. I hear it's quite different?"

"Yes, indeed," Gerald agreed. "And where did you get to on your way here?"

"India," she stated.

"Wow," came the surprised response. "You'll have to tell us all about that when we get home."

For the rest of the journey they spoke mostly about Gerald and Monica's two boys, both pharmaceutical chemists and both married. By the time they reached the Marshall home, Rosa was feeling much more comfortable. "I'll let you into the house," Gerald stated, "Monica can't wait to see you. I'll fetch your case in a minute."

Monica had heard the car and was at the door before Gerald had retrieved his key. "Come in, come in, my dear. I'm so pleased that you're here at last," she gushed, stepping forward; welcoming Rosa with a hug.

As she guided her visitor through to the large sunlit lounge, Gerald could be heard at the front door bringing in the luggage. "I'll be with you in a moment," he called.

Monica excused herself as she went to make a pot of tea. Gerald joined Rosa in the lounge. As soon as Monica returned with the tea, she announced that she had some news for them. Since Gerald had left the house, barely an hour earlier, she'd had a telephone call. "Guess who?" she enthused, addressing her husband.

"I've no idea," Gerald voiced.

"Go on," she teased, "have a guess. You might know too," she added, looking at Rosa.

"I really don't know," Gerald insisted, feeling a little anxious towards their guest.

Rosa sat in silence. How would she know who would be visiting them?

Monica appeared deflated and Gerald a little annoyed.

"It's your brother… Bernard," she stated emphatically.

Gerald sat up straight in his chair then leaned forward towards his wife. "You're joking. Why would he be visiting us?"

"Well, you'll soon know," Monica responded. "He's arriving at teatime today. His flight gets into

Sydney at five o'clock. I said you'd pick him up at the airport."

Turning again to Rosa, she enquired, "Have you not met Bernard?"

"No, I haven't," Rosa was somewhat bemused. Edith never said too much about her younger son, except to indicate that he'd been a bit of a rebel in his youth. She knew that he was now a barrister living in Edinburgh, so surely he must have changed.

"Where's his flight from?" Gerald queried, "just in case it's delayed."

Monica relayed the flight number saying it was from Singapore via Darwin. He had 'phoned from Darwin when the passengers had alighted for custom's checks. "He's taking a year out from his work. He's been hitchhiking around India. So, still the rebel!" she exclaimed.

Rosa looked at Gerald as if needing some support.

"Hm. That's where Rosa's been," he disclosed.

"But not hitching," Rosa stressed, before Monica had time to say anything.

For a few minutes Rosa had been having misgivings about the timing of her arrival. Now, however, she was experiencing a feeling of excitement. A solicitor with a bit of oomph – now, that could be interesting.

Given this piece of news, Rosa decided it best to refrain from telling the story of her travels in India until Bernard joined them. However, she did mention how much she and Josie had enjoyed the week in Cairns –

their first taste of Australia. Being such a popular tourist attraction, she was not surprised that Gerald and Monica had had holidays there. After a pleasant hour chatting, Monica suggested she show Rosa to the guest room, where she might like a little time to herself and perhaps the chance to unpack before lunch.

"When you 'phoned yesterday, we had thought about taking you to Manly Bay this afternoon, but the call from Bernard this morning has rather upset our plans." Gerald nodded in agreement; he would need to leave for the airport around four o'clock to meet his brother. As it was a beautiful day – not insufferably hot as it can be in the summertime – Monica proposed they relax in the garden.

Rosa was happy with this arrangement. Since leaving Scotland she'd hardly had time to draw breath. The opportunity to rest for a while appealed to her – a welcome break in what she anticipated would be a busy schedule in Australia. There was so much that she wanted to see and do.

When Gerald departed for the airport, Monica left Rosa to enjoy the sunshine while she prepared the evening meal. Rosa's offer to assist was firmly rejected. "Another day, perhaps," Monica affirmed, "but certainly not on your first day." Her hostess was adamant: arguing was hopeless.

When darkness fell, Rosa moved inside to the lounge where she sank into a comfortable armchair and quickly dozed off to sleep. She was woken by the sound of voices at the front door – excitement, movement.

Slightly disorientated, it was a moment or two before she realised where she was. "They're here!" she gasped, rising from the chair. Before she got any further, the living room door opened. Gerald appeared, followed immediately by a younger man, similar in looks, though slightly shorter. "This is Bernard," he announced, addressing their guest, "and this is Rosa, a friend of our mother."

"So pleased to meet you," Bernard stated, stepping forward to greet the young woman who was looking a little bemused. "I must freshen up ready for dinner," he apologised, as he turned towards the hall where Gerald was waiting to show him to a second guest bedroom. Rosa was still standing when Monica came into the room. "Do you feel better for your nap?" she enquired.

"I'm so sorry, I must have been more tired than I thought."

"No, no, it's quite all right," Monica responded, "I find sitting out in the sun makes me sleepy. I just came in to tell you I'll be serving dinner in half an hour."

"Oh, okay. I'll get ready."

"You don't need to dress up," her host assured her, "We're not going anywhere, and there'll only be the four of us."

On returning to her room, Rosa sat on the edge of the bed considering whether or not to get changed – not into anything fancy, maybe just a different top: she felt a bit sticky after being in the sun. Then, her thoughts turned to the man she had just met. In looks, he was a younger version of his brother Gerald: dark brown, wavy hair, brown eyes. Not knowing Bernard in the past it was difficult to judge, but he seemed rather thin and drawn. Although his arms and hands were tanned, his face appeared pale.

A glimpse at her watch brought an abrupt end to her daydreaming – twenty-past seven – dinner in ten minutes: barely time to wash, redo her make-up, and don a clean blouse to replace the T-shirt she had worn for the last two days. She was a little flushed as she arrived in the dining room to be greeted by Gerald. "It's okay, you're not late," he quipped, seeing that she had been in a hurry, "We're still waiting for Bernard."

"He looks – well, a bit tired," she faltered.

"Between you and me," Gerald whispered, "I don't think he's too well."

Rosa nodded in agreement just as Bernard appeared at the door. "Ah, I hope I'm not late."

"Right on time," Gerald responded, directing the two guests to be seated at the table as Monica entered carrying a casserole. Gerald disappeared into the kitchen to help bring through the rest of the serving dishes and a bottle of red wine.

He proceeded to pour a glass of wine for everyone and raised a toast, "To our guests from the old country."

"To the old country," Bernard chipped in.

This tribute set the tone for the evening. There was warmth in the atmosphere that had nothing to do with the weather.

220

"So," Gerald remarked, glancing towards Rosa and Bernard in turn, "I believe you have both sampled life in India on your way to this new country of ours. When Rosa told us she had chosen to break her journey in India, we were surprised: now, Bernard, we understand you did the same. So, what was the attraction for you both?"

All eyes turned to Rosa, the most unlikely of the two guests to have chosen the East as a destination. Reluctantly, she began to relate the story of her experience in India with her colleague, Josie. It had been an eye-opener, a cultural revelation, even if not particularly daring. They had stayed in classy hotels, travelled by conventional means, and steered clear of street food. Nevertheless, they had mixed with the locals; they had ventured through the streets and market places, shared crowded railway carriages and local buses and visited Hindu temples, as well as marvelling at the famous sights and magnificent architecture. Rosa's enthusiasm surfaced as she described her experience. She had never been abroad before. India was a personal challenge as was spending six weeks with someone she barely knew before setting out.

"I'm sure my adventures are nothing compared with Bernard's," she commented apologetically, on concluding her tale.

"Maybe not, but it still sounds like an amazing experience," Monica enthused. "From what I've heard and from what you've just relayed, India is a remarkable country."

Attention now turned to Bernard, "I do have quite a different tale to tell," he admitted.

Unlike Rosa, Bernard had been adventurous in his youth. While at university, he had taken advantage of the long vacations to travel throughout Europe – hitchhiking. After qualifying as a lawyer he had spent a year with friends, working in Canada: he was young, he was carefree – he was stupid. That experience had taught him a lesson in life, a lesson that he could never forget. Now, after years proving his worth as a barrister, he had negotiated a year away from his desk. Once again he had an urge to break free, to see the world. He decided to travel independently, without pre-arranged flights, without pre-booked accommodation, and carrying only what was necessary.

"And couldn't you afford hotel bills?" his brother interrupted sarcastically, though failing to hide a smile.

"I wanted the thrill of the open road, a real experience of the people and the countries I visited."

"I thought you said you were hitchhiking in India," Monica queried.

"That's right, I did. But I set out from Scotland, hitchhiking all the way: France; Italy; Yugoslavia; Greece; Turkey… I've been on the road for five months." At this point he produced a photograph from his shirt pocket. It showed a scruffy looking individual with an untamed beard and dishevelled hair down to his shoulders. A large rucksack was slung over his right shoulder. He was wearing sunglasses. "See," he said, passing the image round the table. It was difficult to ascertain the resemblance between the person in the photograph and the neatly dressed clean-shaven man at the table. "I stayed a night in a hotel before I left India. I shaved off the beard and had a hair cut. Well, I didn't want to turn up here looking like a hippie." Rosa suspected that the change might have had as much to do with his forthcoming flight. She doubted his non-conformist image bore any likeness to his passport photo.

Again, Gerald had to smile. A scruffy kid was the way he remembered his younger brother and, though it was obvious that Bernard still had a wild side, it was apparent that he wanted to appear conventional in the company of his brother and sister-in-law. In view of the young woman sitting opposite him at the table, he was relieved that he had left the hippie behind.

"Come on then, tell us about your adventures," Gerald urged: he had always been intrigued at his brother's ability to shock. He might have been considered a rebel, but he was a good storyteller, entertaining his family and, in turn, giving them something to talk about. By the time the meal was over, he was still hitching his way through France, his outlandish experiences capturing the attention of the listeners. Nevertheless, Bernard was flagging – he was tired, jetlagged and feeling unwell. "Enough for tonight," he said at last, exhaustion etched across his pale face. "India will have to wait until another day. Now, if you'll excuse me I must get some sleep."

"Of course," Monica sympathised, "You must be tired after your journey." Despite his effort to be sociable, her brother-in-law was not displaying his usual exuberant personality.

"I must help you clear up," Rosa insisted, "then I'll retire too."

Rosa had thoroughly enjoyed her first day with the Marshall family, wondering why she'd had reservations. Gerald and Monica were so friendly, as was Bernard, although there was something about this younger brother that she couldn't quite understand. Why would a man in his position decide to take a year out to undertake such an outrageous escapade – and to do so alone? Not knowing the man it was difficult to make a judgement, but she sensed all was not well with him. Perhaps it was just jetlag, yet she had a strange feeling it was more than that. Whatever, she wanted to get to know him better and most importantly discover why he was not married.

Considering that she had slept in the afternoon, Rosa was surprised that she had no trouble falling asleep as soon as her head hit the pillow. Yet, when she awoke in the morning, she recalled hearing noises during the night – movement; voices; doors opening and closing. She dressed and went through to the kitchen where Monica was preparing breakfast. "I thought I heard you up and about; tea or coffee?" she offered.

"I'll have coffee please," Rosa replied. "What's happening? Where are the boys?"

"Bernard was very ill during the night so Gerald insisted on taking him to the hospital in Sydney – just to have him checked over. Although my brother-in-law did his best to keep us entertained last night, I could see that he was struggling. Apparently he had some severe bouts of diarrhoea in India – typical Delhi-Belly. He's also tired and possibly feeling the worse for jetlag. Hopefully it's nothing more." Brushing that aside, Monica added, "How would you fancy a ladies day out in the city?"

"Sounds good to me," Rosa concurred.

When they arrived home, after a pleasant morning shopping followed by a leisurely lunch, Gerald and Bernard were back from the hospital. Bernard was looking better – not that he *was* better, but knowing what was causing the problem had perked him up. "I have a tapeworm," he announced, much to the horror of the two ladies. "It's okay," he continued, "I have medication to dissolve the little beast."

"Are you sure you don't want to go and lie down?" Monica suggested, her face paler than that of her guest, "We really don't mind."

"No, no," Bernard argued. "I'm also suffering with jetlag, and the best answer to that is to adapt to Australian time."

Rosa's stomach reacted to Bernard's diagnosis with a double somersault. It made her realise how fortunate she had been on her journey around India. Neither she, nor her travelling companion, had suffered anything more that a few abdominal pains which, in neither of them, had amounted to anything.

The next couple of days were spent enjoying the sunshine and chatting. Bernard resumed the story of his adventures; Monica and Gerald, when he was home from work, spoke about Australia; and Rosa talked more generally about her life in Scotland. Although nothing was said, giving Bernard a chance to recuperate provided the opportunity for the four of them to get to know each another.

Gerald arranged time off work during the following two weeks when they made plans to visit places in and around Sydney. Lake Macquarie was a full day out, as was a trip to the Blue Mountains. After the warmth in Sydney, the chill in the mountains, accompanied by a few flakes of snow, came as a shock. An afternoon at Toranga Zoo on the shores of Sydney Harbour was a delight; marsupials being a special focus. Lunch at Manly Bay, visits to other beaches, including Bondi, and views over the harbour, gave the visitors a real feel for the area. Altogether it was a wonderful fortnight, enjoyed equally by the guests and their hosts.

Towards the end of the two weeks, Rosa began to think about the rest of her stay in Australia, along with the possibility of visiting New Zealand. Guided by Gerald and Monica, she highlighted places that must not be left out: the list was extensive. Bernard had anticipated continuing his travels in the same vein as he had set out. Now he was considering something different... with Rosa. The more time he spent in the company of this young woman, the more he admired her. Although Rosa was a cautious traveller, considering she had never ventured abroad before, her journey had been ambitious: she was feisty, she was amenable and, he had to admit – attractive.

Rosa enjoyed the time spent in Sydney with Gerald and Monica: she could not imagine having more generous hosts. In addition, she had to admit that her stay was enhanced further by the presence of the gentleman who, until just over two weeks ago, she had never met. Brief references to him by his mother, Edith Marshall, were recalled only when she first set eyes on him, looking weary and ill from his travels in India. A rebel – the black sheep of the family – was the way he had been described, a portrayal supported by his older brother when they had met in Fort William. Her first impression, by contrast, was a sick man struggling to be sociable.

As he recovered from jetlag and the unfortunate consequence of his escapade in India, she began to understand the label attached to him by his family. On the one hand he was a barrister, a respected gentleman, down-to-earth; on the other – a would-be hippie with a desire for adventure. He had a sense of humour to match his diversity of character. Rosa wanted to know more about him. What was his story? Why hadn't he married? She liked him. Well, to be truthful, it was more than that. As they both prepared for their departure from Sydney, she realised that she had feelings towards him; she would miss him.

Finding her alone in the lounge a few days before parting, Bernard sat down beside her. She was planning the next stage of her journey – a flight from Sydney to Uluru, thence to Alice Springs. From there, she hoped to board the Ghan Train to Adelaide.

"How would you like some company on your travels to the outback?" he asked.

For a moment Rosa was silent. Was he earnest? His request had come without prior warning. There had been no discussion, not a hint that he might desire her company.

"I'm serious," he continued, as if reading her thoughts "We both want to see more of this vast country, so why not see it together?"

Without giving it further consideration Rosa responded, "Yes, why not."

"That's settled then," Bernard quipped. "I'll book myself on the same flight." Without another word, he was gone.

Rosa was stunned. *What have I done*, she thought, as her own words of acceptance echoed in her mind? He had been blunt; the whole episode was over in a matter of seconds: the commitment was made. Monica appeared at the door. "Dinner's ready," she announced. There was no time for reflection.

Two days later, the pair waved good-bye to their hosts and, much to the amusement of Gerald, boarded the same plane to Uluru. "Well," he stated, "my brother may have adapted to the status of a respected barrister in Scotland's capital, but he still has the rebel in him."

"I hope he doesn't lead Rosa astray," Monica remarked, "She's such a delightful young woman, I feel guilty for introducing them."

"Rosa's quite capable of looking after herself," Gerald retorted. "She's in her thirties; she's not a young kid. Besides, it's not as if we orchestrated their meeting."

"Hmm, I suppose you're right," Monica affirmed, although she was not convinced.

Rosa was filled with nervous excitement as she ascended the steps of the plane bound for Ayers Rock. Bernard had secured a seat next to her so, never having spent more than a few minutes alone in each other's company, they were now side by side, and destined to be together…

*****

After visiting Uluru, the travellers hitched a lift to Alice Springs, where they spent several days gaining an insight into the town's unique features: the Alice Springs Telegraph Station; the School of the Air; the Royal Flying Doctor Service. From there, as Rosa had planned, they travelled on the Ghan train to Adelaide. Hiring a car, they explored the surrounding area and headed east to Melbourne. From Melbourne they sailed to Wellington, North Island, New Zealand, where they hired a camper van. It was the best way to see the whole country at their leisure – a beautiful country, with magnificent scenery, friendly people and glorious spring weather. For three months, they toured both the North Island and the South Island. In the Golden Bay area, at the north of south island, they discovered a Hippie Commune. For two weeks Bernard and Rosa camped nearby, learning something of the alternative lifestyle the group had adopted – producing artwork to sell in order to supplement living off the land and fishing. Having exhausted New Zealand, the pair returned to Australia, flying into Brisbane. They spent a week in a hotel on the Sunshine Coast, relaxing, before hiring a car and making their way south down to Sydney where they had arranged to spend another week with Gerald and Monica.

Rosa was more nervous returning to the Marshall household than she had been on her first visit.

"Don't worry," Bernard quipped, "You are now one of us."

She took a deep breath as she stepped out of their hire car and approached the house, holding tightly onto her husband's arm.

PART 3

NO MORE SECRETS

CHAPTER 21
Rosa and Bernard

It was early spring 1976 when Rosa and Bernard arrived home from their trip around the globe. After leaving Bernard's brother and his wife in Sydney, they flew to Perth in Western Australia to spend a few days with Josie before continuing their travels, visiting South America, Hawaii and California. Bernard had contacted his firm to let them know he wished to extend his leave by three months: he was on honeymoon! After a welcome home/wedding celebration in Fort William, Bernard returned to Edinburgh with his wife.

As they had been getting to know one another in Australia, Bernard disclosed that, although he had never married, he'd had a romance in his youth – a dalliance was the way he referred to this episode. His confession came before his proposal of marriage to Rosa: he didn't want them to have secrets from each other…

Along with several graduates, he had gone to Canada for some work experience. During that time he had become involved with a fellow graduate, a teacher from the UK. The result: a baby daughter. As both were about to embark on their careers, neither was ready to make such a commitment. Moreover, they were by no means devoted to one another. It was a holiday 'fling'; they'd had fun but – a baby – that was a mistake. So, by mutual consent, they arranged for the child to be adopted. A wealthy, middle-class couple became the parents, providing much better prospects than the young graduates could offer. Bernard hinted that he had felt sad on his departure from Canada, leaving the little girl behind, despite not having seen her since a few days after the birth. In retrospect, he admitted that he had been selfish. Giving his daughter away was the price he had paid.

Now well in his forties, Bernard had not entered into any serious relationship since that unfortunate episode. Until the unexpected meeting with Rosa, he had shied away from pursuing any attachment with the opposite sex. Being so ill on their first encounter he thought he had missed his chance for, to be truthful, his desire for this young woman occurred immediately he set eyes on her. The coincidence was bizarre. Here was a fellow Scot, a friend of his mother, sitting opposite him in his brother's dining room at the other side of the world. And here he was feeling so wretched. Still, it had worked out in the end.

On the one hand, Rosa appreciated Bernard's confession: it was much better to put any failings behind them before moving forward in a relationship. However, she now faced a dilemma. How did her misdemeanours compare to his? Should she disclose her guilty secrets and risk losing him, or should she keep them to herself and carry the guilt alone – forever? *I'm not an innocent child,* she thought. *He must realise that I too have made mistakes.* She decided to take a chance. She'd tell all… or maybe not quite all – that would be too painful. So slowly, carefully, she began to relate her actions as a midwife in Glasgow, swapping the babies. For a terrible

234

moment she thought Bernard was going to get up and walk away. *Was that his barrister's look?* He seemed so serious; so remote.

"That took a lot of courage," he stated at last.

Rosa was unsure what he meant, "The action, or telling you about it?" she asked.

"The confession," he confirmed, "The action was spontaneous, it was a response to a crisis. It wasn't premeditated and it probably saved a great deal of heartache for both mothers."

"But it doesn't make it right, does it?"

In response, Bernard took hold of both her hands, drew her close and kissed her gently on the lips.

Rosa sighed. She was relieved, although she knew she could not be completely exonerated, not unless she shared her deepest, darkest secret and that, she decided, she could never do.

***

For more than fifteen years the couple stayed in Scotland's capital. At first, they had hoped for a family but even at the age of thirty-four, when they had returned from their travels, Rosa was older than most new mothers. As time slipped by, pregnancy became less of an option; it was too risky. Ultimately, Rosa and Bernard resigned themselves to life without children; not such a hardship: they were in love; they were content in each other's company.

Rosa had no trouble securing a position as a nursing sister in Edinburgh where, for ten years, she was in charge of a maternity unit. It was a job she had always loved.

When, in 1988, Anna came to Edinburgh to study, Rosa was delighted. For three years, aunt and niece, who had always been close, met regularly. Then Rosa and Bernard moved to Fort William, as had always been the plan. Edith Marshall, now elderly, with no family close by, had opted to go into a care home. She was delighted when her son and daughter-in-law moved to the town, enabling them to visit her every week. Rosa's mother, although approaching eighty, still lived in the big house. With a housekeeper, a gardener and her younger daughter close by, she was not short of helpers. She had always loved her home and was determined to stay there for as long as possible.

Although Rosa enjoyed life in Edinburgh, she was thrilled to be back in her hometown. Both she and Bernard relished the outdoor life. They quickly settled into their new home. It was close to the big house and to her sister and brother-in-law. Ellie and John had a son, Jonathan, born in 1976, before Rosa and Bernard returned from their travels. From across the world, Rosa had worried about Ellie's pregnancy, hoping and praying that, this time, there would be no traumas to ruin the event. How thankful she was to learn that there were no problems... not before, during or after the birth. Jonathan, at fifteen, was a fine young lad who would eventually inherit his grandfather's estate. His father, though keen on outdoor pursuits, had no interest in becoming a laird: he had a thriving business in Fort William.

***

When Rosa discovered that Anna, at the age of twelve, had formed a friendship with Marie McInnes while at the High School in Fort William, she was troubled. The McInnes family had moved to Glasgow soon after Marie's birth. Why had they come back, she wondered? *What if they find out? What if Marie meets Ellie? I hope Anna doesn't introduce her to me.* Fortunately, while Rosa remained in Edinburgh, there was little chance of such a meeting. Although Anna and Marie were friends at school and enjoyed the same extra curricular activities, they rarely met at other times and, if they did, it was to go out as friends or with other girls, not with parents. Rosa, of course, had no control over the situation. She tried to forget about it, to put it to the back of her mind but she fretted, not daring to bring the subject up for fear of arousing suspicion. Needless to say, she was relieved to learn that Marie had moved to the Isle of Bute with her family straight after her standard grade exams. Two years later, when Anna came to university in Edinburgh, Marie McInnes was never mentioned. Anna had too much to relay about life as a student. She was thrilled to be away from home for the first time despite sometimes feeling homesick. She was excited about meeting new friends yet daunted by her new lifestyle. Her aunt became her confidante, a shoulder to lean on when she was anxious. It was a sad day for Anna when, after three years, Aunt Rosa and Uncle Bernard moved away. However, by that time she was well established in the capital and decided to stay there as she embarked on her career in teaching. Not until several years later, when Anna returned to her hometown, did the name of Marie McInnes come up again…

***

Anna was excited: she was going abroad for the first time, meeting her boyfriend at Glasgow airport. Neither her mother nor her Aunt Rosa were enamoured by her latest beau. Not that they had ever met him, and therein lay the problem. They were not convinced that this man cared about Anna. A divorcee, he continually made excuses for not visiting her in Fort William. According to Anna, on the one hand he showered her with affection, begging her to come back to Edinburgh so that they could spend more time together; on the other, he spoke incessantly about his young daughter yet did not want them to meet. He claimed that he wanted to keep the two aspects of his life completely separate. How, she pondered, could she maintain a secure relationship with a man who was seemingly obsessed with his daughter but refused to introduce her to the woman he professed he loved? Nevertheless, there was no point in either her mother or her aunt dissuading her from her forthcoming holiday. Anna's mind was made up.

Even more worrying for Rosa, her niece decided she would visit her old school friend Marie McInnes on the Isle of Bute, on her way to the airport. She arranged to stay for one night, leave her car at Marie's and travel by ferry and bus to the airport, returning a fortnight later to spend more time with her friend when retrieving her car. What concerned Rosa about this proposal was the possibility that Anna would meet Marie's parents; or rather, her adoptive parents. If names were bandied about, conclusions might be drawn.

For the entire two weeks that Anna was away, her aunt was a nervous wreck. Bernard noticed his wife's agitation. "What ever is bothering you?" he asked on more than one occasion during that fortnight.

Rosa brushed aside his concerns: "I have a headache, it's nothing to worry about," she assured him. How she wished she had told him before they were married, when they had both made and accepted each other's confessions.

Rosa was at her sister's when the telephone rang.

"Would you answer that," Ellie asked. She was washing her hands; she had been out in the garden weeding.

The call was from a very distressed Anna. She was at the police station in Glasgow having been stopped at the airport on her return from Spain. Her car had been impounded. After faltering for a moment, not quite grasping the situation, Rosa offered to drive to Glasgow to pick up her niece. She was sure Anna had intended to leave her car at her friend's house on Bute while she was away, so assumed there must have been a change of plan. Did this have something to do with Marie, or was it Anna's boyfriend?

Trying to remain as calm as possible, Rosa told Ellie that Anna was stuck in Glasgow without her car: she had said she would pick her up.

"Oh, okay, Rosa. Are you sure you don't mind?" Ellie asked.

"Of course not," Rosa replied.

Ellie made no further comments. She was not surprised at Rosa's willingness to help out where Anna was concerned: the two had always been close.

CHAPTER 22
Rosa to the Rescue

The drive to Glasgow took more than three hours. Rosa stopped briefly to leave a message on the answerphone for Bernard. She was anxious to reach Anna as soon as possible. Although the girl perked up when her aunt arrived, it was clear that she was greatly distressed, scared that she would be further detained.

"Don't you worry," Rosa declared, after Anna had described briefly what had happened. "They don't have sufficient evidence to keep you here. I'll sort this out right now." With that, she left the cell to search for whoever was in charge. Again, Anna was alone; her stomach churning in anticipation. Her aunt was forthright but would she succeed in her mission? Anna was unsettled by the day's events – she wasn't sure of anything anymore. As soon as the cell door opened, she leapt to her feet.

"We're going," Rosa announced.

Anna collected her belongings, signed for the items that had been confiscated earlier and left the building. *Thank goodness for Aunt Rosa*, she thought, as she escaped from her ordeal.

When they were clear of the city, Rosa suggested they stop for a meal: both women were ready for a break. Aside from a rest before continuing on to Fort William, it gave Anna the chance to relay the rest of the unfortunate tale to her aunt. As regards Marie, they both concluded that it was a mystery. Anna's car, located in Perth, did not make sense. Rosa was especially troubled by the link between the two friends and this episode. It did not bode well for her. What if the two of them were to discover their real association? To detract from this uncomfortable state of affairs, Rosa changed the subject, questioning her niece about the boyfriend – or was that now ex-boyfriend? She had noticed that there was no sign of William West at the police station and was curious to find out what had happened to him. She was increasingly disgusted as Anna's story unfolded. Still, better that she had recognised this despicable side to his character before making any further commitment. Anna admitted that the relationship was finished. Her aunt hoped that she would not be persuaded to change her mind.

It was late when they arrived in Fort William. Anna declined the offer to stay with her aunt and uncle that night; after her ordeal, she wanted to get back to her own home.

For Rosa, the day had presented a different ordeal. After more than twenty-six years, was her secret about to be unleashed? Surely not, not after all this time. Yet she was uneasy. "Stop it!" she told herself. "Get home, get some sleep, things won't seem so bad in the morning." But for Rosa Marshall, the moment of truth was rapidly approaching.

When she entered her home that night, Bernard was waiting patiently, anxious to know all the details of Anna's detention in Glasgow. After all, his whole career had been spent as a barrister, involved in the law. He was also curious about the afternoon's visitor. Why would a detective from Perth travel to Fort William on a quest to find the relatives of a certain Laura Milne if he wasn't sure of his facts? Something was going on: something that made him uncomfortable.

Bernard listened intently as Rosa relayed the story of her mission to rescue her niece from the police station in Glasgow. Knowing Anna, he could not believe that she was in any way involved in her friend's disappearance. Nevertheless, the police did have reason to intercept her at the airport although, as his wife had rightly claimed, they had insufficient evidence to detain her after questioning. However, the incident was strange. Where was the missing girl, and why was Anna's car in Perth?

When Rosa finished her tale, it was Bernard's turn to divulge the strange visit of the detective from Perth. "He was looking for the family of a young woman by the name of Laura Milne, currently in Ninewells Hospital in Dundee. He seemed to think you would be able to help." Bernard eyed his wife as he spoke. She appeared nervous, unsettled, but when he asked if she was all right, she said she was tired: it had been a difficult day.

Rosa realised that her husband was suspicious – she was not going to be able to keep the facts from him for much longer – he would not be fooled.

The dreaded moment came two days later, on Sunday afternoon. The telephone rang. Bernard answered. He looked grave as he returned to the lounge a few minutes later. "That was Detective Sergeant Boyle," he announced.

"Who?" Rosa sounded surprised.

"Henry Boyle – the man who came here on Friday enquiring about Laura Milne."

Rosa's stomach churned. Although she could have no idea exactly what the detective had relayed to Bernard, clearly it must concern Laura. *Had he unearthed the truth? Did he know? Did Bernard know?* Inwardly, she was panicking. The next few seconds, as she waited for her husband to continue, was like an eternity

"It seems that there has been a mix up," Bernard explained. He spoke slowly, deliberately, looking his wife in the eye, expectantly. "The woman in hospital, thought to be Laura Milne, regained consciousness late on Friday night. Her name is Marie McInnes. That's rather odd, don't you think?"

Rosa had no option. She had to tell Bernard what she had done.

CHAPTER 23
The Confession

"YOU DID WHAT?" The words echoed in Rosa's ears. Barely in their married life had Rosa and Bernard had a cross word. He was her husband, her best friend. The idea that she might lose him was unthinkable.

As she had concluded her story, Bernard was unable to retain his anger. Following his initial outburst, he rose from his seat and, half under his breath, declared angrily, "I'm going out for some fresh air – I need some time to think." The engine revved, the car roared out of the drive. Bernard was gone.

For a time, Rosa sat motionless until, gradually, the tears came... tears of distress, tears of shame. It was wrong – what she had done was wrong. She had known that all along. But what should she have done? The girls were born within minutes of each other: one at the end of 1969; the other as the bells chimed in the New Year, the new decade – 1970. For weeks, Ellie rejected her eldest daughter. How would she have coped with two babies? Nevertheless, Rosa knew that her actions were immoral. For more than twenty-six years she had suppressed the guilt, held her nerve. Now the hour of reckoning had come and, as Bernard had asked, what did she propose to do?

Hours passed. The tears turned to uncontrollable sobs until, at last, no tears were left. It had grown dark outside. Where was Bernard? Never before had he stormed out. Never before had he left her. Her stomach rumbled. It occurred to her that she had missed her evening meal; she felt hungry but the thought of food sickened her. Eventually, with great effort, she forced herself to move, to go through to the kitchen and make a mug of cocoa before going to bed. However, sleep didn't come for Rosa, neither that night nor the night after. When the telephone rang, she didn't answer. All she wanted was Bernard but Bernard wasn't there. By Tuesday afternoon, exhaustion took over. She collapsed onto the sofa in the lounge and slept – and slept. And that is where Bernard found her… twenty-four hours later.

Rosa's confession on Sunday had come as a shock to Bernard. He was stunned. How could his beloved wife have carried out such a deed? More than anything, how could she have maintained the deception for so long? He knew he had to get away; he had to think. Such was his desperation he had driven several miles before he thought about the direction in which he was travelling. When he realised that he was on the road to Inverness, he continued to the Highland capital where he booked into a hotel for three nights. Once the anger had subsided, other emotions began to take over. He was deeply hurt. Why, when she made her confession about swapping the babies in the maternity hospital in Glasgow, hadn't she revealed this too? He understood they had been honest with one another before they made their wedding vows. He loved her… he would always love her, although right now, just at this moment, he was disappointed.

246

Only after he had battled with these feelings, did he begin to consider the actions from Rosa's perspective. He was aware that, at the age of eleven, she had helped deliver her sister, Ellie. Her mother had denied the pregnancy and, after the traumatic birth on the bathroom floor, had evaded her responsibilities, leaving her own mother and Rosa to care for the baby. Audrey continued to rely on her elder daughter until Ellie was five years old. Under similar circumstances, when Ellie was widowed during her pregnancy, Rosa once again was left with the job of caring for her sister as well as the new baby; a child that Ellie initially rejected. It had been a difficult, intense time for the family, which Rosa had managed admirably. How would they have coped with twins?

Bernard tried several times to telephone his wife, without success: he was worried. How relieved he was, therefore, to find her asleep on the couch when he returned home. Nevertheless, he was alarmed at her dishevelled state. Her tear-stained face was pale, her hair tousled, her clothes crumpled. Unaware of how long she had slept, he did not disturb her immediately.

It was early evening when Rosa finally stirred. Opening her eyes she was, at first, disorientated. It took a few seconds before she was aware of the familiar surroundings. Reality struck – the nightmare had not gone. Glancing at the clock on the mantelpiece, it was after six o'clock. She must have slept for several hours – or so she thought. As she swung her legs round in an effort to get up, she heard noises – someone was in the house, someone was wandering around upstairs. She sat still, petrified, hardly daring to breathe. Then she heard footsteps descending the stairs. A moment later Bernard's head appeared round the door. "You scared me," was all Rosa managed to say as she sank back onto the sofa.

"Not half as much as you scared me," Bernard answered. Walking slowly over to the couch, he reached out his arms, bidding her to take hold of his hands. Gently he raised her up. "Dinner's ready," he stated, "I thought you might be hungry." Little was said over the evening meal; there would be time for explanations later.

Rosa was bewildered on discovering that she had slept round the clock – a sign of the fatigue caused by the trauma experienced on disclosing her secret. Further, if Bernard's reaction was an indication of what was to come, how would she cope? After all, her husband was not intrinsically involved. How would the girls react? Would Ellie speak to her again? And, what about her mother-in-law? Ever since that Halloween evening when they had met at the telephone kiosk, Edith Marshall held her in high esteem. Although now in her mid-nineties, the elderly lady was mentally aware – and as astute as ever.

Bernard was by nature a patient man. That night, he held his wife in his arms as she slept. When she woke she clung to him, closer than ever, reluctant to let him go. Would he stay by her side, she wondered, or would he leave her?

CHAPTER 24
Running Away

Rosa was not by nature a deserter but on this occasion she could not cope. In the past, facing the difficulties life had thrown in her direction, she had stayed to help and support those close to her. To them, and others who knew her, she was a kind, caring, thoughtful person – the Good Samaritan – who had not turned her back on trouble. How could she bear to lose that respect, to be found out for who she really was? She had to get away, to evade the wrath of those she had rallied around in times of need. She had to escape from her family, from the people who held her in high esteem. In truth, she had to escape from herself, from the lie that, deep down, had plagued her for more than a quarter of a century.

The day after his return from Inverness, Bernard was participating in a golf tournament; he would be away from home until at least mid-evening. Although reluctant to leave his wife, given her current state of mind, the game was a particularly important annual event. "I'll be fine," Rosa assured him, seeing his reluctance to go; and making a special effort to convince him that all was well. Bernard kissed her lightly on her forehead, said he loved her, and departed.

Peeping out through the bedroom window, Rosa watched as her husband drove slowly out of the drive and onto the main road. She showered and dressed, packed a suitcase, grabbed a bite to eat and rang for a taxi. Half an hour later, with her passport safely tucked in her handbag, she was on her way to Edinburgh airport. Long before Bernard returned home, she would be high above the clouds – flying as far as it was possible to go, escaping to a new life, to a place where no one would think to look… no one, that is, apart from Bernard. She telephoned him from the airport.

Bernard enjoyed his day on the golf course. He loved the open air, the camaraderie and the not too energetic exercise. As the tournament got underway, the worry he had felt as he left his wife alone in the house had lifted. Rosa was tough. She was resilient. Somehow she would find the courage to face her demons. Tomorrow they would have a talk about it: together they would work something out, of that he was sure. How wrong could he be?

As soon as he entered the house he sensed that all was not well. "Rosa," he shouted from the hall, "I'm home." There was no reply. Taking his time, he went first into the lounge, half expecting to find her asleep on the settee. All was quiet – there was no sign of her. He looked into the other downstairs rooms, went into the kitchen where he opened the back door and called out across the garden, "Rosa, where are you?" Still there was no reply. He crept upstairs, thinking she must be in bed. Panic began to set in. "Rosa," he called, now in desperation. Back down in the hallway, he noticed the flashing light on the answerphone. On pressing the button, Rosa's voice, though low, echoed in the silence.

"Bernard, I'm so sorry. I never meant to hurt anyone. Please forgive me for leaving without saying goodbye. Some day, when this is all over, I hope we can start again. I love you so much – there'll be no more secrets. I needed to get away. I stuck a pin in the map.

Although Bernard's heart sank as he listened to his wife's voice, he felt the warmth in her message and recognised her sincerity. There would be no more secrets between them. He knew exactly where she was going. When they married all those years ago, he had quipped, "If we stuck a pin in a map as far from home as possible, this would be the place." His immediate instinct was to follow her, to book a seat on the next available flight, but he hesitated. What good would that do? She needed some time to herself. Yes, he would follow her but not yet. In a way he felt guilty, blaming himself for her reaction. After all, when she had revealed the truth he had bolted. No wonder she had taken flight.

**

Determined to be brave, Rosa focused on her journey. She was going to New Zealand; she was travelling as far from her Scottish home as possible – twelve and a half thousand miles – to the spot where Bernard had proposed, to the place where they had made their vows. It had been exhilarating: they were in love. They had come together against all the odds, two people born within a few hundred yards of each other, meeting coincidentally many years later as each followed their own dream. Somehow, Rosa yearned to return to that

251

moment, the moment when she had escaped her mundane existence and found true love. It was a carefree time when she had managed, or almost managed, to leave her guilt at the other side of the world. Could she do that again?

After three consecutive flights, Rosa arrived in Christchurch. It wasn't quite her final destination, but she needed a few days to cast off the remnants of her old life and take on a new identity – a change of hairstyle, a change of clothes. An alternative lifestyle required a different attitude. She must look the part. Gone were the suitcase, the trench coat and court shoes, replaced by a rucksack, an Afghan coat and walking boots. The last flight took her from Christchurch to Nelson, at the north of South Island. From there she hitched a lift to Golden Bay, around sixty miles away, further north, beyond Tasman Bay. It was winter, it was cold, not the same as when they had been there all those years ago in the summer. But the sky was clear and the sun was shining. The snow on the mountain tops glistened in the light. For the first night she booked into a small hotel in Takaka. An indication, perhaps, that she wasn't quite ready for this. "Where are the hippies?" she asked the landlady as she checked out the following morning. If she expected a strange look she was disappointed.

"You hoping to join them?" the woman quipped, "You look like you would take to the lifestyle."

Looking down at her attire, Rosa realised that she had made a good job of changing her appearance: no one would guess that she was a 'respectable', middle-aged lady from a rather affluent family, not that she ever regarded herself in that way.

Following the instructions from the landlady, she headed towards the road over the hills. "It'll take a couple of hours to get there on foot," the woman had warned. Rosa had imagined it to be a little closer to the town, but recalled that when they had visited more than twenty years ago they had a camper van. They had parked a short distance from the Commune, maintaining their own privacy while spending time with the members during the day. The feeling of love and friendship exhibited at that time provided the inspiration that encouraged her and Bernard to marry. Impulsive maybe, yet it had been the right decision: the best decision of her life in fact and, as Bernard often pointed out, his too.

This time was different. Hoping to find some trace of the community she remembered from so long ago, she intended to stay for longer, to be involved with the people. Perhaps she would meet up with some of those she had met on that memorable journey. She was not disappointed.

Entering the vicinity of the Commune, Rosa felt vulnerable. There were dwellings scattered around that she could not recall; many seemed more permanent, less makeshift than before, although there was an old bus and a few dilapidated huts. As she wandered along the rugged path a woman, probably ten years younger than she, approached. "Hi there, my name's Miriam," she called, "Are you looking for someone?"

"I-I-I was here around twenty years ago," Rosa stuttered. "I'd like to stay for a while."

As she said the words, Rosa felt she must sound ridiculous. She hung her head, unable to look the woman in the eye. Undeterred by the request, Miriam stared at the stranger, "Do I know you?" she asked.

Slowly Rosa raised her head, "I'm Rosa," she answered, "I came here in the mid-1970s with a fellow traveller. We married in Takaka."

"I do know you. I remember now; your companion, er…husband, Bernard, was it? Unusual name. He was fine fellow. Oh, I'm so sorry; did things not work out for you? Is he…?" Miriam stopped. Seeing Rosa's eyes glaze over she wondered – had she said too much?

"It's good to see you, Rosa," she continued in a welcoming tone, before enquiring as to the whereabouts of her vehicle.

"I've walked here," Rosa stated.

Observing the look of bewilderment on Miriam's face, she added, "I mean I've walked from Takaka, not Scotland." Both women smiled, relieving any tension that remained.

"Come," Miriam urged, "You look cold and I'm sure you're hungry. I was just about to prepare some lunch; you must join me."

For the next two hours the acquaintances, from such different walks of life, chatted about the years that had passed since they had waved good-bye. Miriam and her boyfriend had eventually married. They had two sons

254

who both attended the secondary school in Takaka. "As young boys we taught them here," Miriam explained. "There was such a wealth of knowledge amongst the Commune members, it seemed pointless to send them away for their early education. However, as they reached high school age, it was different; we accepted they needed to be involved in the wider community, to be able to make up their own minds about the type of lifestyle they wanted for themselves. Our elder son is studious. He's talking about going to university. The younger one is much more keen to pursue the outdoor life, although whether he will stay here, we're really not sure.

"And what about your husband?" Rosa enquired.

"Ah, well, Bill's teaching. He's at the same school as the boys – the only school in the town. He was, of course, qualified before we came here and, much as we both still love it, we had to be realistic."

Rosa nodded. In a way she was a little disappointed, yet she admired the thoughtfulness behind their reasoning.

"We're still very much a part of the Commune," Miriam interjected. "We all help with the crops and the animals and, as you can see, I do a lot of craftwork." The rugs, wall hangings, colourful beads and ornaments had drawn Rosa's attention as soon as she stepped inside. Along with the hand made furnishings and the heavy smell of perfume, this living space was far from conventional.

"There's a weekly market close to the town where I sell my wares," Miriam added, before turning the conversation on the stranger from the past. "What about you?" she queried. "What brings you here on a cold winter's day?"

Although Rosa was tempted to reveal her whole sorry tale to Miriam, she refrained. After all, her life with Bernard had been good – better than anything she could have hoped for when she'd set out on her original adventure: a spinster in her mid-thirties, with no life to call her own. So in the meantime, she dwelt on the happy times, avoiding the reason behind her sudden departure from her beloved Scotland and doting husband. "It's a long story," she responded, when the inevitable questions came, "I'll tell you another day." Faced with a further questioning look, she added defiantly, "I haven't left Bernard."

Declaring her desire to be a part of the Commune, at least in the short term, Miriam guided her to the backpackers lodge. "The building is for tourists visiting the Commune – mostly students on vacation who are interested in finding out about our lifestyle," she explained. "It provides accommodation, giving us an income, which helps sustain the Commune. At the moment it's empty, being out of season, so you'll have the place to yourself. If you decide to stay with us we'll make alternative arrangements. Have you brought any supplies with you?"

"Well, not really," Rosa confessed. "I called at the bakery in Takaka, so I'll not starve for the next day or two."

"I'll be going into the town tomorrow for groceries along with a couple of others. Perhaps you should join us and get to know how things work."

"I'd like that," Rosa responded.

"That's sorted then."

After showing Rosa round the lodge she left her to settle in, agreeing to meet up at ten o'clock in the morning.

As she lay in bed that night, Rosa wasn't quite sure what to think. From what Miriam had said, the Commune was not quite the alternative lifestyle that it had set out to be. It seemed they relied on tourism to exist. They were no longer a group occupying some spare ground; they now had ownership. Miriam's husband was working to support his family should they seek a traditional way of life. Perhaps others were doing the same. Rosa remembered the place buzzing with activity. There didn't appear to be much of that today. However, given that it was still winter, maybe it was not surprising.

Over the next two weeks, Rosa gained a clearer idea of what was going on. There *was* a community spirit here, albeit a little less 'hippie' than in the 1970s. For the most part, the group consisted of those who had been there from that time. Now, they were middle-aged. Mostly, their children had departed preferring to join the so-called rat race that their parents had abandoned, although they all returned for holidays. According to the original stalwarts, none of their offspring had resented their upbringing.

The Community accepted Rosa. She adapted to their lifestyle, participating as if she had not known any other way. When she was with them she tried hard to focus but there were times when her mind drifted, when she was overcome with remorse. Ironically, it was not the guilt of her secret that weighed on her so much as running away from Bernard. The longer she was away, the heavier the burden of her actions became. How could she have done such a cowardly thing? He loved her; he would have been there for her. Three months after her arrival at the Commune, Miriam asked the same question she had posed on that cold winter's day when Rosa appeared, unannounced, on the site: "Are you sure you don't want to tell me why you left your home in Scotland? I don't mean to pry Rosa, but you don't look well. I'm not the only one concerned for you."

Rosa shook her head. If she confessed, she would feel trapped – as if she had brought her problems with her instead of leaving them behind. That night Rosa cried. She had not escaped – she could never escape. For almost a week, she didn't leave her room. She had reached the depths of despair; there was nowhere else to run. Added to her guilt was the love she received every day from her friends in the Commune: people she barely knew who had rallied round to make her welcome. Just as she felt she could no longer carry on living, someone was knocking on her door. "Telephone for you," a voice called out…

CHAPTER 25
Troubled

Anna was angry. It seemed that nothing was right with her life. The mystery surrounding what she hoped would be a rekindled friendship with her old school friend, Marie McInnes, was unfathomable. The realisation that her supposed boyfriend was an uncaring creep left her feeling worthless. Why oh why was her choice of men so disastrous? And now, somehow worst of all, her favourite aunt – well, the only aunt she knew – had disappeared off the face of the earth. What was going on?

Talking to her mother was useless. It wasn't that she didn't get on with her; rather, Ellie seemed remote, looking through her. It was as if her head was somewhere else. She wasn't like that with Jonathan. Anna's half brother was growing into a fine young man. He was destined to follow in the footsteps of his grandfather – a laird. Anna's stepfather, John Scott, the only father she had ever known, did not aspire to such a position. He was happy for his son to take over the family estate. He enjoyed the life he had in Fort William; running a business, organising the mountain rescue team and spending time with Ellie. John doted on his wife and stepdaughter, and Anna, in turn, loved this man who had been a part of her life for as long as she could remember. Maybe she should talk to him.

"I don't know," was John's simple answer to his stepdaughter's query. "I do know that your mother loves you very much, just as she loved your father. Maybe you remind her of him. Perhaps she feels as if she is looking into the past. That's all I can think."

"Thanks Dad. Perhaps you're right but it's hard, and there are other things troubling me."

"Come on, spill the beans," he cajoled, placing a friendly arm around her shoulder."

"How come Mum finds two good men in her life but I can't find any? My love life's a complete disaster."

"Now, now, Anna, it's not a disaster. The right man will come along one day."

Still not reassured, Anna continued, hardly allowing herself time to draw breath.

"Why did Marie desert me, and what about Aunt Rosa? Where is she?"

John listened. He did his best to comfort his stepdaughter but in truth he didn't have answers to her questions.

"I'm here for you," he stressed, "and so is Uncle Bernard, he's suffering too. One day we'll have answers to these questions.

John, of course, was right. Anna had had a difficult few weeks, no wonder she was stressed. As far as Marie was concerned, it occurred to her that she must be patient. If her friend really *was* a friend, eventually she would hear from her. There would be an explanation. Aunt Rosa was family. Somebody must know where she'd gone. Anna decided she would call round to see

Uncle Bernard. William West was another matter. If she had any sense, she would forget about him.

***

Marie McInnes felt guilty. How could she have treated her school friend with such disregard? Anna had done nothing to deserve that. The thought that her friend had been stopped and questioned by the police filled Marie with horror. Although Jack understood why Marie had behaved so irrationally, he could not condone her actions. "I think you owe your friend an apology," he stated, once his girlfriend had fully recovered.

"I think so too," Marie agreed, "I'm just not sure how to go about it. Why would she even agree to speak with me again after what I did?"

"Well," Jack began slowly, "We still haven't done what we set out to do on our holiday."

For a few seconds Marie did not quite understand what he was saying, so much had happened since the day of her accident. "I set out in search of my birth mother," she remembered, at last. "That was part of the problem, it was the reason I didn't tell Mum and Dad where I was going or what my intentions were."

"I think you should tell them now," Jack urged, "Maybe you're fretting unnecessarily."

Marie wasn't convinced, "I can't ask for more time off work just now, it's particularly busy at this time of year, " she argued. It was an excuse to avoid conflict with her parents. After all, her recent break from work was hardly a holiday: she'd spent most of it in hospital.

261

Ignoring her comment, Jack continued, "There's a good chance you'll find Ellie Milne in Fort William, and isn't that where your friend lives? Surely it would be the ideal opportunity to sort things out between you.

Jack was right. Nevertheless, she felt she needed to get back to work, to some kind of normality. Unable to face another challenge so soon, she promised to take some time off towards the end of September.

"Okay," Jack agreed, hesitating somewhat. There were other things on his mind – things that would affect them both: the time was fast approaching when he would have to return to Australia.

"We need to talk," he declared a few days later, looking earnestly at the woman he had set his heart on being with for the rest of his life "My mission in Britain is rapidly drawing to a close; I need to make plans to return home."

"Of course," Marie replied, desperately trying to think of an excuse to delay the moment. As they were about to address the question that would seal their future the 'phone rang…

"I'm afraid your mother is seriously ill. I think you should come as soon as you can."

"Dad, where are you?" Marie responded.

"We're at the infirmary in Glasgow."

"B-b-but when, w-why, what's wrong?"

"It doesn't matter. Just get here."

Marie sensed the panic in her father's voice. Whatever was wrong with her mother was serious.

"I have to get to the hospital in Glasgow," Marie called to Jack, echoing her father's anxiety.

"What's wrong," he responded, moving quickly from his seat at the dining table. Marie was shaking: her face was pale.

"Mum's ill. She's at the infirmary in Glasgow. I don't know any more than that except, judging by Dad's tone, it must be serious."

"I'll come with you," Jack stated firmly. Looking at his watch, he added. "We should make it onto the last ferry."

Within a matter of minutes, having thrown a change of clothes and wash bags into a case, Marie and Jack were on their way to the ferry terminal in Rothesay.

"I'll drive from here," Jack insisted, as they made their way down to the car deck on approaching Wemyss Bay. From there, no words passed between them until they drew into the hospital car park. Marie was trembling. At the reception desk, they were directed to the ward where Chrissie McInnes lay, barely conscious. Her husband was sitting by the bedside gently holding her hand. So focused was he on his wife, he didn't notice Marie until she appeared by his side. Jack stayed back at the door of the ward not wishing to intrude on the small family unit. Colin looked gravely at his daughter, "She's not going to make it," he mumbled, his eyes glistening with half shed tears.

"What happened?" Marie probed.

"She took a turn for the worse in the early hours of the morning."

"B-b-but what do you mean?"

"The cancer – she knew she was dying, but we thought she might last a few more weeks."

"Cancer?" Marie swallowed hard. "I knew she wasn't well, but she never mentioned anything about cancer. Why didn't you tell me?" Marie's voice rose higher with each word she spoke.

"Hush," her father urged, "We didn't want to upset you. Besides, you've not been well yourself."

Hot tears rolled down Marie's cheeks as she looked down at the frail, diminished figure of her mother. This could not have happened over night. How had she not noticed Chrissie wasting away? Too busy immersed in her own troubles; that's why.

"She asked for you," Colin commented.

"When?"

"About half an hour ago she opened her eyes – only for a few seconds. 'Where's Marie?' was all she said."

Marie bent over and kissed her mother gently on the cheek. "I'm here, Mum," she whispered.

Chrissie's eyelids flickered, "Jack's a good man," she murmured, "He'll take care of you."

Chrissie slipped quietly away later that night as Colin, Marie and Jack sat by her bedside.

***

As Bernard Marshall listened to his wife's message on the answerphone, he was, at once, devastated that she had made such a drastic decision, yet relieved

264

that he knew where she was heading… even if it was the other side of the world.

A feeling of guilt enveloped him, as if he were to blame for her reaction. Maybe if he'd stopped to think before storming off, things would have been different. He had been disappointed with his wife, as much as angry: he'd trusted Rosa; he thought they shared everything. It had taken a few days for him to come to terms with her deceit. Why, oh why could she not have told him? Yet, deep down, he knew why – he understood that she had not been able to tell anyone, not even him. Gradually, he forgave her. He rushed home believing, at first, that everything would be fine. Then, only a day later, she was gone! The temptation to follow was difficult to ignore for, as well as yearning for her, it now occurred to him that he was left to deal with the consequences. Sooner, rather than later, the whole sorry tale would surely come to light. He must wait until that happened and defend his wife as best he could.

When, a week after Rosa had left, he answered the door to come face to face with Anna, he believed the moment of truth had come.

"Where's Aunt Rosa?" Anna demanded, having made several unsuccessful attempts to contact her by telephone.

"Come in, Anna," Bernard invited, "Maybe we need to chat."

Fully expecting Anna to have discovered her aunt's secret, he was surprised, and relieved, when he realised that she was as yet, unaware of the situation.

"Where is she?" Anna pleaded. "Why didn't she tell us she was going away?"

It was tricky for Bernard to be diplomatic. He didn't want to lie to the girl yet he could hardly convey the truth while her mother remained in the dark. If he was to reveal anything, Ellie must be the first to know.

"Your aunt needed some time to herself," he began, "She has gone to visit some old friends of ours."

"I see," Anna remarked, although she did not see at all. "If she wanted to be by herself, why is she visiting friends?"

"Erm…" Bernard faltered, "I mean, she needed to get away for a while."

"Away from what?" Anna challenged, "Away from you?"

"She hasn't left me, if that's what you're thinking."

It was obvious that Bernard was hiding something. It was also clear that he was upset: he looked pale and a little thinner, far from his usual cheerful self. Anna decided to back off. In the pause that followed Bernard offered her coffee, which she accepted. When he returned from the kitchen with two steaming mugs, uncle and niece were more at ease.

"So, you had a bit of a hard time in Glasgow, I hear."

"Yes," Anna admitted, "It was a disastrous end to a not particularly great holiday. I haven't heard from my boyfriend since, and I'm not sure that I want to."

"You deserve better than that, Anna. Some day, somewhere, you'll meet the man of your dreams. I wasn't looking for anyone when I arrived at my brother's in Australia to find your aunt. She's the best thing that ever happened to me."

"Hmm," Anna muttered, "I hope you're right. I'm sorry for barging in on you like this. Aunt Rosa disappearing when my school friend and my boyfriend had deserted me was all a bit much. I'm feeling abandoned."

"It'll all work out," Bernard assured her. "Often in life, challenges come in quick succession. Maybe things will get worse before they get better, but they *will* get better."

Bernard was surprised by his own words of wisdom, considering how low he felt. Rosa's departure, however much he tried to reassure himself, seemed like a separation; he hoped he was wrong. Having Anna for company that afternoon was a pleasure; in a strange way it had helped him. He hoped he had helped her.

CHAPTER 26
Marie and Anna

Marie was shocked by her mother's death. Although glad that she had made it to the hospital before Chrissie died, the loss seemed brutal. Now that she was gone there were so many things that she wished they had spoken about. However, her mother's blessing regarding Jack comforted her. Marie's unfortunate accident may have caused much anxiety at the time but it had allowed Jack to reveal his true feelings to her adoptive parents.

Chrissie's funeral was conducted on the Isle of Bute within ten days of her death. With the help of his older brother, also a widower who lived on the Island, Colin managed all the arrangements. Marie found relief being back at work on the farm. Jack returned to Edinburgh to prepare his final reports on farming in Scotland.

Towards the end of September, six weeks after Chrissie's death, Marie and Jack set off to Fort William, this time with her father's knowledge and blessing. Armed with her original birth certificate, as well as her adoption papers, Marie was hopeful of tracing Ellie Milne, her birth mother. Her other quest, to make amends with her friend Anna, had troubled her ever since she gained consciousness after her fall. She had wanted to 'phone her friend to explain, but somehow she had always found an excuse to delay making contact. The telephone seemed such an impersonal way to communicate something so important as a friendship – a friendship that she so desperately wanted to renew.

Leaving from the north end of the Island on the Colintraive ferry, the couple continued their journey via the west coast. It was a beautiful, leisurely drive – hurrying not being an option on the winding coastal route. Besides, the scenery was too picturesque to miss.

Now that they were on their way, Marie was anxious to contact Anna, hoping her friend would agree to meet up over the weekend. Being Friday, it was likely that she would be out for the evening or perhaps away for the weekend. Since Anna would be teaching, the call would have to wait until late afternoon. Marie was decisive, "I'll ring Anna when we reach our hotel," she voiced out loud.

"Okay," Jack agreed. "That sounds like a good idea."

The hotel was a mile or so south of the town, with views across the water. Once settled in their room, Marie lifted the telephone receiver to ask the receptionist for an outside line. "Just press 9 and listen for the dial tone," came the response; "the information is written on the 'phone."

Marie reddened – she hadn't noticed. With hands shaking, she reached for her address book and began fumbling through the pages.

"Calm down," Jack urged, taking the book from her hand. "I'll read the number out for you. What's the name?"

"Milne, it's Anna Milne."

Jack gave her a strange look but made no comment. Marie pressed 9 on the keypad. On hearing the dial tone she nodded for Jack to begin. Slowly he read out the numbers. "Keep calm," he repeated as she keyed the last figure. The ring tone sounded.

Marie's mouth was dry. When Anna answered, no words came.

"Hello, hello," came the voice at the other end of the line, "I can't hear you."

"I-I-It's Marie."

"Marie, is that you?" There was a hint of concern as well as surprise in the tone.

"I-I-I'm sorry. I'm so sorry."

"Where are you?" Anna asked.

"Here, I'm here in Fort William. I wanted to say sorry for all the trouble I caused."

More than two months had passed since the fateful incident. Although Anna had recovered from her ordeal she had longed for an explanation, willing her friend to get in touch.

"I'll be at the bus station in the centre of the town tomorrow morning at ten o'clock. Is that okay with you?"

"I'll be there," Marie assured her friend.

Replacing the receiver, she turned to Jack, "Is that okay with you?"

"Of course," he stated emphatically, "isn't that what you wanted?" As if pondering, he waited a few moments before making the reference to Anna's name. "Your friend is Anna Milne?"

"That's right," Marie concurred.

"That's strange. If your mother is Ellie Milne, then your real name is also Milne."

"Yes, but not really strange," Marie argued. "Milne is a common name in these parts. I've never thought about it, but I'm sure there's no connection."

Marie was relieved at the outcome of the 'phone call. She had been so stupid behaving the way she had. Hopefully, tomorrow morning would seal the friendship she had come so close to throwing away.

Anna was thrilled that her old school friend had at last made contact. It was obvious that she was upset at what she'd done. Anna was sure she could forgive her whatever the circumstances leading to her bizarre behaviour. Sitting in her lounge, watching the news, the evening stretched out in front of her. She couldn't settle. She was excited about the meeting in the morning. *I'll go round to see Bernard,* she decided. There had been no word from Aunt Rosa, no communication with William West – the 'phone call from Marie was the only news. She had to tell someone. *My life really is a bit sad*, she thought briefly, before putting on her coat and heading for the front door.

As usual, Bernard was delighted to see his niece. The news that she was meeting Marie the following morning caused mixed emotions. He understood how Rosa had felt by the threat of her secret being disclosed, yet he longed for the truth to come to light. It was the reason he had not followed Rosa to New Zealand. He could handle it. He could deal with the outcome, hoping that once the worst was revealed, the healing process could begin and open the way for Rosa's return. To Bernard that was what mattered most in his life. He cared for Anna but in the end she would have to deal with her own problems. "Let me know how you get on," he entreated as she left that evening, rather later than she had intended.

Anna was slightly unnerved by her uncle's keenness in her relationship with Marie, despite having visited him solely on that pretext. *Perhaps he's just lonely; missing Aunt Rosa,* she reasoned. Still, she would do as he asked, she would 'report back'.

Anna and Marie met at the bus station in Fort William as planned. On seeing each other they hugged, thus breaking the ice that might so easily have dampened the next two hours. Anna invited Marie to her home for coffee, feeling that the privacy of her apartment would be more appropriate than her initial idea of a café in the town.

Considering the disastrous consequences of their previous encounter, the two women were remarkably relaxed in each other's company. As the result of her actions in the summer, followed by the death of her mother, Marie had learned some hard lessons: she needed to be more honest with those around her; she needed to be rational, to think before acting. Other people had problems too. Understandably, for much of the morning the conversation dwelt on the events of their last encounter. It was difficult for Anna to accept Marie's excuse for taking her car, the reason for her subsequent anguish. Yet it was clear that Marie was genuinely regretful for this irrational act. "I was frantic," she claimed. "My car wouldn't start, yours was there with the key on the passenger seat. I was half way to Loch Lomond before the seriousness of what I had done struck me: I realised I had committed a crime. I'm so sorry Anna – it was an awful thing to do. Please forgive me."

Anna drew a deep breath. Marie was right; her impulsive action was criminal. It had caused much grief. Yet in a curious way, Anna was drawn towards this woman, this school pal from years ago. She wanted her friendship. The fact that Marie faced her after what she had done was admirable: it must have taken courage.

After filling each other in on the events of the two weeks following the day of Marie's accident and Anna's departure to Spain, there was little time left for further exchange of news. Glancing at her watch, Marie was surprised that it was almost one o'clock. "I must get back to the hotel," she declared. "Jack will be waiting."

"How long are you staying in Fort William?" Anna asked.

"That depends," Marie replied. "I'm searching for my mother." Seeing the enquiring look from Anna, she quickly explained. "I'm adopted – my adoptive mum died six weeks ago. I'm looking for my birth mother. I had set out in search of her on the day of the accident, when everything went so badly wrong."

"Oh, okay, I just thought it would be nice to see you again before you go home. Perhaps introduce me to Jack."

"I'll give you a ring," Marie promised.

Marie was glad that Anna was understanding, and hoped she'd have the chance to see her again before returning to Bute. Equally, Anna was thrilled that Marie had visited and, of course, she had forgiven her friend.

Not until half way through the afternoon did Anna remember the promise she had made to Uncle Bernard.

It was Saturday: Bernard was having a game of golf so missed Anna's visit. She called round again on Sunday morning.

"We'll go out for lunch," he announced, taking his coat from the hallstand without waiting for a response. Anna was delighted to be taken out – her social life was practically non-existent at the moment so any company was welcome.

Her uncle listened intently as she relayed the events as told by Marie the previous day. He was already aware of part of the story from Rosa: this completed the puzzle. However, the information he sought was not forthcoming. He wanted to know much more about this young woman, this 'friend' of Anna's, but he dared not ask – he didn't want to make his interest too obvious.

"So, your friendship is intact," he commented when she had finished the tale.

"Yes, very much so," Anna smiled. She didn't like to be at odds with people. Enough problems had come her way, without any provocation on her part.

"Have you heard from Rosa?" she asked.

"No I haven't," he answered, barely disguising the sadness he felt. He realised that his wife's disappearance made no sense to Anna, but how could he explain?

"I don't understand," she admitted. "It feels like she's abandoned all of us. Why would she do that?"

"Your aunt will be back. I know that she's all right," he added, in a poor attempt to justify the situation.

In order to divert the conversation from Rosa, Bernard asked Anna how long Marie was staying in Fort William and whether they would have the chance to meet again before she left.

"Ah, well, that's another story. Marie's mother – her adoptive mother – died a few weeks ago. Marie is searching for her birth mother."

CHAPTER 27
Revealing the Secret

That was the news Bernard wanted, yet dreaded. There was no doubt in his mind that Marie would be successful in her search. It was apparent that the girls had not discussed the issue further. Why would they? Now, it seemed, sooner rather than later the truth would be out. Guilt – Rosa's guilt – enveloped Bernard. He had to do something. Was it too late to talk to Ellie? Would Marie get to her first?

Bernard attracted the attention of the waiter to request the bill. It seemed an abrupt end to the afternoon. Anna sensed her uncle's unease. She assumed the mention of Rosa had unsettled him so made no comment. Besides, she had lessons to prepare for her classes the next day.

Back home, alone in the lounge, Bernard sank down into an armchair. *I must think,* he sighed. *I have to do something. I have to talk to Ellie.*

From the information he had discovered through the detective he concluded that Marie knew her mother was Ellie Milne. He rang Ellie.

Unusually, it was her son Jonathan who answered the 'phone.

"I'm sorry Uncle Bernard, Mum and Dad are visiting my grandparents today." Came the polite response. "I'm not sure when they will be home."

"Okay," Bernard replied. "Perhaps you could ask your mother to give me a call."

"I will," Jonathan assured him.

Bernard resumed his seat in the armchair, more concerned than ever about this predicament. He desperately wanted to see Ellie before Marie contacted her. For the rest of the day, until well into the evening he attempted, unsuccessfully, to focus on other things. Between watching TV, reading, and listening to the radio, he paced the room, not daring to move far from the telephone for fear of missing a call from his sister-in-law.

When, by ten o'clock, his call had not been returned, Bernard decided to ring again. Surely Jonathan must have forgotten to relay his message. This time Ellie answered.

"Ah, you're home. I'm sorry it's so late."

"No, no. I'm sorry. I should have called you. Jonathan's out, but he did leave a note to say you'd 'phoned. We've had a rather hectic day."

"I w-w-wondered," Bernard fumbled for words, "W-w-would it be possible to call round to see you tomorrow?"

"Y-y-yes," Ellie hesitated. "Can you manage in the morning?"

"Yes. Is ten o'clock okay, or maybe earlier?"

"Anytime after nine-thirty suits me." Ellie sounded more decisive before adding… "I'm expecting a visit from my daughter in the afternoon."

"I thought Anna was at work tomorrow?" Bernard queried.

"Yes, that's right, she is. I mean my other daughter."

After an uncomfortable pause, Ellie continued, "I'll see you in the morning Bernard. It's been a long day."

As he replaced the receiver, Bernard was more puzzled than ever. Clearly, Ellie was tired, but there was no sign of stress in her voice: she didn't sound upset. Now he would have another long wait until the morning. In the meantime, there was nothing more he could do.

Bernard was at his sister-in-law's by nine-thirty in the morning: he'd had an unsettled night. Having rung the doorbell, it seemed to take forever before he heard Ellie's footsteps approaching. Slowly the door opened.

"Come in, come in. It's good to see you." Ellie appeared more cheerful than usual as she directed Bernard towards the large kitchen where he took a seat at the oak dining table. "Tea or coffee," Ellie offered. "The kettle's just boiled."

"I'll have coffee please," Bernard answered.

"I'll join you," Ellie replied.

As they settled with their coffee Ellie looked curiously at her brother-in-law. He seemed a shadow of his former self. It was obvious that he was missing his wife yet she wondered if that was all. "Have you heard anything from Rosa?" she asked.

"No, not yet," he answered.

"I thought perhaps that was the reason you wanted to come round."

"No, it was nothing to do with Ro…" he stopped for a moment. "Well, I suppose it has everything to do with Rosa. I wanted to talk about your daughter – your other daughter."

"Ah, Laura. I guessed you must know something."

"Yes, but when did you find out?"

"I think I've always known, although I put it to the back of my mind. You see, at the time I couldn't cope with one baby, let alone two. I was ill. I was muddled. For weeks I rejected Anna, thinking she must belong to Rosa."

"When did you know for sure?" Bernard persisted, already recognising the irony of the whole affair.

"I was at a parents' open evening at the High School, waiting to see Anna's form teacher. Two women behind me greeted one another like long lost friends. One commented she didn't realise the other had a daughter that age. In response the other whispered, 'She's my adopted daughter. Remember my brother Paul who was killed? Well, it's his daughter.'

At that moment I was called in to see the teacher. Snatching a brief glance at the pair, I vaguely recognised my sister-in-law – I hadn't seen her in fifteen years. As far as I was aware she had moved away from Fort William soon after Paul's death. Anna always performed well at school so I suppose my interview with her form mistress was positive. I left straight after, trying to make some sense of what I had overheard.

Rosa was away in Glasgow at the time otherwise I might have challenged her. The next time I saw her, I had come to terms with the news. As I said, deep down I'd always known. The night of the birth was a blur – it was something I wanted to forget, not to remember, yet I recall Rosa's anxious tone as she shouted over the racket that was going on... 'Just one more push!' I thought it was all over. Rosa said it was the afterbirth."

"Why did you never ask Rosa about it?" Bernard was curious.

"Rosa's the best sister ever. She looked after me. I didn't want to upset her. Besides, when I calmed down after learning that I really had had a second baby and Paul's sister had adopted her, I was pleased. I knew that my little girl was in the best possible hands. Honestly Bernard, I couldn't have coped with twins."

"So... Laura contacted you?"

"Yes, she rang yesterday soon after we arrived home. I believe she wanted to see me to break the news face to face, but I'd had a call from a detective a few weeks ago asking about a Laura Milne, so her request was not a complete surprise. At the time, I'd denied all knowledge of this person. After all, I didn't know the name of my estranged daughter."

"Hmm," Bernard muttered. It was apparent that Ellie was not aware that the name Laura was the girl's birth name but not her adopted name. Did she realise that she was Anna's friend Marie McInnes? Should he tell her?

"Does Anna know she has a twin?" Bernard asked, almost sure he knew the answer.

"No, although I suppose I'll have to tell her."

Bernard shuffled uncomfortably in his chair. "I think there's something else you should know before you see Laura," he muttered, as if he was about to make a confession.

"Oh, what's that?"

"Well, Laura Milne is your daughter's birth name, but it's not her adopted name, it's not the name that she is known by." There was a pause, why did he not just tell her instead of delaying the moment.

"Laura is Anna's friend, Marie McInnes," he revealed at last.

Now it was Ellie's turn to be stunned. "So maybe Anna does know."

"I'm certain she doesn't," Bernard assured her.

"I'll make some more coffee," Ellie offered. There was another problem that must be broached while the two had each other's attention.

***

"Where's Rosa?" Ellie asked, "And don't tell me you don't know."

"She's in New Zealand."

"Why? Why has she left you?" Ellie was serious. She was baffled when her sister had gone away without any explanation, especially since Bernard was evasive whenever her name was mentioned. Now she suspected the reason. Rosa, she recalled, had disappeared at the time the detective was asking questions about Laura. The pieces of this puzzle were beginning to fall into place. "It's about this, isn't it?" she persisted.

"Yes," Bernard confessed, "She couldn't face it. The guilt was too much."

"So, am I understanding this correctly? Rosa has fled because she's worried about me discovering what she did more than twenty-six years ago?"

"That's right."

Ellie sighed deeply, sitting back in her chair. "But she only did what she thought was best."

"Well, it *was* reckless," Bernard commented, realising, as soon as the words were out, that it was an odd way to defend his wife's actions… or maybe he was defending his own. "When Rosa confessed to me, I stormed out of the house. I stayed away for two nights. Seeing my reaction might well have prompted her decision to leave."

"You didn't consider following her?" Ellie asked her brother-in-law.

"Yes, of course. But, how would that have helped? I decided to stay behind and face the consequences for her. Oh Ellie, what have I done? I miss Rosa so much. The last few weeks have been unbearable. I'm so sorry."

Changing the subject slightly, Ellie quizzed Bernard about Marie McInnes. "What else do you know about her?"

Much to his surprise, Bernard knew more about the girl than Ellie, who had never extricated the full facts of Anna's holiday drama from her daughter. However, he refrained from giving too much detail, believing it was not his prerogative. He did mention that Marie's adoptive mother had died recently – information that saddened Ellie.

As he was leaving, his sister-in-law commented that he would, no doubt, be interested in the outcome of her forthcoming meeting with Marie, as well as the reaction of both young women to the news of their relationship.

"I'm concerned for Rosa," he sighed. "I want her home safe."

CHAPTER 28
Marie meets her birth mother

Ellie was more anxious about meeting her second daughter than anyone would judge from her calm manner: her worry was impacted further following Bernard's visit. Her initial reaction on speaking with Laura the previous afternoon had been excitement – albeit nervous excitement. Although she had always suspected the truth, until she'd attended the parents' evening she had not been sure. Even then there remained a question mark over the whole situation. For many months after giving birth, she had been very ill. Darkness had crept over her when Paul died – she'd spent months in hospital. Frightened, disorientated, engulfed in sadness, how could she possibly know what was happening around her? What she did remember was her sister's love. Rosa was there for her; Rosa would never have done anything to harm her. Unlike Bernard, it did not occur to Ellie that she had anything to forgive Rosa for.

Unsettled after the visit, it was a while before Ellie made a move. *Get a grip*, she told herself at last. Resuming her practical side, she prepared lunch, ate, washed the dishes and went upstairs to tidy herself up. At half past two, the doorbell rang. She steadied herself, taking a deep breath as she walked, sedately, to the front door.

Marie stood on the doorstep, as if on the edge of a precipice. Was she really doing this? Was she really Laura Milne, about to meet her birth mother? The death of the woman who had raised her so lovingly was so recent, so fresh in her mind: barely six weeks had passed. How could she do this so soon? Well, she reassured herself, it had been on her mind for a long time. Now it was crucial. She had to discover her roots before her imminent trip to Australia – something else she could no longer delay.

Slowly the door opened: the two women looked at one another. Then, taking her daughter's hand, Ellie guided her over the threshold into the hall where they hugged. "I'm so glad you searched for me."

It was all that needed to be said. Marie, so vulnerable after the trauma of recent weeks, was more fragile than she had realised. With tears in her eyes, she followed her mother into the lounge, where they relaxed in each other's company oblivious to the passing of the afternoon.

A door opened and closed in another part of the house: noises; footsteps; someone moving around; a voice called out, "Mum." Before there was time for an explanation, the lounge door opened and Anna Milne stepped into the room.

"Anna!"

"Marie! What are you doing here?"

Without time to think, Ellie had little option but to introduce her two daughters, blatantly revealing the truth.

"B-b-but how can that be?" Anna contested. "We were both in the same year at school: there's only a day between us."

"You're twins," came the next admission.

"Did you know about this?" Anna demanded, turning to Marie.

Jumping to her younger daughter's defence, Ellie responded, "She had no idea, any more than you did… until now."

Anna flopped down on the settee.

"But *you* knew?" she stated emphatically, turning on her mother.

"I didn't know that your friend Marie was my daughter – not until Bernard told me this morning."

"And what's this got to do with Uncle Bernard?"

Ellie sighed deeply; she had not considered all the implications until this moment. "Bernard knew nothing about it," she explained, "not until three months ago when a Sergeant Boyle came to talk to Rosa. I was ill when the two of you were born. Rosa registered the births and arranged for the adoption. She named the second baby Laura. I know it sounds impossible but I didn't know I'd had twins."

Both girls gasped in disbelief. There were so many unanswered questions. Anna was the first to speak.

"Sergeant Boyle – I recognise that name. He was the man I saw in Dundee about my stolen car."

"And," Marie interjected, "it was Sergeant Boyle who came to see me when I was in hospital, where everybody called me Laura. Apparently, my wallet was

287

stolen when I had my accident but my original birth certificate was in the zipped compartment of my handbag. I was supposed to be meeting Jack and coming to Fort William. I'd set out in search of you when I had the accident."

Glancing at the clock, Ellie ended the conversation. "I'm sorry girls, John and Jonathan will be home soon, I need to prepare the evening meal. You're both welcome to stay, of course."

"I must get back to the hotel, Marie answered, regretfully. "Jack will be waiting for me."

"I'll stay," Anna replied. "I don't think I can concentrate much on preparation tonight."

Before leaving, Marie intimated that she would be in Fort William for the rest of the week. Ellie suggested she meet Uncle Bernard and also John and Jonathan. "After all Jonathan is your half-brother," she commented, adding, "Hopefully we will see you again in the next few days. Give me a ring once you've had a chance to talk to Jack."

It was Anna who showed Marie out, walking down to the main road where her car was parked. "I hope I didn't appear rude," she stated apologetically. "All this has come as a bit of a shock."

"Me too. I've always known I was adopted but I'd no idea I had a sister. There's something else you should know… my adoptive mother, Chrissie, was your – our – father's sister? I was so angry when I found out. I couldn't understand why she didn't keep in touch with her sister-in-law – my mother. Now, I think I know why.

By the way, who is Rosa? She seems to have a lot to answer for."

"Aunt Rosa is amazing, you'll love her. But oddly, she disappeared a few weeks ago. Uncle Bernard knows where she is, but he's not saying anything."

"Goodness, this gets more intriguing by the minute."

"Why don't you come round to my place after tea on Thursday? In the meantime, I'll try to uncover as much information as I can."

"Okay, thanks Anna."

***

Both Anna and Marie needed time to come to terms with the situation although, as yet, neither was in possession of all the facts. When Marie told Jack that she and Anna were twins he expressed surprise, while hardly resisting a grin. "I know, I know," she affirmed, registering the look on his face, "you did question that we might be related. Honestly, we've been friends for so long, it didn't occur to me." Wisely, he refrained from comment.

"How did you get on with your mother?"

"Brilliant, everything was going smoothly until Anna walked in."

"So that was a problem?"

"It was a shock. We were both stunned at first but parted amicably. I'm going round to see her early on Thursday evening. By that time she may have gleaned more information and," she continued, gazing longingly at her partner, "in the meantime we can enjoy a few days holiday."

By Thursday evening, Marie was ready for a chat – sister to sister – with her erstwhile friend. It seemed strange knocking on Anna's door knowing that, given the recent revelations, the relationship between them had changed forever. Since their encounter the previous Monday, Anna had wangled as much information as she could from her mother – all of which she now shared with her twin.

Marie explained that in Chrissie and Colin she'd had the best possible upbringing: they were devoted parents. She would never resort to referring to them as Aunt and Uncle; they would always be Mum and Dad. Yet she was comforted by the fact that they really were close family. Nevertheless, the thought that her own mother abandoned her had always irked. How could any mother give away her child? Now, of course, she realised that was not the case. Ellie, it seemed, had been unaware of the drama going on around her at the time of the birth. This Aunt Rosa, whoever she was, had been responsible. Where was she now? Was she afraid to stay around to face the consequences of her deeds?

"I was abandoned too," Anna explained. "You do know our father was killed at work before we were born?"

"Yes."

"Well, Mum was devastated. She didn't want us – either of us. She'd no idea she was having twins: only Aunt Rosa, who was a midwife, knew that. Ellie wouldn't entertain anyone else near her. After we were born, Mum refused to have anything to do with me – she wouldn't look after me, she wouldn't feed me. Initially, Rosa took over the responsibility. In the end, Mum was hospitalised. I was put into hospital with her but it was many weeks before she accepted me. Somehow, Aunt Rosa succeeded in having you adopted by our father's sister and her husband who didn't have any children of their own. That's as much as I know. Until Aunt Rosa reappears it's as much as any of us knows except, perhaps, Uncle Bernard. Believe me Marie, I knew none of this until Monday evening when I prised it, bit by bit, from our mother."

"Where was Ellie's mum, our grandmother? Why didn't she offer to help?" Marie questioned.

"Apparently, her father died around that time, so Audrey (our grandma) went to Inverness to look after her mother."

Marie shook her head. She knew that families could be complicated… this, she concluded, was extreme.

Having discussed what their mother had so far revealed, Marie changed the course of the conversation. "What happened with your boyfriend, the one who was with you on holiday in Spain?"

"I dumped him," Anna retorted, decisively.

"Oh."

"He deserted me. Left me languishing in a cell at the police station in Glasgow."

"You're exaggerating."

"Actually no, I'm not."

Marie gaped at her sister. "And it was all my fault."

"I admit that being stopped by the police at the airport did have something to do with you. However, the fact that William walked off and left me didn't. In a way the incident served to show what a jerk he is. So… maybe you did me a favour."

"Well, that's one way of looking at it, I suppose," Marie smiled. "So, I take it you saw him again since you say you dumped him."

"Well no. I mean I've finished with him in my head. I'll not entertain him again. If he comes calling, I'm not available. What about you? How did you manage to find such a seemingly gorgeous hunk, stuck out on a lonely Scottish Island?"

"I'd hardly call it that. Nevertheless, you're right to wonder. One day, as he was walking along the road, he happened to see this fair maid working in the fields. He eyed her with admiration and immediately fell in love."

Anna looked inquiringly at her sister, "You're really not joking, are you?"

"Really, I'm not. We're going to Australia at the end of the month. His family have a farm that he will one day inherit." In a low voice, she added, "We plan to marry, but please keep that to yourself for the time being."

"Of course," Anna promised.

"And what about you?" Marie asked. "Is there anyone else on the scene?"

"I'm afraid not." There was sadness in Anna's eyes as she thought of all her failed relationships but, most especially, of the successful one – the one that had somehow slipped through her fingers. Why had she not offered to go with Dan instead of agreeing with him when he said she must follow her own ambitions? Ultimately, she had returned to her hometown, to a career that was fast loosing its appeal? What was the point in working hard when there was no one to share her life with?

"I'm sorry Anna, I didn't mean to pry. It's just you seem to have had so much going on in your life – moving to the capital, going to university, having a profession."

"You're right, but love doesn't come when you're looking for it – not to me anyway"

Changing the subject again, Anna advised, "Mum wants us to get together on Saturday to meet the rest of the family. It seems a bit soon but if you're planning to go home on Sunday, and flying off to Australia in two weeks, it might be the only opportunity we'll have for a while. Jack must join us too."

"That sounds good to me."

"Lunch will be around one o'clock. However, I wondered if the two of us could meet earlier? There's someone else I'd like to introduce to you"

"Another mystery?"

"Not exactly. It's Edith Marshall, Bernard's mother. She knew Rosa long before her son."

"She introduced them?"

"No, no, that's another story."

"Edith is in a residential home. She must be ninety-five, at least, but still very alert. She's always had a great admiration for Rosa."

"Okay, where shall we meet?"

"At the home," Anna suggested. She wrote down directions for Marie.

It had been a productive evening, although Marie remained dubious about Aunt Rosa. Understanding her sister's doubts was the main reason behind Anna's desire to take her sister to visit Edith. As for her aunt's disappearance, that was as much a mystery to her as it was to Marie. Bernard, she decided, must be challenged on that issue at tomorrow's gathering. She was sure Edith Marshall would know nothing about it.

On Saturday morning, as Marie made her way to visit this elderly lady, she wondered just what it would achieve. Anna greeted her on the front steps at the main entrance to the building, a single storey purpose built establishment. On entering, there was a slight whiff of disinfectant in the air: the whole interior was immaculate.

"Mrs Marshall's in the lounge," a matronly figure called out as they made their way along the main corridor.

"Thanks, we'll find her." Anna was familiar with the geography of the home.

Going through to the lounge, she pointed to the far end of the room, "She's over by the bay window, reading a book."

Edith Marshall turned and smiled as she heard the two women approaching from behind, "Anna! It's so good to see you, and I see you've brought a friend. Bring up a couple of chairs for yourselves."

Seated comfortably in a small circle the three of them chatted casually for a few minutes. Edith, with the sharp inquisitive eyes of a much younger woman, was attentive to every word. "So, this is your friend, and it's a pleasure to meet you my dear." Turning to Anna, she continued, "How is it that you've never brought any of your friends to see me before?" she asked. Even at ninety-five Edith Marshall was no fool. She sensed that this was more than a casual visit.

"W-w-well Edith, Marie isn't just my friend. Last weekend we discovered that we are sisters – not just sisters, but twins."

"I see," Edith answered, with slightly raised eyebrows, yet no evidence of surprise in her voice. "It's good to have a sister. Rosa was the best sister your mother could have had."

"How did you meet Rosa?" Marie enquired. "Anna tells me you've known her for a long time."

"Yes, that's right. It's quite a story. Do you have time to listen to an old woman?" she grinned. "I'm not sure how much of this *you* know, Anna?"

"I'm listening, Edith."

"It was Halloween, 1952. I went out to the telephone box, just across the road from my house. I'm not even sure who I was going to ring. Anyway, a man was in the kiosk and a young girl was in the queue. She was trembling. I asked if she was all right. Wiping away tears, she told me that her mother had just had a baby. No preparations had been made and the girl didn't know what to do. She had a telephone number to call for a midwife. I stayed with her as she made the call, and remained with her for the rest of the evening until her grandparents arrived. Mother and baby were taken to hospital. The girl was Rosa – she was just eleven years old. She had come home from school that afternoon to find her mother on the bathroom floor, giving birth. She helped deliver the baby – Ellie – your mother. When, after two weeks, Audrey and her baby were discharged from hospital, it was Rosa and her grandparents who cared for Ellie. Gradually, with much coaxing, she came to accept and love her daughter but it was a real struggle. Quite what would have happened if it hadn't been for Rosa I'm not sure."

Both Marie and Anna were aghast at the story. As with their mother, her mother before her had endured the trauma of losing her husband while pregnant. Neither had coped well. Both, it seemed, had Rosa to thank.

Before they left, Anna thanked Edith for sharing the story. Neither Anna nor Marie judged it wise to question the elderly lady about their birth, despite being sure that Rosa had confided in her.

"Time for a quick coffee before we join the party?" asked Anna.

"I think so," Marie agreed.

***

The afternoon get-together included Bernard, John and Jack. Jonathan put in a brief appearance before

296

departing for a badminton tournament. Marie was, understandably, self conscious at her introduction to three strangers as a close member of the family. She could imagine how much talk must have been going on in recent days to explain her appearance although, without Rosa, much would remain a mystery.

After they had eaten and settled in each other's company Anna, as she had decided, challenged Bernard. "Where's Rosa?" she demanded.

"She's in New Zealand," he answered. "I did tell your mother the other day."

"You didn't tell me where in New Zealand, and you didn't say why she'd gone," Ellie commented, seeing the look on Anna's face, as if she'd committed a crime by not telling her straight away.

"She's gone to the Commune in Golden Bay, the place where we were married. She is so sorry for what she did. When she realised that the two girls had met up and the police had discovered that Laura Milne and Marie McInnes were the same person, she knew it was only a matter of time before the truth was discovered. She couldn't cope with the guilt; she couldn't face the people she had deceived – her family."

"Have you heard from her?" Anna asked.

"I'm going to Australia next week," he announced. "I've booked my seat on the plane and arranged to stay with my brother in Sydney before travelling to New Zealand."

"But she has been in touch?" Anna persisted.

"W-w-well, not exactly."

Anna sighed. It was useless. Bernard was not going to convey any more information.

"We're going to Australia in a couple of weeks," Marie declared, looking fondly at Jack.

"Yes, it's my home," Jack professed. "I'll be introducing Marie to my family. We have a farm, so hopefully she'll feel at home too," he smiled.

"So you're emigrating?" Ellie turned to the daughter she hardly knew.

"We'll see how things go in Australia," Jack intervened. "I've grown quite fond of Scotland."

"I assume you're in the south west?" Bernard queried.

"No no, our place is in New South Wales."

"I'll give you my brother's address," Bernard offered. "If you're showing Marie the sights of Sydney you might take a run out to Northbridge. You'd be most welcome."

"When are you going back to Bute?" John asked. He'd had little part in the afternoon's deliberations, but had taken to Jack with his Aussie twang and obvious admiration for Marie, the stepdaughter he'd not met until today.

"We had planned to head off tomorrow," Jack answered.

"Pity, I thought you might like a trek up Ben Nevis since you're so close – or perhaps you've already scaled Scotland's highest mountain?"

Marie and Jack looked at one another. "I think we could manage another day," Jack replied, speaking for

298

them both. "Our hotel's not busy, I'm sure they could accommodate us for another night."

"That's decided then; I'll be your guide. Maybe Jonathan will join us."

Climbing Ben Nevis proved exhilarating as well as satisfying for Marie and Jack. Feeling a little guilty that she had neglected her boyfriend in the past few days, Marie was pleased to see that he was so readily accepted. As they intended an early start on Monday morning the pair did not linger for long following their descent. A brief good-bye to Ellie as John dropped them off to retrieve their car from outside the house, was all they managed. The parting of mother and daughter, albeit fleeting, was filled with emotion. "Please keep in touch," Ellie urged, "and let me know how you get on in Australia."

CHAPTER 29
Rosa Reunited

Scarcely a week after the reunion, when the scattered family had come together without the drama that Rosa had anticipated, Bernard was on his way to Australia. It wasn't his destination but it was a place to relax; to recover from jetlag before continuing, refreshed, to be reunited with his beloved wife. A message on his answerphone and a postcard on her arrival in Takaka was all the news he had received. It was enough for him to know where she was.

However, on arrival at Gerald and Monica's, he was not feeling well. He had expected to be tired and maybe a little disorientated after the flight: not in agony with stomach pains as he was suffering now. "It's not a tapeworm," he assured his brother in a feeble attempt at humour, "I didn't stop off in India."

Nevertheless, on this occasion, as on his visit more than twenty years ago, hospitalisation was required. This time it was urgent – an ambulance was called. An immediate operation to remove his appendix was undertaken before he'd had the chance for a good night's sleep. He was detained in hospital for over a week and only released on condition he rest for a month. Frustrated was hardly the word to describe his anguish. "I need to see Rosa," he pleaded.

"You're going nowhere until you're fully recovered," his sister-in-law stressed.

"And that's final," Gerald chipped in.

Had he really felt 100% fit, Bernard would have persisted in arguing, but to be truthful he knew he needed more time to recuperate.

Two weeks after his release from hospital, there was a knock on the door. "There's someone to see you," Monica called from the hall. Bernard rose from his armchair and moved cautiously to the hall where he stood, momentarily bewildered, before recognising Marie and Jack expectantly gazing into the relative darkness of the interior.

"Come in, come in," he invited excitedly whilst introducing the couple to a rather bemused Monica.

"Yes, come in," Monica reiterated, leading the visitors into the lounge. "Bernard has told us all about you."

"We weren't sure that you would still be here?" Marie looked questioningly at her uncle.

"Well my dear, that's another story."

Over tea and cake the couple intimated that they had arrived almost a fortnight ago and, having met Jack's family and made herself at home, they had decided to spend a few days in Sydney. Bernard, in turn, relayed the story of his untimely illness. Since they had booked into a hotel in the city for two nights, Monica insisted they stay for an evening meal and meet Gerald who, she was sure, would be delighted to meet them, and most upset if he missed out on their visit.

During the course of the evening Marie, seeing her uncle's distress at his forced sojourn in Sydney, suggested she fly to New Zealand to meet her aunt. At first Bernard rejected the offer but on consideration, realising that he could not make the journey for at least another two weeks and maybe not even then, he decided to give it some thought.

"Let's leave it for a day or two," Jack interjected. "We'll call in on our way home the day after tomorrow and, if you think it's the right thing to do, I'm sure we can make the necessary arrangements."

In consultation with his brother, Bernard had to agree that travelling to New Zealand, especially to a relatively isolated spot, would not be sensible. "And supposing Rosa has already left and is heading home?" Monica questioned.

"She wouldn't do that," Bernard argued, "She's harboured too much guilt for too long. Until she realises her family understand the decision she made – that no one has suffered as a result – she will not return."

"Odd isn't it? You're all far more upset that she's left."

"I want her to come home; I miss her so much. I wonder if she will accept Marie's forgiveness? After all, she's never met the girl."

"You're worrying too much, Bernard," his brother consoled. "From what I hear, Marie is totally immersed in the family, and that goes for Jack too: he is so supportive. Maybe the news that no one is blaming her, coming from the one person who has been most affected, is a good idea. Besides, Marie is anxious to meet this mysterious aunt who, after all, ensured that she was adopted by relatives whom she knew would give her the best possible upbringing." Bernard relented. Gerald and Monica were right.

***

Within two days, Marie and Jack were on their way to New Zealand. Marie had tried to persuade Jack that she would manage on her own. "You're so patient; you've done so much for me already."

"And I suppose you think you've done nothing for me," he teased, "except travel half way round the world to meet my relatives."

Jack would not take 'no' for an answer. Hopping over to New Zealand to visit friends or family in Christchurch might have been acceptable – journeying out into the 'sticks' was not. They boarded an early morning flight from Sydney to Christchurch, where they joined a domestic flight to Nelson. In Nelson they booked into a hotel for the night and hired a car the following day. Making enquiries in the town, they discovered that the Commune had become a popular stopover for hikers. Accommodation – a lodge – had been built where travellers could spend a night or two. Booking was advised. Marie made a note of the telephone number. Although they did not intend to stay there, it was comforting to know that she was only a telephone call away from her aunt. "I'll ring when we get to Takaka," she decided. Jack agreed.

It was late morning when they reached Takaka, some sixty miles from the town of Nelson. They found a

B&B where they checked in for the night before setting off on their mission to find Rosa. Spotting an information centre, they went in to ask directions. A public telephone was available near the centre from where Marie called the Commune.

Tentatively, she asked if she might speak to Rosa Marshall. For a moment or two she held her breath, half expecting to be told that they knew no one of that name. "Ah, Rosa, I think she's in her room. I'll ask her to come to the 'phone. May I ask who's calling?"

Marie hesitated, unsure of how to respond. "I'm her niece," she answered at last.

***

"A telephone call!" Rosa exclaimed, as she hastened to answer the door, in response to the messenger. "Who?"

"Your niece."

"My niece?"

"Hurry, the caller is ringing from a pay phone."

Rosa couldn't think how her niece could be calling. No one, as far as she knew, had the telephone number. Her next thought, Bernard: something must have happened to Bernard.

Hurrying as fast as she could, she reached the office and grabbed the receiver. Panic had already set in. "Anna," she panted, catching her breath, "What is it? What's wrong? Is it Bernard?"

"Is that you Rosa?"

"Yes."

"Nothing's wrong, nothing at all. Bernard's fine. I'm in Takaka. I've come to see you."

"Oh Anna. I suppose you know what I did, I'm so sorry." Tears welled up at the thought of a visit from her niece.

"Rosa," Marie repeated slowly. "I'm not Anna, I'm Anna's sister, Laura."

"Laura!"

"It's all right Rosa. Can I come to see you?"

"Now?"

"Yes, as soon as I can get there. I have a car – it shouldn't take long."

"I'll see you then; I'll see you soon. I'll be waiting for you." Rosa replaced the receiver.

Bewilderment would hardly be the word to express Rosa's confusion on hearing Laura's voice – the voice of the young woman she had not set eyes on since handing her over when she was just a few hours old. Why hadn't she realised straight away that it wasn't Anna? Her accent was completely different. After dawdling in the office for several minutes, somewhat disorientated, she announced to the receptionist that her niece, Laura Milne, would be arriving soon. "Please direct her to my room."

"Of course," came the polite response.

Rosa returned to her room, totally flummoxed. "I must tidy myself up," she muttered to herself. "Whatever is going on?"

Twenty minutes later, after a wash, a change of clothes, and having put a brush through her hair, Rosa felt marginally better. At least now I'm presentable, she

306

thought. Unable to settle, she wandered down towards the office where she waited in anticipation. Ten minutes later a young woman, casually dressed with a mass of thick, brown, untamed curls, approached. "Laura," Rosa called, intercepting her before she reached the building.

"Yes."

"I'm Rosa," her aunt introduced herself. She smiled, a tear in her eye, before stepping forward to hug the stranger… a gesture readily reciprocated.

"My adopted name is Marie McInnes," Laura responded, with a friendly grin.

"Of course it is," her aunt acknowledged, "I'll call you Marie."

Rosa led Marie to her room where the two of them chatted over a coffee. Marie gave a brief resumé of the events leading to her meeting with Ellie in Fort William. Rosa, thoroughly ashamed of her actions, was relieved to learn that the outcome had not turned out badly – as she had feared.

"I take it you've met Bernard?" Rosa enquired. "He's the only one who knew I was here. I thought, perhaps, he would come after me, although that's not what I wanted him to do – not until things were sorted. I really am a coward, leaving him to deal with the mess."

"Honestly Rosa, it's not a mess. Ellie has known the truth for years and Anna and I are delighted to be sisters." Her aunt raised her eyebrows in surprise.

"Ellie knew!" she exclaimed. "How did she know?"

"Aunt Rosa, it's a long story. There's much to tell… on both sides." Marie hesitated before adding, "My boyfriend's waiting in the car."

"Boyfriend – your boyfriend's here? Why didn't you say, he could have joined us for coffee."

"No, no. He thought it best I see you alone first, but he'll be delighted to meet you."

"So you've come all the way from Scotland to find me?"

"Well, not exactly. Jack is from Australia. I came over to meet his family."

As they strolled over to the parked car, Rosa asked about Bernard. "I shouldn't have left him. I've been so worried."

"Bernard is in Australia staying with Gerald and Monica. He's waiting there for you."

Rosa's eyes lit up. Bernard – Bernard *had* come looking for her. Her head was spinning as they reached the car. She gazed at the swarthy figure with the warm, friendly smile, waiting patiently by the hire car. "Hi, Jack Todd, pleased to meet you, ma'am." His accent clearly identified him as Australian.

"Pleased to meet you too." Rosa was distracted from her thoughts by this charming man who was obviously in love with her niece.

"So, are you coming home with us?" Jack asked, observing this unconventionally dressed, middle-aged woman. Recent months in New Zealand had given her a weathered look, indicating that she had spent much time out of doors adapting to life in the Commune. Yet he detected a deep sadness in her eyes: she was not as settled as her outward appearance seemed to suggest.

Rosa glanced at Marie. Nothing had been said about travelling back with them. Nevertheless, it was understood.

"We've booked into a B&B in Takaka for the night. Would you like us to pick you up tomorrow morning?"

Rosa was decisive, "Yes please, that will give me time to say 'good-bye' to everyone and pack my things."

As the hire car disappeared down the track, Rosa wasted no time preparing to leave the Commune. Miriam must be the first to know. She had been a true friend since the moment Rosa had arrived three months earlier. "I'm glad," was her immediate reaction, "although I will be sorry to see you go, as will everyone else." Rosa had fitted in well but Miriam had noted a change in her mood in recent weeks. The inner sadness, always present in the new resident, had given way to depression. The arrival of this niece had triggered a remarkable transformation. "Join me for breakfast in the morning, before you leave," she invited.

The rest of the farewells were relatively easy. The packing took little time as Rosa had few possessions. The Bohemian style attire that filled her wardrobe would have to suffice until she had time for a shopping spree in Australia. Bernard would be amused.

The journey to Christchurch, where they stayed overnight, passed without incident. The onward flight to Sydney was similarly straightforward, although Rosa was nervous with anticipation. Marie had, in the meantime, brought to her attention the fact that Bernard had undergone surgery to remove his appendix – the reason he had not completed the journey to New Zealand as originally intended. Rosa was alarmed. "He's making a good recovery," Marie assured her, "there's nothing to worry about, but he does need to take things easy for a while." Rosa relaxed – just a few more hours to go.

The reunion was emotional, not only for Rosa and Bernard but also the young couple, who were delighted to see the change in the older relatives. Monica insisted that Marie and Jack stay with them that night, before returning to the farm. Bernard contacted Ellie and Anna to say that he and Rosa would be staying in Australia for a few weeks, expecting to return to Scotland in time for Christmas.

Marie's father, Colin, was flying out to Australia to be with his daughter and her partner for the festive season. So far, they had made no plans either for staying in the southern hemisphere or returning to the UK. Of one thing they were sure – whatever the decision on location, they did plan to marry.

After all the excitement – discovering that her friend, Marie, was her twin sister and her beloved Aunt Rosa had fled in shame – Anna attempted to settle back into what now seemed a rather mundane existence. Each day she set off in the gloom of the approaching winter, returning in the shadow of darkness to her empty flat. Then, one day, as she walked along the corridor towards the staffroom for the mid-morning break the secretary

310

intercepted her, intimating there was something for her in the office. Mystified, Anna followed the young girl as directed.

"These arrived for you this morning, Miss Milne," she waved her arm in the direction of the filing cabinet on top of which lay a beautiful bouquet of flowers.

"For me?" Anna mouthed, in surprise.

"For you."

Anna moved towards the array of blooms.

"Who are they from?'

"I don't know." Anna poked around delicately, not wishing to disturb the arrangement. "There doesn't appear to be a message with them. Is it okay if I collect them at the end of the afternoon?"

"Sure, Miss. I'll look after them."

Anna left the office, elated. Someone was thinking about her... but who?

It wasn't her birthday; it wasn't Valentine's Day; it was no day in particular. It occurred to her that it must be William. She had not seen or heard from him since that fateful day at the police station in Glasgow. Maybe he was truly sorry; maybe he wanted to make it up to her. So desperate was she for company, it even crossed her mind that it wouldn't do any harm to give him a second chance.

When she returned to the office at the end of her last afternoon class, the secretary looked up from her desk. "Ah, Miss, I found this envelope behind the door."

Anna picked up the small white envelope from the desk, opening it to reveal a card with the words:

I'm back in Edinburgh. Please contact me if you're free. Much love, Dan x.

Anna was trembling as she picked up the flowers and walked out of the office.

About the Author

Louie Elizabeth Parker was born in Kingston Upon Hull in 1947, where she lived until the age of twenty. In 1968 she moved to Leeds and trained for the teaching profession. For more than six years Louie taught at a primary school on an estate designated as an education priority area. It was a challenge! At the end of 1977 she moved to Aberdeenshire, where she spent the next thirty-nine years. During that time she taught in country and village schools, lectured at the Northern College and gained the Degree of Master of Education. For the last seven years of her career she was Head of the Lower School at Albyn School for Girls in Aberdeen.

louieelizabethparker.com

THE ANDERSON FAMILY SAGA

SISTER PEGGY
(The First Book in the Anderson Family Saga)

Sister Peggy is the first book in the Anderson Family Saga. It is a prequel to The Chris-Cross Episode and sets the scene of the Anderson family. It begins with the meeting of Thomas Anderson and Elizabeth (Lizzie) Anderson from two unrelated Anderson families.

As she stepped out onto the road, Lizzie was knocked sideways by a noisy rabble of men anxious to be on their way home. A young man in the crowd, apparently in less of a hurry than the others, caught her by the arm, saving her from stumbling to the ground. In the time it took him to ascertain that she was okay, the crowd was beginning to thin out. "You look shaken hen," he said. "Can I walk you home?"

She was about to say 'No' when, looking up into his clear blue eyes, she changed her mind. "Yes, please," she responded, angelically. "It's not far from here."

As they drew close to her home, they stopped. Turning to face one another, the young man introduced himself as Thomas Anderson. Taken by surprise, Lizzie announced, "And I'm Elizabeth – Elizabeth Anderson," she grinned coyly, "But everyone calls me Lizzie."

"Well, I hope we're not related," came the light-hearted response from Thomas, followed by a polite request, "Can I see you again?"

Sister Peggy traces the events of the Anderson family when, after twelve contented years, tragedy strikes this once happy household.

THE CHRIS-CROSS EPISODE
(The Second Book in the Anderson Family Saga)

A baby is abducted, but unbeknown to the kidnappers it is the wrong baby.

The Chris-Cross Episode follows the lives of two children, one the nephew and the other his unfortunate uncle who is taken, in error, from his pram when just a few weeks old. Stuart Anderson, the ill-fated child, is the youngest son of Alexander (Sandy) and Kathryn (Kitty) Anderson. Raised by his supposed paternal grandparents hundreds of miles from his birthplace in Aberdeen, he never feels that he truly belongs in their home. Meanwhile, the couple's real grandson, Crispin Nigel Leadbetter, who is also the grandson of Sandy and Kitty, enjoys a very different lifestyle in North East Scotland.

As a result of a few moments of passion in his youth, Timothy Campbell, a solicitor and a laird takes a special interest in the Anderson Family. Aware of the tragedy that has befallen them he sets out to discover the truth.

It is a tale of love and loss, arrogance and selfishness, estrangement and reunion.

THE MIXED FORTUNES OF STUART ANDERSON
(The Third Book in the Anderson Family Saga)

The lives of three young men changed forever when the mystery of the kidnap of Stuart Anderson in 1940 was solved fourteen years later.

When the respectable Mr and Mrs Leadbetter organised the kidnap of their grandson, they never suspected that the abductors would take the wrong child. For fourteen years they brought up the boy as Crispin Nigel Leadbetter, the supposed offspring of their only son who was killed in the Second World War. A chance encounter between a Scottish Laird and the victim of this heinous crime eventually led to his rescue. The innocent Stuart Anderson, uncle of the real Crispin Nigel Leadbetter, is reunited with the family from whom he had been estranged since he was just a few weeks old.

However, the solving of the mystery of his disappearance was not the end of his troubles. The Mixed Fortunes of Stuart Anderson continues the saga of the ill-fated victim who cannot escape from his past. A past closely entwined with his nephew, the real target of the kidnap and heir to the Leadbetter family fortune. But there is someone else lurking in the background – a man who has an axe to grind – a man with an illogical sense that Stuart Anderson is the source of all his troubles.

Another publication from the author:

TWENTY YEARS FROM HOME
by Louie Elizabeth Parker

Twenty Years from Home follows the life of a young child seemingly abandoned by her irresponsible parents who, as students, are tempted by a hippie lifestyle. Her widowed grandmother, determined not to make the same mistakes she feels she must have made with her daughter, decides to go back to 'basics'. She leaves her middle-class existence in the city to bring up the child in a run-down cottage in the Scottish countryside. For twelve years they have no electricity, no telephone and only a cold-water tap in the kitchen. The toilet is an outside privy.

But what has happened to the parents? Why did they desert their families, their precious offspring and their promising careers?

It is a story of kindness and cruelty; love and foolishness; revenge and shame.